Witch Is Where Rainbows End

Published by Implode Publishing Ltd
© Implode Publishing Ltd 2021

Chapter 1

"Penny for them," Jack said.

It was Sunday, and Jack and I were having lunch in the village pub, The Middle. Florence had been at Wendy's house most of the morning.

"I was just wondering where to start my search for the first of the guardians."

"I thought Martin had given you her name."

"He did, yeah: Madam Rodenia, but she could be anywhere."

"Have you tried the Candlefield phone book?"

"She won't be in the phone book."

"Why not?"

"Because she's one of the compass stone guardians."

"I still think it's worth a shot."

"Have you decided what you'd like to eat yet?" Arthur Spraggs, the landlord, had appeared at our table.

"I'll have the Sunday roast, please, Arthur," I said.

"Which meat?"

"Beef, please."

"Same for me," Jack said. "But with chicken, please."

"Two Sunday roasts it is. I assume you've heard that the police have charged her brother with Marcy Drinkwater's murder?"

"Hmm." I was trying to forget about that fiasco.

"He sounds like a nasty piece of work," Arthur said. "I wonder what's going to happen to the tea room now."

"When I spoke to the Peeps, it sounded like they'd still be interested in buying it."

"I hope someone does. It would be a shame for it to close. I'll take your order through to the kitchen."

"So?" Jack said.

"What?"

"Are you going to check if Madam Rodenia is in the phone book?"

"Okay, but only to get you off my case." I took out my phone and called Aunt Lucy.

"Jill, have you called about the lido?"

"The lido?"

"I take it Grandma hasn't spoken to you yet?"

"No, I haven't seen her today. What's all this about the lido?"

"I think I'd better let her tell you that."

"Fair enough. Do you happen to have the Candlefield phone book handy?"

"Yes, it's right here."

"Would you check to see if there's an entry for someone with the surname Rodenia, please?"

"How are you spelling that?"

"R-O-D-E-N-I-A."

"Just a sec, I'll see. P, Q, R. Roberts, Robins. No, It doesn't look—oh, hang on, yes. There's only the one, though: A. Rodenia. Do you want the number?"

"Yes, please. And the address, too."

When I came off the call, Jack was smirking. "Was I right? Or was I right?"

"It's probably not her."

"Are you going to call the number?"

"It won't be her."

"You won't know if you don't give it a try."

"Okay, okay, I'll call her." The number rang out. "No answer. It's probably not her."

"It might be."

"I'll go to the address after we've finished lunch."

"Thanks, Jack, you're so clever," he said to himself. "Don't mention it, Jill."

"I'm telling you; it won't be her."

***

By the time we'd finished our meals, it was almost time to collect Florence from Wendy's house.

"You can head home if you like, Jack. I want to tell Donna about the unicorns."

"Okay. Oscar said he might pop over later, so I ought to show willing and stick at least a few stamps in my album."

Donna must have been looking through the window because she'd opened the door before I'd even had a chance to knock.

"I was hoping you'd be the one who came over, Jill."

"Is everything okay? Is Florence alright?"

"Yes, the two of them are upstairs playing with Bob."

"Who's Bob?"

"My father's brother. He's staying with us for a couple of days. He's great with kids."

"Hang on. Are you saying that your father's brother is called Bob?"

"Yeah. Why?"

"That means *Bob's your uncle*," I laughed.

"I know he is. I just said so."

"But I mean, *Bob's your uncle*."

"Yeah. So?"

"Never mind, it doesn't matter. Has Florence behaved

herself?"

"She's been as good as gold, as always. There is one thing, though, Jill — "

"Yeah?"

"She said something to Wendy about the two of them going to see a unicorn. I wasn't sure what to make of that. I assumed Florence was joking."

"Actually, it's true. I recently did some work for the queen of the unicorns. When I'd finished on the case, I asked Ursula, that's the queen, if it would be possible for Florence to pay her a visit. She agreed, and even said that Florence could take a friend with her."

"That's fantastic. When is this?"

"I didn't mention it before because I'm waiting for a call back from Ursula, to confirm that next Sunday will be okay. Will you be around then?"

"We'll make sure we are. Wendy won't want to miss the opportunity to meet a real unicorn. Do you want to come in for a cuppa?"

"I'd love to, but I have stuff I need to do."

"Okay, I'll call the girls." She went back into the house, and shouted up the stairs, "Wendy! Florence's mum is here."

A few seconds later, the two of them came rushing down the stairs, followed by a man.

"Jill, this is my Uncle Bob," Donna said.

Somehow, I managed not to laugh.

"I'm pleased to meet you, *Uncle Bob*. I hope Florence hasn't worn you out."

"Not at all. I love playing with the kids. They're lots of fun."

"Come here." Donna called Wendy to her side. "I've

just been talking to Florence's mummy and it's true, you will be able to go and see a unicorn."

"Yay!" Wendy did a little jig around the hall. "When?"

"We don't know for sure yet," I said. "But it's probably going to be next Sunday. I'll let your mummy know as soon as I can."

"I told you, Wendy, didn't I?" Florence said. "Ursula is the queen of the unicorns, isn't she, Mummy?"

"That's right, and she lives in a big palace."

"Mummy," Florence said, much more serious now, "Wendy and her mummy have been practising their dance for next week's competition. Why haven't we?"

I turned to Donna. "Are you actually going to take part in that thing?"

"I don't really have a choice." She shrugged. "All the other mums are."

"Will you, Mummy?" Florence pleaded. "I want to be in the competition too."

"Err, yeah, okay. I suppose so."

"Cool! Can we practise our dance when we get home?"

"I have to work this afternoon, so why don't you come up with a dance for us to do? Then, when I get back, we can practise it together."

"Okay, Mummy."

Oscar was already at the old watermill. He and Jack were in the kitchen, looking through Jack's stamp album.

"Hi, Oscar, Jack said you might be popping over. I know he was looking forward to showing you how his collection is taking shape."

If looks could kill, Jack would have struck me down on the spot.

"Hi, Jill." Oscar had what looked like toothpaste on his chin. "While I'm here, I also want to finalise the details for our trip to StampCon."

"Jack's talked about nothing else, have you, darling? When is it, Oscar?"

"Next month. On a Saturday."

"You should come with us, Jill," Jack said.

"I'd love to, but you know Florence has her dance class on Saturdays. In fact, she and I are taking part in a dance competition this week."

"Since when?" Jack looked gobsmacked. "You said you—"

"Since always. I'm really looking forward to it."

"Mummy says I can make up a dance for us to do," Florence chipped in.

"Did she, pumpkin? You should make it really complicated because Mummy loves a challenge."

"Sorry, Oscar," I said. "We're interrupting. You and Jack will want to make your plans for StampCon."

"I'm really looking forward to it this year. My friend, Phil and his wife, Natalie, are going to come with us."

Florence went upstairs to plan our dance routine, and I went through to the lounge where I stayed until I heard Oscar leave.

"Are you really going to take part in that dance competition?" Jack said. "I thought you didn't want anything to do with it?"

"Of course I do. Florence and I are bound to win."

"Not if you fall off the stage like you did when you were dancing with Winky."

"Thanks for the reminder. By the way, do you think

Oscar made up those names?"

"Which names?"

"Phil and Natalie."

"Why would he make them up?"

"Just think about it. What are stamp collectors called?"

"Philatelists. So?"

"And collecting stamps is called philately, right?"

"Yeah?"

"Philately." I laughed. "Phil and Natalie. See?"

"Hmm."

**

I'd tried calling the number for A. Rodenia several times, but there had been no answer, so I magicked myself to the address listed in the phone book. Where would you have expected a guardian to live? In a sprawling mansion? In a secret cave? In a castle in the clouds?

None of the above.

The address turned out to be a third floor flat in the seedier part of North Candlefield. This was looking more and more like a fool's errand. Surely, the guardian of the north compass stone wouldn't live here. Still, I'd come this far, so I figured I might as well speak to A. Rodenia, on the off chance that the guardian was one of his relatives.

"He's not in." The man standing in the doorway directly across the corridor was holding what smelled like a bowl of tomato soup.

"*He?*"

"Yeah. He's down the bingo hall."

"Do you happen to know *his* name?"

"Rhodes or something like that."

"Could it be Rodenia?"

"Yeah, that's it. I get post for him sometimes. The posties around here are useless. I'm still waiting for my kite catalogue. They reckon they posted it two weeks ago."

"You don't happen to know the guy's first name, do you?"

"The postman?"

"No. Mr Rodenia."

"I've no idea. We don't talk."

"But you think he might be at the bingo hall?"

"More than likely. He works there."

"Right. Thanks for the help."

"I've got over fifty kites. Would you like to see them?"

"Thanks, but I'm in a bit of a hurry right now."

Candle Bingo Hall looked as though it had once housed a cinema. According to the sign next to the main doors, there were sessions every afternoon and evening, so I followed the stream of punters inside.

"Card?" A young man dressed in a blue suit, yellow shirt and blue bow tie held out his hand.

"Sorry?"

"I need to see your membership card."

"I'm not here to play. I'm just looking for someone. Do you know a man called Rodenia?"

"Yeah. He's the caller."

"*Caller?*"

The young man looked at me like I was stupid. "The guy who calls the numbers."

"Right. Of course. I just need a word with him."

"You still can't come in without a membership card."

"I'm not a member."

"You can join over there." He pointed to a small window.

"How much does it cost?"

"It doesn't. It's free."

"Oh, okay." I walked over to the window and gave the woman my details. A few minutes later, I was a proud member of Candle Bingo.

"How many sets do you want?" the woman asked.

"Sets of *what*?"

"Bingo cards." She held up a card full of numbers.

I'd never actually played cash bingo, although I had once won some bathroom scales on the prize bingo at Blackpool. Seeing as I would have to wait until the caller had finished working, I decided I might as well give it a try.

"How many cards do I need?"

"Most people have a set of six. That way you know you have all the numbers."

I had no idea what she meant, but I decided to take her advice anyway. "Okay. I'll have a set of six."

It was more expensive than I'd expected, but I figured I'd end up with a nice profit when I won.

"Have you got a dabber?" she called after me.

"Sorry?"

She held up an enormous marker pen.

"Oh, right. You'd better give me one of those too."

Even though the bingo hall was busier than I'd expected, there were still several free tables. I'd only been seated for a few minutes when the caller, who I assumed was Mr Rodenia, walked onto the stage. In his late twenties, he was younger than I'd expected. He too was wearing a blue suit, yellow shirt, and blue bow tie. His floppy fringe was so long that it made him look like an Old English Sheepdog, which made me wonder how he managed to see the numbers.

The caller went so fast that I found it really difficult to keep pace. The two old ladies on the next table, who had three sets of six books in front of them, were obviously veterans because they had no such problem.

The first four games came and went, and I didn't get as much as a sniff. But then, on the fifth game, I hit a lucky streak, and in no time at all, I needed only one number to win the full house.

"Come on number thirty-seven," I said under my breath. "Come on thirty-seven."

Just then, my phone vibrated with a text message. I took it out of my pocket, to find that it was just stupid spam. When I looked up at the illuminated board, which was on the wall behind the caller, number thirty-seven was now lit.

"Bingo!" I held my card aloft.

The prize money was one-hundred and twenty-five pounds, which meant this little trip had proven to be worthwhile, even if I drew a blank on my search for the guardian.

Another young man, wearing an identical blue and yellow uniform, came over to my table and took my card. After studying it for a minute, he shouted to the caller, "It's a false call."

"What do you mean, *false call*?" I said. "I've got a full house."

"You don't have the last number called."

"Yes, I do. Number thirty-seven."

"That isn't the last number called. Number twenty-three was called after that."

"But I still have a full house."

"I'm sorry, but the rules are very clear. You must have the last number called on your card." He handed it back to me and the game continued.

Just three numbers later, the woman on the next table shouted, "Bingo!"

And won all of *my* money.

The rest of the games were a total washout. When the session ended, I hurried down the aisle to catch the caller as he came off the stage.

"Excuse me," I shouted.

"If you're about to complain about missing your call, there's nothing I can do about it. Those are the rules."

"It's not that, although I do think that was very unfair."

"What do you want, then?"

"Is your name Rodenia, by any chance?"

"Yes. Why?"

"I'm looking for someone called Madam Rodenia, and I wondered if she might be a relative of yours."

"I don't know anyone who goes by the name of Madam Rodenia."

"Are you sure? You're the only Rodenia in the phone book."

"That's because I'm the only one who lives around here. Since my parents died, that is."

"I'm Jill. And you are?"

"Adam."

"*Adam*? As in, rhymes with *madam*?" Was it possible that Martin had misheard the name?

"Yeah. What is it you want, anyway?"

"I'm looking for the guardian of the north compass stone."

"Oh?" It was clear from his reaction that my words had caught him off guard.

"Do you know something about the guardian?"

He pushed the fringe off his face. "That's me. I'm the guardian."

"You?"

"Yeah."

"In that case, could we have a quick chat somewhere?"

"I suppose so, but I'm absolutely ravenous. I was just about to go to the cafe next door. I could meet you there after I've got changed out of this stupid suit."

"Okay, I'll see you there."

The cafe, which was called Two Little Ducks, was a bona fide greasy spoon. When Adam Rodenia turned up a few minutes later, he'd exchanged his suit for a baggy green and blue tracksuit. As soon as we stepped inside the cafe, the guy behind the counter shouted, "Your usual, Adam?"

"Yes please, Joe."

"And what about your lady friend?"

Adam turned to me.

"No thanks. I've already eaten."

It wasn't difficult to find a table because there were only two other customers in the place.

"Why do you want the compass stone?" Adam said.

"I'm going after Braxmore."

"Are you insane?"

"Probably. Do you know where the north compass stone is?"

"Of course I do. It's my job to know."

"How long have you been a guardian?"

"This gig has been in my family for centuries. It's passed down from one generation to the next."

"If you're a guardian, how come you have time to be a bingo caller?"

"Being a guardian doesn't take up much of my time. All I have to do is make sure I keep the information safe in case anyone asks for it."

"How often does someone do that?"

"You're the first person to ask me. And I know for certain that no one ever asked my father or grandfather. Before that, I couldn't say."

"Do you get paid for doing this?"

"Yeah. I receive a payment into my bank account each month. It's not much, but I can't complain because it's basically money for nothing."

"So where is this information?"

"Back at my flat."

"Can we go and get it?"

"Yeah, when I've finished my egg and chips."

When his food arrived, I began to regret my decision not to partake. The cafe might be a greasy spoon, but the grub looked delicious.

"Can I pinch a chip?" I said.

He had to think about it for a moment. "Okay, but only one. I'm starving."

Tight or what?

When Adam had finished his meal, we made our way to his flat.

"It's a bit untidy," he said.

It was nothing of the sort; it put my house to shame.

"Do you want to grab a seat in there?" He pointed to the lounge. "I'll go and see if I can find the info. I haven't seen the folder for a while, but I think I remember where I put it."

"Okay."

This guy wasn't exactly filling me with confidence. And, fifteen minutes later, when he still hadn't returned, I was beginning to fear the worst.

"Got it!" He reappeared, holding a Manila folder. "I'd put it in the ottoman." He passed me the file.

Inside was a scrap of paper, on which were the words:

Find the north compass stone where the rainbows end

"Is that it?" I checked the folder to make sure there wasn't anything else inside, but it was empty.

"Yeah."

"Are you sure? There must be more to it."

"No, that's it."

Great.

Chapter 2

I hated Monday mornings, particularly when it was pouring down with rain. And as if that wasn't a bad enough start to the day, when I picked up the box of Chococandy Pops, it was empty.

"Who's been eating my Chococandy Pops?"

"You're the only one who eats that rubbish," Jack said.

"What about you, Florence? Did you eat them?"

"No, Mummy, I don't want my teeth to fall out."

"How come this box is empty, then?" I shook it to prove the point.

"Most likely because you put it back in the cupboard like that," Jack said.

That was a ridiculous notion. Someone must have eaten them. Maybe it was Buddy.

"What am I supposed to do now?"

"You're welcome to have some muesli."

"Don't be ridiculous. I'll go and see if they have some at the store."

"Good luck with that." Jack laughed.

I was on my way across the village when someone called my name.

"Grandma, what a nice surprise," I lied. "I'm just on my way to the store for some—"

"I'm not interested in your shopping habits. I want to talk to you about the lido."

"Aunt Lucy mentioned something about that yesterday."

"Candle Lido is one of the great institutions in Candlefield. It's been there forever, but they've just served notice that it will close soon, and is going to be demolished."

"Who are they? Who owns it?"

"That's just the point. No one seems to know. If I did, I'd be hammering on their door to register my displeasure. I want you to find out who's behind this awful decision."

"How am I supposed to do that?"

"Oh, sorry. I was under the impression that you were my granddaughter, Jill, the private investigator. You must be another Jill."

"Very funny."

"So, you'll find out who's behind it?"

"I'll try, but I'm not making any promises."

"Good, and make sure you report back to me as soon as you know something."

"Yes, ma'am."

The two Stock sisters were behind the counter, playing a game of dominoes.

"You can't put that there, Marjorie," Cynthia said.

"Why not?"

"Because it's a blank."

"I know it is. That means I can put it next to any domino I like."

"No, it doesn't. You have to put it next to another blank."

"That's not right. A blank can go anywhere."

Marjorie turned to me. "Jill, will you explain the rules of dominoes to my sister?"

"I'm sorry, but I'm not familiar with them. I just popped in for a box of Chococandy Pops. Do you have any?"

"I'm afraid we're all out of them," Cynthia said. "But we do have Strawberrycandy Pops."

"And Toffeecandy Pops," Marjorie added.

"I haven't tried either of those. Where would I find them?"

"The Toffeecandy Pops are under P for pops."

"Right, and I assume the Strawberrycandy Pops are with them?"

"Actually, no, they're under S for strawberry."

"Of course." Give me strength.

Once I'd tracked down both flavours of the cereal, I returned to the counter where the two sisters were still arguing about the rules of dominoes. Eventually, I managed to get their attention long enough to pay for my purchases, and then I made my way back to the house.

Jack took one look at the boxes of cereal and rolled his eyes. "Really?"

"They didn't have Chococandy."

"Mummy!" Florence tugged at my hand. "When are we going to practise our dance? You said we could do it yesterday, but we didn't."

"I know, darling, and I'm very sorry, but I was really tired last night."

"Can we do it now?"

"There isn't enough time because I have to go to work and you have to go to school, but we can do it when I get home tonight."

"Do you pinkie promise?"

"Yes." We locked pinkies.

"Would you like me to show you the dance now?"

"I—err—"

"I'd love to see it," Jack piped up.

When I'd told Florence that she could come up with the dance, I'd expected something really simple. Like the one Winky and I had done for the pirate competition. How was I supposed to know that Florence was a budding choreographer? The routine she'd come up with lasted for over five minutes and was incredibly complicated.

"Do you like it, Mummy?" she asked.

"It's very good, but it's rather complicated. Maybe you could make a few —"

"It's just perfect as it is," Jack said. "You and Mummy are bound to win."

"Thank you, Daddy," Florence gushed.

"Yeah." I forced a smile. "Thanks, Daddy."

Fifteen minutes later, Florence went upstairs to get ready for school.

"That's a great dance routine she came up with, isn't it?" Jack grinned.

"I'm going to petition them to have a father and daughter competition."

"You should. I've got the moves." He did a weird kind of jig.

"What was that?"

"You're only jealous. I still can't believe that the guardian turned out to be a bingo caller."

"Me neither. I was expecting some kind of exotic creature. Certainly not a young guy with a floppy fringe, calling legs eleven."

"Have you given any more thought to the clue he gave you?"

"Plenty, but I'm no wiser. Where do rainbows end, anyway?"

"Beats me. Isn't there supposed to be a pot of gold at the end of them?"

"Supposedly."

"What are you going to do?"

"Ask around, I suppose. I might go to Candlefield Library to see if I can turn up anything there."

***

Mrs V was sitting cross-legged on her desk. Her eyes were closed, and she was making a humming noise. I wasn't sure if I should say something or just creep past her. I was still trying to decide when she opened her eyes.

"Good morning, Jill."

"Morning. Is your chair broken?"

"No, dear. I've decided to take up meditation."

"You were making a weird humming noise."

"That's my mantra."

"Right. What made you decide to take up meditation?"

"It was one of my yarnie friends, Matilda Moretime, who suggested it. As she pointed out, we live in such stressful times. It's extremely important to relax and recharge our batteries."

"I'd better leave you to it, then."

"It's all right, dear." She eased herself off the desk. "I've finished my session for this morning, and I'll do another one after lunch. You're welcome to join me if you like. There's plenty of room on the desk."

"It's not really my thing."

"You should give it a chance. You always seem so stressed out."

"I'll think about it."

"I have something to show you." She opened her handbag and took out a photograph.

"Is this Pepe?"

"It is. Isn't he a handsome boy?"

"Which end is his head?"

"Very funny. You can see his little face there."

"Oh yes, I see it now. How are you getting on with him?"

"Pepe and I are doing famously."

"And Armi?"

"Unfortunately, Pepe seems to have taken a dislike to him. Whenever Armi comes into the room, Pepe growls at him. To tell you the truth, I think Armi is a little afraid, which is silly because Pepe wouldn't hurt a fly."

"I'm sure they'll become the best of friends. Could I have a coffee, please, Mrs V? I need something to get me going this morning."

"Coming right up. You haven't forgotten that you have an appointment this morning at ten, have you?"

"Of course not." Totally. "What was the name again?"

"It's a Ms Arnold. I have to say, she was remarkably well spoken. It's nice to see we're attracting a better class of clientele at last."

"You're beginning to sound like a snob, Mrs V."

"Not at all. I would just prefer that the riff-raff kept their distance."

Wow!

"Maybe I should put up a sign outside saying no riff-raff allowed."

"That's a good idea. Incidentally, I've put a newspaper on your desk, Jill. There's an article on the front page that I thought you'd like to read."

"Right, thanks."

There was a tent pitched on the floor in the middle of my office.

I walked over and unzipped the flap to find Winky sitting inside.

"This may be a silly question, Winky, but why are you sitting in a tent in my office?"

"It's not big enough for me to stand up in."

"That doesn't make any sense. You're about the same height whether you're sitting or standing — hang on, that's not the point. I meant why is there a tent pitched in my office?"

"It's a dry run."

"For what?"

"Before I venture out into the wild. I wanted to make sure I could remember how to put it up."

"You're going camping?" I laughed.

"Why not?"

"You're much too nesh for the outdoor life."

"Rubbish. I am at one with nature."

"Where exactly are you going?"

"I haven't decided yet. Wherever my compass takes me. You should join me. You look like you could do with some fresh air."

"No, thanks."

"Being stuck in this office all day isn't good for you."

"What is it with everyone, trying to sort out my health? Mrs V just asked me to meditate with her."

"The great outdoors would do you the world of good. You could collect wood, build fires, and cook our food."

"And what would you be doing while I was doing all

that?"

"Keeping a watch out for wild animals."

"In case an elephant should happen to stumble across our tent, I suppose?"

"Exactly."

"Tempting as that sounds, I think I'll give it a miss."

The newspaper article that Mrs V had highlighted related to Phil Black, a client who had hired me to clear his name. Phil had been convicted of the murder of his younger brother and had served several years behind bars. I'd discovered that the young boy was still alive and living with his stepfather, who had allowed Phil to take the blame for a non-existent murder. According to the article, the stepfather was now serving time for the kidnap of his son, and Phil's conviction had been quashed. By far the most pleasing aspect of the article was the news that Phil had been reunited, not only with his younger brother, but also with his estranged mother. That was a testament to his character because Phil's mother had totally disowned him, believing him guilty of his younger brother's murder. She'd refused to visit him in prison, and wanted nothing to do with him after his release. No one would have blamed Phil if he'd held a grudge, but instead, he'd forgiven his mother, and the three of them were happily reunited.

It brought a tear to my eye.

***

Just before ten o'clock, Mrs V came through to my office and pushed the door closed behind her.

"Is Ms Arnold here?" I said.

"Yes, but I fear I may have misjudged her."

"Oh?"

"I'm not sure we should be dealing with the likes of her."

"What do you mean?"

Mrs V walked over to my desk, and said in a hushed voice, "I fear she's one of those Bell's Angels."

"Bells? Do you mean Hell's Angels?"

"Yes. Shall I tell her there's been a mistake and you're too busy to see her?"

"Definitely not. Send her in."

"Are you sure?"

"Positive."

"Very well, but the sooner you get that *no riff-raff* sign made, the better."

The young woman was indeed dressed from head to toe in biker leathers, and she had a crash helmet under one arm. Her black hair was wild, and there was a small tattoo of a dragon on her neck.

"Jill Maxwell?" Her voice didn't match her appearance at all. She spoke as though she had a plum in her mouth.

"That's me."

"I'm very pleased to make your acquaintance." She strode across the room and offered her hand. "I'm Alison. Alison Arnold."

"Do have a seat, Alison."

She put her helmet on the floor. "I think I may have scared your receptionist."

"You could be right. Mrs V was expecting a debutante."

"Been there, done that. It wasn't for me."

"How can I help you, Alison?"

"I'm a member of the Wash-on-Wheels Motorcycle Club. You may have seen us around the city?" She stood up and turned around. On the back of her jacket was a picture of a dragon sitting astride a motorbike. Underneath it were the words Wash-on-Wheels M.C.

"Impressive artwork."

"The club is over thirty years old, and although it has a bad reputation amongst some of the residents of Washbridge, its members actually do a lot of work for children's charities."

"I see. And what brings you here today?"

"One of our members, Killer Cole, has been—"

"Sorry to interrupt, but did you just call him Killer?"

"That's just his nickname. His real name was Cecil."

"*Was?*"

"He died a few weeks ago. He was found, lying in a pool of blood, on the floor of the club's workshop."

"What happened?"

"According to the police, he tripped, fell backwards, and hit his head on the workbench."

"That sounds like an accident."

"We don't believe that for one minute. We're sure this is the work of a rival club from West Chipping. They're known as the Loose Chippings."

"Do you have any proof they're in some way responsible?"

"No, but there's a lot of animosity between the two clubs."

"It's not much to go on."

"I realise that, but I'm willing to pay whatever it costs for you to prove they did it. Your receptionist was right in as much as I do come from a wealthy family, and I inherited a small fortune."

"I see." This woman was beginning to grow on me.

"Will you take the case?"

"I'll be happy to, but I'm going to need a lot more information."

"Of course. Why don't you come and see me at the club's HQ, and we can talk there?"

"Sounds good."

She made to leave, but then turned back. "Just one question, Jill."

"Sure."

"Why do you have a tent in the middle of your office?"

"The tent? I—err—I'm going camping this weekend."

Just then, Winky poked his head out of the tent.

"There's a cat in there." No doubt Alison was beginning to wonder if she'd made the right decision in hiring me.

"That's Winky."

"So-called on account of his one eye, I assume?"

"Correct."

"I love cats. I have three of them: Bill, Ben and little—"

"Weed?"

"Bob. I named him after my uncle Robert."

Chapter 3

"That tent has to go, Winky," I said, once Alison had left. "I could have lost that case because of you."

"Rubbish. She's clearly a cat lover. You should dress in leather. It would suit you."

"I don't think so."

"Sorry, I forgot that you prefer to buy your clothes from The House of Boring."

"There's nothing boring about my clothes."

"If you say so." He yawned. "I could be your personal shopper and give you a whole new look."

"Not a chance. I'm going out now. Make sure that tent has gone by tomorrow morning."

"I hope you told that young woman that you couldn't take her case," Mrs V said.

"I certainly did not. I need all the work I can get at the moment."

"Are you sure you know what you're getting into?"

"Don't worry, Mrs V, I know what I'm doing."

"Hmm?"

Another resounding vote of confidence.

Over the weekend, when I'd spoken to Kathy, she'd mentioned a new shop that had opened on the high street. According to her, the small ice cream parlour sold the best ice cream she'd ever tasted. High praise indeed and definitely worth checking out.

"Welcome to Scream High." The preppy young woman practically bounced to the counter. "My name is Cherry Pop. What can I get for you?"

"I bet you hate that, don't you?"

"What?"

"That they make you use that stupid name."

"It's my real name."

"Yeah, sure."

"It really is." She began to well up. "People are always making fun of it. It isn't fair."

Now I felt terrible. "I was just kidding. It's a lovely name. I really am sorry. Please don't cry."

"Gotcha!" She laughed.

"It's not your real name?"

"Of course not. My name's Toyah Smith."

"You had me going there for a minute. My sister tells me you have the best ice cream in Washbridge."

"Your sister is right. We have over fifty flavours to choose from." She pointed to the glass fronted cabinet.

"What do you recommend?"

"That depends on which size you want. Single, double, quad or maxout."

"How many flavours would I get with a maxout?"

"As many as the cone can hold. Usually nine or ten."

"That's a lot of ice cream."

I know what you lot are thinking. Greedy Jill is going to go for the maxout. Shame on you.

"I'll try the quad, please."

"What flavours would you like?"

"Why don't you choose for me?"

"Sure."

And she did. Who would have thought that rhubarb delight, strawberry shock, mango mash and chocolate cherry would work together? But they did. It was absolutely delicious.

I was walking back up the high street, licking my ice cream when someone said, "Jill? It is you, isn't it?"

The woman standing in front of me clearly knew me, but I didn't have the first clue who she was.

"Hi?"

"This takes me back. You always did like your ice cream. How long has it been?"

"I—err—a long time."

"It must be almost twenty years."

"I guess so." *Twenty years*? That must mean she was someone I was at school with.

"I wish I could stay and chat, Jill, but I have an eye test in five minutes. We must get together and catch up."

"Absolutely."

"Can I take your number?"

"Err, I guess so."

We exchanged numbers and off she went, but I was still no wiser who she was.

***

After checking that she was free, I magicked myself over to Aunt Lucy's house.

"Come in, Jill. I'm just sorting out my cork drawer. Could you pop the kettle on, and I'll be with you in a couple of minutes?"

"Sure."

Cork drawer?

By the time I'd poured out the tea, Aunt Lucy had joined me in the kitchen.

"I'm ready for this." She took a sip. "I've been at that for over an hour."

"Did you say your *cork* drawer?"

"Yes. Surely I've told you about my collection of corks?"

"No. I'm pretty sure I would have remembered."

"I've collected them ever since I was a little girl. Would you like to see them?"

"Maybe another day. I need to get started on something Grandma asked me to look into."

"The lido?"

"Yeah. I didn't even realise there was one here in Candlefield."

"The twins used to love going there when they were kids. It's years since I was last there."

There was a thudding on the stairs and moments later, Barry burst into the kitchen.

"Jill!" He began to run around the table, his tail wagging ten to the dozen. "I haven't seen you for ages."

"It hasn't been all that long, Barry," I said. "Calm down. You're going to break something."

"Can we go for a walk, Jill? Please! I love to go for a walk."

"I'm sorry, but I'm working at the moment."

"I have an idea," Aunt Lucy said. "We could kill two birds with one stone."

"That's not a very nice thing to do." Barry frowned. "You mustn't kill little birds."

"That's not what I meant."

"You said you were going to kill two birds with one stone."

"No, it's just a—err—I promise I'm not going to hurt any birds." Aunt Lucy turned to me. "I was thinking we could take Barry for a walk to the lido."

"How far is it from here?"

"Not far. I really fancy a swim. That's if you don't mind watching Barry while I take a quick dip?"

"They won't let me in there with him, will they?"

"I think so. They always used to allow dogs in the viewing area around the pool."

"Okay, why not? After you've had your swim, you can bring Barry home, and I'll do some sniffing around, to see what I can find out from the staff."

After we'd finished our tea, the three of us set off. I had Barry by the lead, and he was pulling so hard I could barely keep a hold of him.

"Barry, settle down, will you?"

"I want to see the lido."

"You don't even know what it is."

"I know, but it sounds fun."

"What exactly did Grandma ask you to do, Jill?" Aunt Lucy said.

"She reckons they're planning to close down the lido."

"Why?"

"No one seems to know. Grandma suspects they may try and build houses on there."

"That would be a terrible loss. By the way, the twins told me that Martin is back."

"He is."

"You must tell him to come and see me."

"I will, but I'm not sure if he'll be able to make it because he's only ever over here for a few minutes at a time."

"Where has he been, and what's he been up to all this time?"

"Keeping an eye on Braxmore."

"What's that evil monster up to now?"

"I have no idea."

There was no way I was going to tell her about the threat hanging over Florence because there was no point in her worrying too.

The lido was next door to Candle Park. I'd never noticed it before because I'd always used the gate at the opposite end of the park.

"Is it all right if we bring the dog in?" I asked the man on the turnstile.

"Yes, but you must keep him on the lead and make sure he doesn't go anywhere near the pool. Will you both be swimming today?"

"Only me," Aunt Lucy said. "Jill's just here to watch."

"It's four pounds for swimmers and two pounds-fifty for those watching."

We paid our money and made our way inside.

"I'll go and get changed, Jill, if you're okay with Barry."

"Sure."

Aunt Lucy headed for the changing rooms, which were on the opposite side of the pool, and I found a sun lounger as far from the pool as possible.

"I want to go in the water." Barry tugged on the lead.

"You can't. You heard what the man said: Dogs aren't allowed in the pool."

"Not fair."

"Those are the rules, I'm afraid. Here, eat these." I gave him a few Barkies, which I'd put in my pocket, just in case. They seemed to take his mind off the pool.

Aunt Lucy appeared a few minutes later, wearing a multicoloured swimsuit.

"Wow, Aunt Lucy, I like your costume."

"Thanks. I bought it last year while we were on holiday. I'd better go and test the water."

She walked over to the pool's edge, dipped in her toe, and then dived in.

"It's lovely, Jill. You really should give it a try."

"Maybe another day." No chance.

Aunt Lucy was a much stronger swimmer than I'd expected. She was soon ploughing up and down the pool, length after length, without once stopping to rest. There was no way I could have managed that.

Fortunately, Barry had found himself a friend. The woman on the next sun lounger had a little poodle, and the two of them seemed to have hit it off. It was just as well because I didn't want to have to pull him out of the swimming pool.

After half-an-hour or so, Aunt Lucy climbed out, and went to the changing rooms to get dressed.

"I feel so much better for that," she said.

"I was very impressed with your technique. And your stamina."

"Did I ever tell you that I used to swim for Candlefield in my youth?"

"No, I had no idea."

"I won several medals for my backcrawl. I really should start to come here regularly. That's assuming they don't close the place down."

"Would you be okay to take Barry now? I'm going to talk to the staff, to see what I can find out."

"Of course. Come on, Barry, it's time to go home."

He wasn't thrilled at having to say goodbye to his new friend, but he soon succumbed to the offer of a few more

Barkies. When the two of them had left, I went over to have a word with the lifeguard who was seated at the deep end of the pool.

"Excuse me."

"Yes?" The young wizard had ginger hair and a tiny nose.

"You don't happen to know who owns the lido, do you?"

"No, sorry. The manager might, though."

"What's his name?"

"Duggan. Doug Duggan."

"And where would I find him?"

"His office is over there, behind the changing rooms, but I don't think he's in today. If not, you could try his assistant, Debbie Debbins. She normally uses Dougie's office when he's not here."

"Okay, thanks."

I walked around the pool, past the changing rooms, and came to a small office with the word Manager on the door.

When I knocked, a female voice shouted from inside, "Come in!"

The young witch behind the desk was wearing a tracksuit top over a swimming costume.

"Debbie Debbins?"

"That's me."

"I was actually hoping to talk to Doug Duggan, but I understand he's not at work today."

"That's right. It's his day off. Can I help?"

"I'm trying to find out the name of the owner of the lido."

"I'm afraid I don't know."

"Surely you must know who pays your wages?"

"I can tell you the company name that appears on the wage slip if that helps."

"That would be a start."

"It's Reptile Holdings. We used to get paid by a company called Candlefield Lido, but then last month it changed."

"Do you know anything about Reptile Holdings? Anything at all?"

"No, sorry. When this place belonged to Candlefield Lido, the old guy who owned it used to pop in about once a month, but I haven't seen him since the change of ownership."

"Okay, thanks. Just one more question: I've heard rumours that the lido might be closing down. Is that true?"

"I honestly don't know. We've heard the same rumour, but there hasn't been an official announcement either way. It's all a bit disconcerting because this is my livelihood."

"If I leave you my number, would you ask Doug to give me a call?"

"Sure."

I handed her my card.

"Jill Maxwell! I thought it was you. I'm a big fan."

"Thanks."

"I can't wait to see Doug tomorrow. He'll be green with envy when I tell him you were here."

She really was a big fan because she seemed to know about every tournament that I'd ever taken part in, and she insisted on recounting them all in great detail. There was a danger that I would never get away, so I started to walk slowly backwards out of the office, towards the pool. Unfortunately, that didn't stop Debbie who followed me outside.

"I couldn't believe that time in the Levels tournament when — look out, Jill!"

The next thing I knew, I had tumbled backwards over something furry, and landed in the pool. When I surfaced, I found Barry and Aunt Lucy staring down at me.

"I'm really sorry, Jill," Aunt Lucy said. "He got away from me."

"You look funny." Barry chuckled when I climbed out of the pool, soaking wet.

"You'd better come back with me." Aunt Lucy had a straight face, but I was pretty sure that she was laughing inside. "I still have some of the twins' clothes, you can change into those."

***

After an awful day, I was looking forward to a nice, quiet evening, but it wasn't to be.

"No, Mummy!" Florence said. "You did it wrong again."

"No, I didn't. I put my left foot in, just like you said."

"It should have been your right foot that time. It's left foot, then right foot, then right foot again."

"Oh, okay."

The two of us were in the bedroom, practising the incredibly complicated dance routine that Florence had devised. We'd been at it for almost an hour, and I still hadn't mastered it.

"We'll have to start again." Florence was clearly exasperated by my feeble attempts to follow the steps.

"Okay, but it'll soon be bedtime."

"We have to get it right, Mummy, or we won't win the competition."

Just then, I heard a snorting sound coming from behind the door, which was partially open. In the full-length mirror mounted on the wall, I spotted Jack's reflection. I'd given him strict instructions not to come upstairs while we were practising, but he was crouching behind the door.

"I can see you, Jack."

He stepped into the room. "Sorry, I was just on my way to the loo."

"No, you weren't. You were spying on us. How long have you been there?"

"Long enough to realise you don't know your left foot from your right."

"I'd like to see you do any better."

"How's it going, Florence?" he said.

"Mummy is rubbish. We've practised lots and lots, but she gets it wrong every time. She puts her left foot in when she should put it out. And her right foot out when it should be in. And then she always forgets to shake it all about."

"I'm doing my best, Florence," I said in my defence. "It's only Monday. We've got lots of time until the competition."

"It looks like you're going to need it." Jack grinned.

"I think you should go downstairs," I snapped.

"Can't I stay and watch?"

"Goodbye, Jack."

"I might be able to give you a few tips."

"Goodbye, Jack."

I could hear him laughing all the way down the stairs.

I'd get my own back on him. You see if I don't.

"Are you ready to try again, Mummy?" Florence said.

"As ready as I'll ever be."

The only positive thing to come out of the dancing was that by the time we'd finished, Florence was exhausted. As soon as her head hit the pillow, she was fast asleep.

When I came downstairs, Jack was grinning like a Cheshire cat.

"What's tickling you? As if I didn't know."

"I was just thinking that you should definitely get your entry in for Strictly."

Chapter 4

I'd promised to call in at Kathy's house on my way to the office, so I decided to skip breakfast.

"We have to practise our dance again tonight, Mummy," Florence said, as I kissed her goodbye.

"I shall look forward to it all day."

"Don't forget to swot up on which is your left foot, and which is your right," Jack said, through a mouthful of muesli.

"You'll get them both up your backside if you're not careful." I grabbed my bag. "I'll see you both tonight."

Kathy had decided to give herself the day off. It seemed that sister of mine never did any work these days. She just stayed at home and calculated all her profits.

Jealous? Me? Of course I was.

As I walked up the driveway, Kathy tapped her watch. "I thought you said you'd be here for eight o'clock."

"Relax, it's only ten past. It's not like you have to be anywhere."

"I just got a cryptic text from Jack. He said I should remind you to shake it all about. What does that mean?"

"Nothing. He thinks he's funny."

"Come in. I thought we could have our tea in the orangery."

"If you say so." While Kathy made the drinks, I went through to the *conservatory* and took a seat by the window. Outside in the garden, the two gnomes spotted me, and gave me a little wave. Kathy walked in just as I was waving back to them.

"What is it with you and those gnomes? The last time

you were here, I caught you talking to them. Now, you're waving to them."

"Don't be ridiculous. I wasn't waving to them. I was—err—I was just swatting a fly. I hope you're rotating the gnomes, like you promised you would."

"I'm not sure why you would care, but yes, Pete does it once a week." She handed me my tea.

"There's sugar in this."

"Sorry, I forgot that you'd stopped taking it. Do you want me to make you another one?"

"No, it's all right. I'll soldier on."

"I have custard creams." She held out a plate full of them. And much to my relief, they had not been mixed with other, inferior biscuits.

"Thanks, Kathy." I took a bite. "Ugh, this is soft."

"No, it's not."

"I'm telling you, it's soft. Where did you get these from?"

"I picked up a box of them from the local cash & carry. They were half the normal price."

"I'm not surprised. Have you checked the sell-by date?"

"No one takes any notice of those. Eat it and stop moaning."

Just then, I heard a clomping sound out in the hallway, and then Lizzy came in on crutches; her left leg was in a cast.

"Lizzie? What happened to you?"

"Hi, Auntie Jill. I broke it last Friday, playing netball."

I turned to Kathy. "How come you didn't tell me?"

"She's fine. Aren't you, Lizzie?"

"Yeah, but the doctor says it'll be a few weeks before the pot comes off."

Kathy's phone rang. "Sorry, I need to take this. It's the manager of one of the shops."

She disappeared out of the conservatory.

"Auntie Jill, while Mum's not here, could I have a word?"

"Sure. What is it?"

She hobbled a little closer, and said in a hushed voice, "Do you remember when I was little, and I used to see ghosts?"

"Your mum told me that you'd come through that phase."

"It wasn't a *phase!*" Lizzie said, clearly much louder than she'd intended. "I still see them. I've just stopped talking about it. Mum and Dad never believed me, and Mikey made fun of me."

"I'm sorry. I had no idea."

"I was wondering if I might be able to talk to that friend of yours again. The one who's into ghosts."

"You mean Mad?"

"Yeah. Would you ask her if she'll talk to me sometime?"

"What about your Mum? I'm not sure she'd approve."

"I'm not going to tell her." Lizzie was close to tears. "You won't, will you?"

"I—err—"

"Please, Auntie Jill."

"Okay. I'll have a word with Mad and see what she says."

"Thanks."

Kathy walked back into the room. "What have you two been talking about?"

"Lizzie was just telling me how she broke her leg."

"I'm going up to my room now, Mum." Lizzie hobbled out of the conservatory.

"Hey, Jill, you'll never guess what Pete and I are thinking of buying." Kathy drank the rest of her tea.

"Please tell me it isn't more gnomes."

"Definitely not, although Pete would buy another twenty of them if I let him. I told him I don't mind having a few more garden ornaments, as long as they're not gnomes."

"If it isn't gnomes, what is it that you're going to buy?"

"A holiday home."

"What! You must be raking it in if you can afford to do that."

"We're doing okay."

"Whereabouts?"

"We thought the south of France, maybe."

"I'm clearly in the wrong line of business."

"You, Jack and Florence will be able to go there too."

"How much will you charge us?"

"Nothing, of course. What do you think I am? By the way, you'll never guess who I bumped into in town at the weekend."

"It wasn't a squirrel selling donuts, was it?"

"I really do worry about you sometimes, Jill. It was Rita Reed."

"You say that name as though I should know who she is."

"Of course you do. She lived across the road from us when we were kids. You must remember RiRi."

"RiRi! Yeah, I remember her now. Come to think of it, I bumped into someone on the high street yesterday. She obviously knew me, but I had no idea who she was. I reckon that must have been RiRi. We exchanged phone numbers."

"You gave your phone number to someone you didn't recognise?"

"I was embarrassed to ask her who she was. Wasn't she the one with the metal detector?"

"Yeah, she was always up in the meadows with that thing. It looks like it paid off for her, though."

"How do you mean?"

"She was telling me that she's a coin collector now. She's just opened a small shop in town."

"Sounds exciting." I yawned.

"Talking of rare coins, did you hear about that boy scout who found that rare ten-pence?"

"I heard something about it."

"It sounds like someone must have given it to him when they bought his cookies. I bet they're kicking themselves. Still, it's gone to a good cause. I love feelgood stories like that, don't you?"

"I can't get enough of them."

***

When I arrived at the office, I was confronted with a sight I never thought I'd see. Mrs V was sitting, cross-legged, on the desk, but that's not what took me by surprise. Seated next to her, was Winky. He too appeared to be meditating, and was making a strange noise, which I assumed was the feline equivalent of a hum. Neither of them had noticed me, so I crept on by to my office.

There were four pigeons on the window ledge: Bobby had one wing around Briana, and Bertie was cuddled up to Bianca.

"Hi, guys. How's it hanging?"

"Life's really good, thanks to you, Jill," Bobby said.

"We wanted to thank you for reuniting us," Bertie chirped.

"It was my pleasure. It's nice to see you two boys looking so happy."

"The thing is, Jill," Bobby said. "We have some bad news."

"What now?"

"I'm afraid Bertie and I will be moving out."

"Where are you going?"

"We're going to move in with Briana and Bianca on their ledge. I hope you don't mind."

"I'll miss our little conversations, obviously, but I'm really pleased that the four of you have found true love."

"If there's ever anything we can do for you, Jill," Bertie said. "You only have to whistle."

"Thanks, I'll keep that in mind."

Thirty minutes later, the door opened and Raymond Double, AKA Rock, walked in. I really wasn't in the mood for a confrontation, but if he'd come to argue the toss about paying my bill, he was going to get short shrift. I'd put in the hours and uncovered the person who had been sabotaging his lookalikes business. It wasn't my fault if he was too stubborn (or stupid) to accept my findings.

As he approached my desk, he smiled, and produced a bunch of flowers from behind his back.

"I hope you'll accept these by way of an apology."

"Thanks. They're lovely."

"I'm sorry I was so dismissive of your findings. It's just

that I've known Wayne for such a long time, and I didn't want to believe he'd do something so despicable."

"I assume something has happened to change your mind?"

"After I'd had time to reflect on what you'd said, I began to wonder if I was giving him too much benefit of the doubt, so I set up a little trap."

"What kind of trap?"

"I waited until I was sure he and I were alone, then I pretended to take a booking for a Ruby Red lookalike. Normally, I enter all bookings into the register, but I deliberately didn't do that this time. That way, I knew the only two people who knew about it were me and Wayne. The booking was meant to be for The Rhubarb Club."

"The *what* club?"

"Rhubarb. It's a small jazz club here in town. Haven't you heard of it?"

"No, but then jazz isn't really my thing."

"The owner is a friend of mine. He'd agreed that I could use his club's name, and he promised to let me know if anyone contacted him about his 'booking'. Sure enough, the next day, some guy turns up and offers to provide a Ruby Red lookalike for half the price that I was charging. That was all the proof I needed because the only person who could have tipped him off was Wayne."

"What do you intend to do about it, Rock?"

"I've already done it. I've kicked Wayne off my books.'"

"Do you plan on telling the police?"

"No, I still can't bring myself to do that. He's just lost his livelihood. I don't want to pile on the agony by taking him to court as well."

"That's very generous of you. A lot of people would."

"I guess I'm just a big softie. Anyway, like I said, I'm sorry I didn't believe you."

"Consider it forgotten."

"Thanks." He turned to leave, but then hesitated. "I have to ask, Jill. Why is your receptionist sitting on the desk, humming, with a cat by her side?"

"She left her dog at home."

***

I was a little nervous about my visit to the HQ of Wash-on-Wheels Motorcycle Club. I'd followed Alison's directions to a crumbling building, on a quiet back street near to the old gas works. From the outside, there was nothing to identify the building, and I wasn't even sure I was at the right place. The door was locked, so I pressed the red button next to it and waited. A minute later, the door sprang open and a tall guy, clad in biker gear, stepped out. He had long greasy hair, and a cigarette stub wedged behind his ear.

After looking me up and down, he said, "Hello, sweetcheeks. If you're looking for the beauty spa, it's on the next street."

"Actually, I'm looking for Wash-on-Wheels."

"You sure about that?"

"Tony, move out of the way." Alison stepped out of the door. "Sorry about him, Jill."

"Who is she, anyway?" Tony took the cigarette stub from behind his ear, popped it into his mouth and lit it.

"Jill's here to see Chains," Alison said.

"No one tells me anything." He stepped aside.

"Come in, Jill." She led the way inside.

I'd expected the room to smell like motor oil and sweaty armpits, but surprisingly it had the aroma of potpourri. At the far end of the room, a couple of men were playing pool. In one corner, a game of cards was in progress. The others, mainly men but a few women, had all fallen silent and were staring at me.

Alison led the way to a door behind the pool table.

"I'm going to introduce you to Chains."

"I'll go out on a limb and guess that's not his real name."

"You'd be right, but it's what everyone calls him. He's the club leader."

"Okay."

There were three people inside the small room. I assumed the man seated in the centre was the aforementioned Chains because his leather jacket was covered in them. In his mid-forties, his hands were stained with nicotine. Seated to one side of him was a woman, with piercings in her nose and lip, whose hair was a strange shade of orange. On the other side of him was a younger guy who could have been a model if he hadn't been so ugly.

The big guy broke the silence. "I'm Chains. You must be Jill?"

"Yeah, Jill Maxwell."

"This is Fi. She's my lady. And this is Sid, my second in command. Ali reckons you might be able to find out who murdered Killer."

"I'll do my best."

"I'll be straight with you, Jill, I wasn't keen on the idea of bringing you in. We normally prefer to fight our own battles."

"We've talked about this, Chains," Alison said. "If we have any more trouble with the cops, they'll close this place down for sure."

"Keep your hair on, Ali, I've agreed to talk to her, haven't I?" He turned back to me. "Grab a seat, Jill, and tell me what you need to know."

"Alison told me that you believe your colleague was murdered?"

"Colleague?" He grinned. "That's a bit posh for the likes of us. Killer was a mate. But yeah, we're sure he was murdered, and if the police had a brain cell between them, they'd have realised that."

"And you think the murderer might be a member of the rival club from West Chipping."

"I'd bet my old lady's life on it." Fi snarled at him. "Only kidding, doll." He grabbed her and the two of them began to explore each other's tonsils with their tongues.

Gross!

"Those Loose Chippings guys are all nutters," Sid said.

"I take it there's bad feeling between the two clubs, then?"

"You could say that." Chains had come up for air. "In the good old days, we'd have gone around there to sort this out ourselves, but we can't do that nowadays with all the surveillance equipment the cops have at their disposal. There's CCTV everywhere, and they can trace your phones."

"Is there any particular reason you believe Loose Chippings wanted Killer dead?"

"Yeah, because of the competition."

"Sorry? What *competition*?"

"Didn't Ali tell you?"

"I thought I'd let you do it," Alison said.

"There's an annual competition held between the local motorcycle clubs. It's been running for almost twenty years."

"A race, you mean?"

"No. It's a competition to make the best custom bike; all the big clubs take part. We've won it for the last two years and we were all set to win it again until what happened with Killer."

"I take it he was working on your club's bike?"

"Yeah, the guy was a genius. I reckon the Loose Chippings guys decided to take him out, so they'd have a shot at the cup."

"But to kill him? That's a bit extreme, isn't it?"

"Like I said, those guys are crazy, particularly that new leader of theirs. His name is Ray Rainer, but everyone calls him Slugger. The guy is insane. It wouldn't surprise me if he was the one who did it."

"I plan on taking a close look at the Loose Chippings guys, but I'll also need to speak to whoever here was closest to Killer."

"That would be the three of us around this table."

"In that case, I'd like to take your phone numbers?"

"Why don't you just talk to us now?" Chains said.

"Because I'd like to speak to you individually, in private."

"Fair enough. Give Jill your numbers, guys."

"I assume if I want to speak to any of the other members, that'll be okay too?"

"Sure. If anyone gives you any hassle, come and talk to me. I'll sort them out."

Chapter 5

When I arrived at the office, Mrs V was back in her chair, knitting.

"Jill, were you here earlier?"

"Yes, but you were meditating at the time, and I have to say that I was a little surprised."

"Because I was meditating? I did tell you that I'd taken it up. In fact, you saw me doing it yesterday."

"No, I meant that I was surprised to see Winky sitting next to you on the desk."

"What?" She looked horrified. "Are you sure?"

"Absolutely. I assumed you knew he was there. He appeared to be meditating too."

"I had no idea. If I'd realised, I would've kicked him off the desk in double-quick time."

"Have there been any calls for me?"

"Just the one. Someone was asking if you were Jill Maxwell the quantum physicist. I told them I didn't think that was you. It's not, is it?"

"Err, no. I could never get along with physics at school. All those atoms and stuff left me cold."

Winky was lying on the sofa.

"Okay, out with it, Winky. What were you up to?"

He looked around. "Are you talking to me?"

"I don't see anyone else in here."

"I haven't done anything."

"I saw you on the desk next to Mrs V. What were you doing?"

"I would've thought that was obvious. I was meditating."

"Don't give me that nonsense."

"It's true. I happened to walk through the outer office, and saw the old bag lady on the desk, so I decided to join her. With all the stress I'm under, I thought it might help."

"Stress? You? You don't know the meaning of the word. You have the life of—"

I was interrupted by my phone ringing.

"Is that Jill?"

"Yes, Jill Maxwell speaking."

"It's Rita Reed."

"Hi there. I was actually over at Kathy's this morning, and she told me that she'd bumped into you too."

"I was just thinking that it would be nice if the three of us could get together for a girls' night out. We could talk about the old days and catch up on what we've all been up to since then. That's if you can make it."

"A girls' night out sounds good to me. When were you thinking?"

"One day next week? I'm free every night, so I can work around you two."

"Okay, I'll speak to Kathy and get back to you."

"Great. I'll wait to hear from you."

When I came off the call, Winky was rolling around in hysterics. "What's so funny?"

"You are. A *girls'* night out? You've not been a *girl* for at least a decade."

"You're no spring kitten yourself. Hey, Winky, you know lots of stuff about stuff."

"That's true."

"What do you know about rainbows?"

"I know that there are some really hot cats over at the Rainbow Club, which reminds me, I've not been there for ages. I reckon it's time I paid it a visit." And with that helpful contribution, he shot out of the window.

I had no idea what the Rainbow Club was, and I was probably better off not knowing.

I'd just started to go through some paperwork when I received another phone call.

"Jill, it's Ursula. I promised to call you about your daughter's visit."

"Is it still on?"

"Of course, I'm looking forward to meeting her. Does she still want to bring a friend?"

"Yes, please. If that's okay."

"That's fine."

"Her friend's name is Wendy. Just one thing, though. Wendy is a werewolf. Is that going to be a problem?"

"Not at all. As long as she doesn't shift while she's here."

"She won't, but please don't give her any jelly."

"Why not?"

"For some reason, jelly causes her to change into a werewolf."

"Right, I'd better make a note of that. No jelly. How does Sunday afternoon at two sound?"

"It sounds good."

"Great, I'll see you all then."

My phone was red hot today. I'd no sooner finished talking to Ursula than it rang again.

"Is that Jill Maxwell?" The woman's voice seemed familiar, but I couldn't place her.

"Speaking."

"It's Debbie Debbins. We met yesterday at the lido."

"Oh, yes. Did you manage to speak to the manager?"

"I spoke to Doug last night and told him that you'd been asking about the owners, and that you wanted him to call you."

"I haven't heard from him yet."

"That's why I'm calling. I'm afraid Doug's dead."

"What? How did that happen?"

"When I got to work this morning, I found him face down in the pool. I called the police, and they've cordoned the place off."

"Was it an accident?"

"I've no idea, but I thought I should let you know."

***

I was halfway home when the glove compartment popped open and both Henry and Henrietta appeared.

"Hello, you two."

"Have you got a minute, Jill?" Henrietta said.

"Sure."

"We've been talking a few things over, haven't we, Henry?"

"That's right." He nodded. "The thing is, Jill, now that Henrietta and I are an item, we don't feel there's enough room in this glove compartment for the two of us."

"I'm sorry, but I can't afford to buy a bigger car."

"We wouldn't expect you to do that. No, we were thinking that maybe we should move to a house."

"Hang on, I thought you two were *car* elves."

"We are, and we've always lived in cars, but we got to thinking: What's to stop us living somewhere other than a car? Who would know? It might take a little getting used to, but we'd definitely have more space."

"That sounds like a great idea. Are you going to move back to Candlefield?"

"No way." Henrietta jumped in. "We both prefer it here in the human world. I could never go back to living in Candlefield where there's no internet. We were actually wondering if we could move in with you?"

"Definitely not." I hadn't intended to be quite so blunt, and felt bad when I saw the disappointment on their faces. "Obviously, I'd love for you to move in with us, but Florence has—err—elfitis."

"What's that?"

"She's allergic to elves."

"I've never heard of it."

"I'm not surprised. It's a very rare condition."

"That's really disappointing." Henry sighed. "I don't suppose you know of anywhere else we could live, do you?"

"Surely, you could live anywhere. It's not like humans can see you, is it?"

"That's something else we've been discussing. It can feel very isolated only being visible to sups such as you. It's as though most of the population is ignoring us."

"That's why I suggested that you go back to Candlefield."

"That's not happening," Henrietta said. "I'd go crazy if I couldn't check my Facebook."

"I'm not sure what you're going to do, then."

"Henrietta came up with a backup plan in case we couldn't move in with you, didn't you, sugar? Why don't you tell Jill?"

"Okay, but you must promise not to tell the rogue retrievers."

"Err, okay."

"I managed to get hold of some Elf-2-Stone potion on the black market in Candlefield."

"What's that?"

"It will allow humans to see us."

"Whoa! Won't that freak them out?"

"No, that's the whole point. They'll just see us as stone figurines."

"As long as we remember not to talk," Henry chipped in.

"Hang on." I was still trying to get my head around this. "Are you telling me that you can turn yourselves into stone figurines?"

"Yes, as long as we keep taking the potion."

"Would I see you as a stone figurine too?"

"Yes, but we'll still be able to talk to you. What do you think, Jill?"

"This Elf-2-Stone stuff sounds like something you've just made up."

"Says the woman who reckons her daughter has elfitis."

Touché.

"If we can't stay at your house, Jill, do you have any idea where we could go?"

"Actually, I might know somewhere."

"Really?"

"Don't go getting your hopes up because it's a longshot."

"When will you know?"

"You're going to have to give me a few days."

"Thanks, Jill. You're the best."

So true.

As I approached the village, I noticed a new poster at the side of the road. It read:

Afternoon tea – Now available ONLY at Hotel First Time

Unbelievable! Did my grandmother have no scruples whatsoever? Of course she didn't.

I drove through the village and parked outside the hotel. As soon as the receptionist saw me, she picked up the phone. "Your grandmother?"

"Yes, please, and tell her it's urgent."

Much to my surprise, just a couple of minutes later, Grandma came hurrying down the stairs.

"I hope you have some news for me about the lido."

"Can we talk in your office, Grandma?"

"If we must. Come on, I have lots to do." As soon as we were in her office, she was on my case. "So, what's happening with the lido?"

"I've no idea. I've not found anything out yet."

"Why are you wasting my time, then?"

"I just saw your poster."

"It's good, isn't it? I have them all over the village."

"It's very distasteful."

'What do you mean, *distasteful*? I designed those posters myself."

"I don't mean the design of the poster. I mean the fact that you've put them up so soon after poor Miss Drinkwater was murdered."

"*Poor* Miss Drinkwater? You didn't even like her."

"That's beside the point. The woman was murdered."

"That's hardly my fault, is it? I didn't kill her."

"The least you could do is to show a little respect."

"*Respect*? There's no room for *respect* in business, Jill. It's dog eat dog, and the sooner you realise that, the better."

"I think you should take them down."

"There's more chance of me being struck by lightning in the next thirty seconds than of me taking those posters down."

The temptation to cast the 'lightning bolt' spell was oh so strong.

"I'm leaving."

"Hold on. What about the lido? What's happening?"

"I spoke to the assistant manager there yesterday."

"You should have talked to the manager, not his sidekick."

"I had planned to, but he was found dead in the swimming pool this morning."

"How did that happen?"

"I don't know. I've only just found out myself."

"That proves it. Something is definitely afoot."

"I know, and I intend to find out what."

"You'd better be quick about it."

I was on my way out of the hotel when someone called my name.

"Psst, Jill, over here." It was Mr Ivers. The very last person I wanted to see. "Quickly, Jill."

"I am rather busy."

"This is urgent." He practically dragged me into what appeared to be a small broom cupboard.

"What are we doing in here, Mr Ivers?"

"I needed to talk to you where no one can hear us. There's something very strange going on in this hotel."

"What do you mean?"

"I know this sounds crazy, but there are some very weird creatures in here."

"My grandmother can be a bit strange, I know."

"I don't mean your grandmother. I saw a vampire."

Oh bum!

"There are no such things as vampires." I laughed. "Someone must have been wearing fancy dress."

"I've seen other creatures too. I saw an elf-like thing and a fairy."

"You've clearly been overworking. Maybe the stress has got to you."

"I know what I saw, Jill."

"I've been all over this hotel, and I can promise you that there are no strange creatures in here. I really think you should take the rest of the day off."

"Your grandmother would kill me."

"Don't worry. I'll clear it with her. Go home and have a lie down."

"Okay. I haven't been sleeping very well lately."

As soon as he'd left, I headed back to Grandma's office.

"That was quick," she said. "Have you got news on the lido?"

"No, I haven't, but I do have disturbing news about Mr Ivers."

"Don't tell me he's gone and dropped dead. How am I supposed to keep this place ticking over if people will insist on dying?"

"He isn't dead, but he did just tell me that he's seen a vampire, an elf and a fairy in the hotel."

"He can't have. The potion wouldn't let him see them."

"Clearly the potion isn't working."

"What did you say to him?"

"I think I managed to convince him that he must have imagined it, and that he was overworked. I sent him home and told him to rest."

"You did what?"

"You can't run the risk of him being here until you sort that potion out."

"Okay. I'll sort it. There won't be any more problems."

"There had better not be. We can't have Mr Ivers telling the world that this hotel is full of paranormal creatures."

***

Jack and a very disgruntled Buddy greeted me at the door.

I glanced around. "Where's Florence?"

"Donna asked if she could go to their house after school, just for an hour or so. She should be back any minute now. Didn't I see you drive past a few minutes ago?"

"I've just been up to the hotel to have a few choice words with Grandma."

"What's she done now?"

"Have you seen those posters of hers all around the village?"

"You mean the ones about the afternoon tea?"

"Yes, that woman is despicable. Miss Drinkwater is still warm in her grave, and Grandma is already trying to drum up trade for afternoon tea."

"What did she say?"

"She ignored me as usual. She said there was no room for respect in business, and that it was a dog-eat-dog world."

Buddy yelped.

"Sorry, Buddy. I only meant that figuratively speaking."

Unimpressed, he turned tail and walked off into the kitchen.

"Oh dear. Looks like I've upset him too."

"You look exhausted, Jill."

"I am. I've had a lousy day, and I've just discovered that a potential witness in the lido case was found face-down in the swimming pool this morning. All I want to do tonight is kick off my shoes, have a nice glass of wine and some chocolates, and fall asleep in front of the TV."

The door flew open behind me, and Florence came running in. Donna and Wendy were behind her, standing in the doorway.

"Come in, you two."

"We won't if you don't mind, Jill," Donna said. "We need to get back for our dinner."

"Was Florence a good girl?"

"Of course. She always is. The two of them played really nicely."

I'm glad you came over because I have some good news for Wendy and Florence."

"What's that, Mummy?" Florence said.

"I've just found out that you can both go to see Ursula, Queen of the Unicorns, on Sunday afternoon." They both squealed with joy and began to jump around. "That's if it's okay with you, Donna?"

"Definitely. Wendy has talked about nothing else. Thanks for arranging this, Jill."

"No problem."

"There's just one thing. Will you warn the queen about—"

"The jelly? I already have."

"Thanks. Come on, Wendy, we'd better get going. Bye, Florence."

Florence waved them both off.

"Did you have a nice time at Wendy's, darling?"

"Yes, Mummy. We found three caterpillars in their back garden."

"That's great. Jack, how long will dinner be?"

"About fifteen minutes."

"Good because I'm starving."

"Don't forget, Mummy, we have to practise our dance again tonight."

"I don't suppose we could miss just one night, could we? Mummy's really tired."

"You promised, Mummy, because you were rubbish yesterday. If we don't keep practising, we won't win."

"Oh, okay then."

"Is it all right if I go and play upstairs?"

"Yes, off you go, darling."

So much for my relaxing evening in front of the TV.

Chapter 6

Jack looked up from his breakfast. "Why are you hobbling, Jill?"

"I twisted my foot when I was practising the dance with Florence."

"You never mentioned it last night."

"You know me. I'm not one to complain."

"Right." Jack practically spat out his muesli.

"It seems to have tightened up overnight."

"Let me take a look at it."

"There's nothing to see. It's internal."

"*Internal*? Right."

"I don't know why you're grinning. It's very painful. If it doesn't improve by Saturday, you might have to take my place in the competition."

"That's. Not. Happening."

"But what if I can't walk?"

"First, the competition is for *mothers* and daughters, so there's no way I can take part. And, second, there's nothing wrong with your foot."

"Just wait until you injure yourself. Don't expect any sympathy from me."

"I'm going to see a unicorn!" Florence came charging into the kitchen. "How many days is it now, Mummy?"

"It's Wednesday today, so how many days are there until Sunday?"

She put up her fingers and counted out the days. "Wednesday, Thursday, Friday, Saturday. Four! That's a really long time."

"It's not all that long, pumpkin," Jack said. "And you have the dance competition to look forward to as well, remember. Mummy was just saying how excited she is about it. How is she doing with the dance practice?"

"She put the wrong leg in twice again last night, didn't you, Mummy?"

"Hmm."

"Sit down, Jill." Jack patted the chair next to him. "Why don't you rest your leg while I get you some breakfast?"

"I can't. I have to call at Kathy's on my way into the office."

"Weren't you over there just yesterday?"

"Yes, but there's something I need to give her, and I want to sort out our girls' night out next week."

"*Girls*?"

"Don't you start." I gave him a peck on the cheek, and then bent down and gave Florence a kiss. "I'll see you both tonight."

I was almost out of the kitchen door when Jack shouted after me, "I'm glad to see your foot seems to be okay now."

Drat! Foiled again.

***

On my way to Kathy's house, I pulled into a lay-by, and opened the glove compartment.

"Henry, Henrietta, could I have a quick word, please?"

"Of course, Jill."

The two of them jumped onto the passenger seat next to me.

"I think I may have found somewhere for you to live."

"Really? That was jolly quick." Henry beamed. "Where?"

"My sister's house, but there are a couple of catches."

"Go on."

"You wouldn't actually be living in the house; you'd be in the garden."

"I'm not sure that will work," Henrietta said. "We're not used to living outside."

"Kathy has a summer house in the garden, so although you'd be outside during the daytime, you'd be able to use that at night and whenever Kathy and her family are out. It's a lovely garden."

"What do you think, Henrietta?" Henry said.

"I'm not sure. The thought of living outdoors scares me a little, but I do like the idea of having all that space. And the summer house sounds great. Maybe we should give it a try."

"I'm up for it if you are. Let's do it."

"You said there were two catches, Jill."

"My sister and her family are humans, so you'll have to take that potion of yours, ElfyStone."

"It's Elf-2-Stone." Henrietta corrected me.

"How long does it take to work?"

"Only a few seconds. When would we be able to move in?"

"If you're both sure about this, I'll take you there now."

"Gosh, this is all very sudden," Henrietta said.

"It'll be fine," Henry assured her. "Just think of all the space we're going to have after being cooped up in here."

"You're right. Let's do it."

I pulled up outside Kathy's house.

"Right, guys, I'm just going to have a quick word with my sister. I'll be back in a few minutes."

"Okay, Jill. We'll take the potion. It should have worked by the time you get back."

Kathy answered the door in her dressing gown.

"Don't tell me you're taking another day off," I said.

"No, but I don't have to be in the shop until ten. Anyway, I'm intrigued. You said in your call that you had something for me?"

"Possibly. You know yesterday when you said you'd like some more garden ornaments."

"I said Pete would."

"Right, well, I might have some for you."

"I hope it's not more gnomes."

"It isn't. I have a pair of garden elves."

"*Elves*? Aren't they the same thing as gnomes?"

"No. An elf is nothing like a gnome. Gnomes are big, ugly things like those in your garden. Elves are small and quite attractive."

"How much do you want for them?"

"Nothing."

"There has to be a catch."

"Why so suspicious? One of my clients popped into the office yesterday, to thank me for some work I'd done for him. He owns a garden centre and he asked if there was anything I'd like, so I got these for you."

"Why didn't you get something for your own garden?"

"With Florence and Buddy, there's a limit to what we can put in there. They're in the car. I'll just go and get them."

When I got back to the car, Henry and Henrietta had turned to stone.

"Are you two okay?"

"Yes, but it's not easy to talk like this," Henry mumbled.

"That's probably just as well."

Kathy studied them for a minute. "You're right. They're much more attractive than the gnomes. Why don't you go and put the kettle on while I put them in the garden?"

"Will do."

By the time Kathy came back in the house, the tea was ready, so we went through to the conservatory.

"Look, I've put them over there by the summer house."

"Good idea. That's exactly where I would have put them. By the way, I had a phone call from RiRi yesterday. She suggested that the three of us have a night out next week."

"Great idea. I'd definitely be up for that. It's ages since we went out on the town."

"What days can you do?"

"Any, except for Monday."

"Shall we make it the middle of the week? Wednesday?"

"That works for me."

"Okay, I'll give RiRi a call later. Once I know the details, I'll get back to you."

As I was about to drive away, I spotted Lizzie in the upstairs window, which reminded me that I needed to have a word with Mad.

***

In Washbridge, I parked in my usual spot, but instead of going straight to the office, I took a walk down to Vinyl Alley. The place was buzzing. Brad was busy behind the counter, serving a customer, but there was no sign of Mad. I waited to one side until Brad had finished, then I managed to catch his eye.

"Hi, Jill. Sorry, I didn't see you there."

"Business seems to be good."

"It's suddenly gone crazy. If it carries on like this, I might have to set on an assistant. You don't know anyone who's looking for a job, do you?"

"No, but I'll keep my ear to the ground and let you know if I hear of anyone. I was hoping to grab a quick word with Mad. Is she around?"

"She had some paperwork to do, so she's gone down to Coffee Animal. Why don't you pop down there?"

"I'll do that. Thanks, Brad. See you later."

I'd just arrived at Coffee Animal when Mad stepped out of the door.

"Brad said I'd find you here. Are you on your way back already?"

"No, I only got here a couple of minutes ago, but I don't plan on staying."

"Why, what's wrong?"

"Guess what the animal of the day is."

"Don't tell me it's snakes again."

"No, even worse than that. They're handing out skunks! It stinks in there. The owners must be out of their tiny minds."

"We could go to my office and get a drink there if you like."

"I've got a better idea. Have you seen that new coffee shop at the other end of the high street?"

"I can't say I have."

"It's only been open for a couple of days. It's called Coffee Rock. Do you want to give it a try?"

"Sure, why not?"

Coffee Rock was only half the size of Coffee Animal. Even from the outside, it was clear that the theme was fifties rock and roll. The interior resembled an American diner with a classic jukebox in one corner of the room. The walls were covered with framed photos of stars from that decade.

"Why don't you grab a table, Mad? I'll get the drinks. What do you want?"

"I'd love a green tea, please."

"Are you serious? Since when did you drink green tea?"

"Brad got me into it. I love it now."

The young woman behind the counter had her hair in a ponytail, and was wearing a cardigan that appeared to be on back to front.

"Hi, welcome to Coffee Rock. Is this your first visit?"

"It is, yeah."

"In that case, you're entitled to buy one drink and get one free."

"Great. I'll have a caramel latte and a green tea, please."

"Anything to eat with those?"

"No, just the drinks, thanks."

"Rather you than me." I handed the green tea to Mad. "That stuff looks horrible."

"Your problem is that you have no sense of adventure. You should try new things."

"Why would I want to do that?"

"Because you might find something that you like?"

"That doesn't make any sense. I already know I like caramel latte, so why would I try another five drinks just to find out I don't like any of them?"

"You might discover that you *do* like one of them."

"But then I would still have had four drinks that I didn't like."

"You're a hopeless case." She sighed.

"I don't want to take up too much of your time. Brad told me you had some paperwork you needed to sort out."

"That's what I told him." She grinned. "I do have a couple of things I need to do, but mainly I just needed a break. The shop's been absolutely crazy this last couple of weeks."

"How about the ghost hunting? Is that still quiet?"

"It has been, but I had a call yesterday from my boss, warning that a big case is going to land on my desk any time now."

"Did he say what it was about?"

"No. I tried to push him, but he wouldn't give me any details. If that does happen, I'm going to be rushed off my feet. I think we're going to need an assistant at the shop. You don't know anyone who wants a job, do you?"

"Brad asked me the same thing. If I hear of anyone, I'll let you know. Anyway, I wanted to talk to you about Lizzie."

"Kathy's girl?"

"Yeah. Do you remember a few years ago when she said she could see ghosts?"

"Of course."

"She hasn't mentioned it for a while, and I assumed that was because she no longer saw them. When I asked Kathy about it, she said it was a phase and that Lizzie had come through it. But then yesterday, I was over at Kathy's, and Lizzie was there because she broke her leg playing netball."

"Oh gosh. Is she all right?"

"She's fine, but when Kathy was out of the room, Lizzie told me that she still sees ghosts. Apparently, she never stopped seeing them. She just stopped talking to Kathy and Peter about it because they didn't believe her. She wondered if she could talk to you about it sometime."

"Of course, I'd be happy to chat with her. When and where?"

"I don't know. Maybe I could give her your number and she can call you. Perhaps you can arrange something between the two of you. She's old enough now to come into town by herself."

"Sure, that's fine. Tell her to call me anytime."

***

"I'm going to kill him," Mrs V said, as soon as I walked into the office.

I was fairly sure I knew who she was talking about, but on the off chance that I was wrong, I thought I'd better ask for clarification.

"Going to kill who?"

"That cat of course. I knew he was up to something when you told me he'd been sitting on the desk next to me."

"What's he done?"

"He's stolen my yarn. That's what he's done."

"But I thought it was locked away in the linen basket?"

"It is."

"You're surely not suggesting that he somehow managed to pick the lock?" I laughed. "He's a cat."

"You may think it's funny, Jill, but that yarn cost me a lot of money, and some of it is very rare and will be impossible to replace."

"I'm sorry, Mrs V, I didn't mean to laugh. I'm just trying to understand what's happened."

"I'll show you." She got up and marched across the room to the linen basket. After entering the combination, she threw open the lid. "See?"

The basket was almost full to the top with yarn. "There still seems to be an awful lot of yarn in here."

"That's as maybe, but where has all the yellow gone?" She shuffled the wool around. "There's green. There's blue. Red, purple, and orange. Every colour under the sun except for yellow."

"Are you telling me you think Winky somehow managed to unlock the basket, and then steal all of your yellow yarn?"

"That's precisely what I'm telling you, and I won't stand for it. The time has come for you to get rid of that cat."

"Don't you think you're being a little harsh? We don't know for sure that he's responsible."

"Who else could have done it? I expect you to do something about this."

"Like what?"

"You can start by finding my yellow yarn."

"Right."

Winky was sitting on the window ledge, whistling, and enjoying the view.

"Hey, you, I want a word," I snapped.

He jumped onto my desk. "What can I do for you?"

"You can give Mrs V her yellow yarn back."

"Sorry, you've lost me."

"Don't come the innocent with me. It won't wash."

"I have no idea what you're talking about."

"I should have realised that something was going on yesterday when you were pretending to meditate. You sneaked into Mrs V's yarn basket while she had her eyes closed, didn't you?"

"No, I did not. I was just meditating. Nothing more. Nothing less."

"Cobblers!"

"You can't say that to me."

"I just did. Either you return the yellow yarn by end of business on Friday, or you can find yourself a new home."

"That's ridiculous! You can't just throw me out onto the street."

"Just watch me."

Chapter 7

It was time to turn my attention to the compass stones. To find the first one I would need to decipher the cryptic clue that Adam Rodenia, the bingo caller, had given to me. The clue simply read:

Find the north compass stone where the rainbows end

People had been searching for the end of a rainbow for years, but to the best of my knowledge, no one had ever found a pot of gold. But what if it was different in the paranormal world? Maybe it would be possible to track down the end of a rainbow in Candlefield. I needed to do some research, and what better place than Candlefield Library.

There was a young wizard behind the information desk, dressed in a long purple robe and a matching purple hat. It was unusual to see someone wearing such formal clothes except at tournaments.

"Good afternoon," I said.

"Sorry, I didn't see you there. I've been sorting out these books all day."

"That's okay. I was just admiring your robe and hat. Are you wearing them for a special occasion?"

"No, I wear these most days. I wish more people would do it. It's a tradition that sadly seems to have fallen by the wayside."

"Don't you find it a little uncomfortable, wearing that hat all day?"

"Not at all. I'm Alexander, by the way, but everyone calls me Xela."

"That's an unusual name."

"It's Alex backwards."

"Right. Of course."

"How can I help you?"

"I'm hoping to find a book on rainbows."

"Did you have a particular book in mind?"

"Not really."

"I'll see what I can find." He sat down and began to tap on the computer. "Rainbows. Let's see what we have. Okay, we appear to have three. The first one is called Raising Hamsters by Lucy Rainbow. Hmm, that's no good. What about this one? It's called How to Make the Perfect Rainbow."

"That's a strange title."

"This other one might be better. It's called Everything You Ever Wanted to Know About Rainbows."

"That sounds promising. Where can I find it?"

"It appears to be in the children's section."

"Oh? It might be worth a look, I guess. Where is the children's section?"

"Turn around, walk straight down the aisle behind you, to the very end. All the books are in alphabetical order."

"Thanks. I'll go and check it out."

It didn't take long to locate the book in question, but I knew before I took it from the shelf that it wouldn't be any use because it was a child's board book. Its contents were remarkably simple:

Rainbows are very colourful.

Rainbows appear in the sky when it rains while the sun is shining.

Rainbows are very pretty.

At the end of the rainbow, there is a pot of gold.

Despite the beautiful illustrations which accompanied

the text, this clearly wasn't what I was looking for, so I went back to the information desk where Xela was busy sorting out another pile of books.

"Was that book what you were looking for?" he asked.

"I'm afraid not. It's a young child's board book. What was the other title you mentioned?"

"How to Make the Perfect Rainbow."

It doesn't sound very promising, but I may as well take a look. Which section is that one in?"

He checked his screen. "Food and drink. Turn to your left, walk past the first three aisles, and then take the next one on your right. You can't miss it."

"Thanks."

Another bust. It turned out that the *full* title of the book was actually How to Make the Perfect Rainbow Sponge.

"No good?" Xela said.

"Not really. Are there any more books on rainbows at all?"

He checked his computer again. "The only other titles listed here all relate to rainbow fairies. Sorry."

***

After my visit to the library, I was feeling a little dispirited, and I needed something to cheer me up. What better than a blueberry muffin?

One of the assistants was behind the counter in Cuppy C, which was incredibly quiet. The twins were seated at a window table, poring over some papers. Whatever it was had them thoroughly engrossed because they hadn't even noticed me. Once I had my coffee and muffin, I went over to join them.

"Room for a little one?"

"For a little one, yeah, but I'm not sure there's room for you." Pearl grinned.

"You're so funny. Not." I grabbed a seat and took a look at their scribbled notes on the writing pad.

"Been swimming recently?" Amber said, and the two of them exploded into laughter.

"I take it you've heard about my little mishap?"

"It made our day," Pearl said through tears of laughter. "It's just a pity Mum didn't think to take a photo."

"I'm glad I was able to brighten your day. So, what are you up to, anyway?"

"We're brainstorming."

"Oh dear. Not another madcap scheme I hope."

"What do you mean, *another*?"

"Do you really want me to list them all?" I glanced around. "It's very quiet in here today."

"Don't we know it." Pearl sighed. "It's been like this for a couple of weeks. We're starting to get a bit worried."

"Any idea why trade should suddenly have dropped off?"

"Not a clue. I wish we did. That's why we're brainstorming. We're trying to come up with an idea for what to do with the space upstairs. Since we closed the creche, it's just standing empty."

"Have you considered reopening the creche?"

"We're not going to do that. It was more trouble than it was worth. Plus, it turned out to be a money pit. We need something that's going to make us money, not lose it."

"What ideas have you come up with so far?"

"We haven't." Pearl shook her head. "What about you, Jill? Can you think of anything?"

"Sorry, I don't have any bright ideas. Have you thought about asking Grandma?"

"*Grandma*?" Amber looked like I'd just asked her to suck on a lemon. "Why would we ask *her*? She's old and past it."

"You say that, but she's run a number of successful businesses, including Ever Tea Rooms. And she's never short of new ideas."

The two of them exchanged a glance, then said in unison, "Nah."

"We'll come up with something ourselves," Pearl said.

Which was precisely what worried me.

"I've just been to the library."

"Pretending you can read again?" Pearl laughed.

"I've been trying to find information on rainbows."

"You could have saved yourself a journey. We could have told you that they're those colourful things you see in the sky."

"You're hilarious. Maybe you should open a comedy club upstairs. I went to the library because I wanted to find out if rainbows work differently in the paranormal world."

"Work differently? What do you mean?"

I pulled the scrap of paper from my pocket and put it on the table. "I have to figure this out."

"Is this from a case you're working on?" Amber said.

"Err, yeah."

"Where's the rest of it?" Pearl picked up the paper.

"What do you mean?"

"The rest of the clue. It looks like this piece of paper has been torn. Maybe there's more to the clue than this."

"I don't think so. It's pretty obvious that I have to work

out where rainbows end."

My phone rang.

"Is that Jill Maxwell?" a woman's voice said.

"Jill Maxwell speaking."

"Are you the private investigator?"

"That's right. Who am I speaking to, please?"

"My name is Elizabeth Duggan. My husband, Doug, was the manager at the lido."

"Oh, hi." I hadn't been expecting a call from her, and particularly not so soon after her husband's tragic death.

"I hope you don't mind me calling you, Jill."

"Not at all."

"It's just that I wondered if we could meet."

"Of course. When would work for you?"

"I can't do today. How about tomorrow morning at ten?"

"That'll be fine."

"Okay. I'll give you my address."

"Who was that?" Pearl asked when I'd finished on the call.

"The widow of the manager of the lido.

"Wasn't he found dead in the pool?"

"Yeah. His assistant found him. He was supposed to be giving me a call the day he died."

"What about?"

"Grandma asked me to try and find out who owns the lido because she's heard they're going to close it down and sell it off. I talked to his assistant, but all she could tell me was that she was paid by a company called Reptile Holdings. Have you heard of them?"

"Sorry, no."

***

Back in the human world, I was on my way to meet with Chains, leader of Wash-on-Wheels Motorcycle Club. I'd called him the previous evening to set up the meeting, and although he'd seemed a little hesitant at first, he'd eventually agreed. I was probably guilty of stereotyping, but I'd expected him to live in one of the more rundown areas of Washbridge, but it turned out that he lived in Upper Wash.

The drive over seemed eerily quiet now that I no longer had Henry or Henrietta to keep me company. I wondered how they were getting on. Hopefully, they weren't getting too amorous in Kathy's summerhouse.

When the satnav announced I'd reached my destination, I thought it must be a mistake because I was outside a quaint cottage. This couldn't possibly be where Chains lived. Perhaps he had a caravan parked around the back of the property.

The immaculate front garden put mine to shame. There were hanging baskets on either side of the door, and a welcome mat with a picture of a cat on it. By now, I was convinced I was at the wrong place, but I thought I'd better make sure, so I knocked and waited. A couple of minutes later, an elderly woman, wearing a floral dress, answered the door.

"Hello, young lady. What can I do for you?"

"I'm sorry to trouble you. I think I must have the wrong address. I was actually looking for someone called Chains."

"You mean Norman."

"Do I?"

"Norman is my son, but he does sometimes go by that horrible name. Why he can't use his given name, Norman Rupert Masters, is beyond me."

"Norman Rupert? That's a fine name."

"Mum!" Chains' voice came from somewhere in the house. "Is that for me?"

"Yes, there's a young woman to see you, Norman." She turned back to me. "Sorry, I didn't catch your name."

"Jill Maxwell."

"Her name's Jill Maxwell," she shouted.

"Show her in, would you, Mum? I'll be there in a minute."

"He's in the loo. He's had a bit of an iffy tummy all day. Let's go through to the parlour and I'll make a nice cup of tea. My name's Hettie, by the way."

"It's very nice to make your acquaintance, Hettie."

She led the way into the small parlour where everything, and I mean everything, was floral: The wallpaper, the carpets, the curtains, the tablecloth, and even the radio.

"Take a seat at the table, Jill, and I'll go and make the drinks."

A couple of minutes later, Chains (or should I say Norman?) appeared. I barely recognised him. Instead of his leathers, he was wearing corduroy trousers, a checked shirt, and slippers.

"Hi, *Norman*." I grinned.

"I thought Mum would be out this afternoon." He rolled his eyes. "But her bridge club was cancelled."

"She seems really nice."

"She's the best."

"I like your outfit, Norman."

"Mum doesn't approve of my biker gear. Or my nickname."

"Do the rest of the club know you live with your mother?"

"I don't live here. Not normally, anyway. I was living with my girlfriend up to a week ago, but then she found out about Fi and threw me out."

"Oh dear. Couldn't you have moved in with Fi?"

"She sort of still has a boyfriend."

"Your life is extremely complicated, Norman. Or should I call you Chains?"

He glanced at the door. "You'd better call me Norman while Mum is around."

"Here we are." His mother appeared with a cup of tea in each hand. I wasn't sure how many sugars you took, Jill."

"None for me, thanks."

"I've put four in yours as usual, Norman."

"Thanks, Mum."

"I'll leave you two to it. It was nice to meet you, Jill."

"Likewise."

Once we were alone in the room, Norman seemed to relax a little.

"Your Mum has a lovely home," I said.

"She's always been very houseproud."

"Why don't you tell me about Killer?"

"Sure. Where should I start?"

"Wherever you like."

"He used to be a member of the Loose Chippings Motorcycle Club."

"Really?"

"Yeah. For several years."

"Is it normal for a member to swap clubs?"

"No, it's very rare. In fact, I don't know of anyone else who's done it."

"Why did he defect?"

"Killer was never really interested in the biker lifestyle, just in the bikes. He was a real petrol head. He loved messing around with cars and bikes, but mainly bikes. There was nothing he didn't know about them. Loose Chippings is a much smaller club than ours, and they didn't have the funds to allow Killer to be as creative as he wanted to be on the competition bike. Out of frustration, he reached out to me, to ask if I'd consider allowing him to join our club."

"How did you feel about that?"

"I was delighted. I'd been aware of Killer's reputation for years, and I knew he could help us to land the trophy."

"So, you agreed?"

"Yes. I didn't hesitate."

"Was there any bad feeling?"

"Plenty. On both sides. The Loose Chippings guys felt that Killer had betrayed them, and there were a small number of our members who didn't think he should have been allowed to join."

"Did he get any abuse?"

"Lots of it. And threats."

"How did he react to that?"

"He wasn't bothered. He never took it seriously. And besides, Killer could handle himself."

"Can we talk about the days leading up to his death? Did anything unusual happen?"

"Err, no. Not really."

"You don't sound sure."

"It's just that Killer was usually the life and soul of the party. He was always laughing and joking, but on the last couple of days before he died, he was unusually quiet. I asked if anything was wrong, but he said he was just feeling a bit under the weather. Looking back now, I wonder if there might've been more to it."

"Apart from the three of you that I met at the club, was anyone else particularly close to Killer?"

"There's Andy. He's a mechanic too. He's not as talented, but he worked on the bike with Killer sometimes."

"Do you have his contact details?"

"Sure. I'll let you have them before you leave."

Chapter 8

The three of us had just finished breakfast when there was a knock at the door. A visitor at this hour of the morning usually meant bad news, and today proved to be no exception.

"Great-Grandma!" Florence yelled when I opened the door.

"Hello, my little poppet." Grandma gave her a gentle pat on the head. "You're looking even more beautiful than ever. I can't think where you get your good looks from."

Thanks.

"What brings you over here at the crack of dawn?" I said.

"The *crack of dawn* was several hours ago. I've been for a three-mile walk already this morning."

"That's great, but we are kind of busy."

"What's my little poppet been up to lately?"

"Mummy and I are in the dance competition on Saturday."

"Are you now? Isn't that exciting?"

"Would you like to see our dance, Great-Grandma?"

Oh bum! Please tell me Florence didn't actually say that.

"I'd love to see it." Grandma grinned.

"Why don't you take Great-Grandma into the kitchen, Florence, and show her the dance?"

"No, Mummy, we both have to do it."

"Yes, *Mummy*." Grandma was enjoying this way too much. "I want to see both of you do the dance."

Florence grabbed my hand and dragged me into the kitchen.

"Hello, Jim," Grandma said. "I didn't realise you were

home."

"It's Jack."

"Same difference. Florence and Jill are going to show me their dance."

"Are they?" Jack's face lit up. "Cool. I'd like to see that too."

"We can't dance in here because we don't have the music." This was my last, pathetic attempt to get out of it.

"I'll go and get the iPod." Florence dashed upstairs.

"I'm looking forward to this." Jack sat back in his chair.

"Are you ready, Mummy?" Florence came charging back downstairs with the iPod.

"As ready as I'll ever be."

The music started and we began our (not so short) routine. I kept my eyes shut until we'd finished because if I'd seen the smirks on Jack's or Grandma's face, I'd have totally lost it.

When we'd finished, Florence took a bow, and said, "Did you like it, Great-Grandma?"

"I thought you were excellent. You're clearly a natural."

"Do you think we'll win the competition on Saturday?"

"I'm sure you will, but only if your mummy puts in a lot more practice."

"We're going to practise again tonight, aren't we, Mummy?"

"Yes, darling. Now, Grandma, did you come over for anything in particular?"

"I did. Do you think I might have a quiet word in the lounge?"

"Sure." Once we were in there, I closed the door behind me. "What is it?"

"Before I get into that, you do realise that you'll have to

use magic if you want to win the dance competition on Saturday. You have three left feet."

"I'm not all that bad."

"You're worse. I've seen camels with more grace."

"I have no intention of resorting to magic. What kind of example would that be to set for Florence?"

"If you don't, you'll probably come last. She won't be very happy then."

"I'm not going to use magic and that's final. Now, what was it you wanted to talk to me about?"

"I just wanted to let you know that I've resolved the Ivers problem."

"Are you sure?"

"Positive. Do you remember what I told you about how the potion was administered?"

"You said it was in a fine mist that was sprayed onto any human who came through the main entrance."

"That's right."

"Clearly it isn't working properly, otherwise Mr Ivers wouldn't have been able to see the paranormal creatures, would he?"

"I'd tested that system thoroughly, so I couldn't understand why it wasn't having the desired effect, but then I discovered Ivers doesn't always use the front entrance. He occasionally comes in the back way, which meant he wasn't being sprayed with the mist."

"How do you propose to rectify that situation?"

"I've already done it. The mist system has now been installed on all entrances to the hotel, so no matter which way Ivers comes into the building, he'll always be sprayed by the potion. The same applies for any other human who ventures into the hotel. Am I a genius or am I a genius?"

"If you were a genius, you'd have set it up correctly the first time."

"There's no pleasing you, is there?"

"Let's just hope it's not too late." I was about to leave the room when Grandma said, "Isn't it time that human of yours, John, or whatever his name is, found himself a job? It isn't right that he should stay at home all day while you have to work."

"Wow! Where do I even begin? First, he is not *that human of mine*; he's my husband. Second, and as you very well know, his name is Jack, not John. And Jack works from home."

"If you ask me, he's playing you for a mug."

"Here's the thing, Grandma. I didn't ask you. And if I ever need your advice on my marriage, I'll — scrub that — I will *never* need your advice on my marriage."

"Please yourself, I was only trying to help." She stormed out of the house in a huff.

"Great-Grandma didn't say goodbye to me." Florence pouted.

"She had to go back to the hotel straight away, but she told me to tell you again how much she liked your dancing."

"Did she like yours, Jill?" Jack said.

***

Mrs V still wasn't happy.

"I'm not happy, Jill."

See, what did I tell you? It's almost as though I have a sixth sense.

"Are you still upset about the missing yellow yarn?"

"Yes, that yarn is simply irreplaceable. I wish I knew what that cat had done with it."

"We don't know for sure it was Winky who took it."

"Who else could it have been?"

"Maybe someone sneaked into the office while you were sleeping—err—I mean, meditating."

"That's ridiculous. Who would want to steal a few balls of wool?"

"Hang on. How is it that you think that's ridiculous, but you're prepared to believe the cat did it?"

"He has history."

"Maybe you should meditate. It might take your mind off it."

"I tried earlier, but I can't focus. Every time I close my eyes, I can see those balls of yellow yarn disappearing out of the door. I even had a nightmare about them last night."

Winky was sitting on the sofa, filing his claws.

"Where is it?" I demanded.

"Where is *what*?"

"The yellow yarn you stole, of course."

"I told you yesterday. I had nothing to do with taking the old bag lady's yarn."

"You do realise that time is running out for you, don't you? If that yarn is not back here by five o'clock tomorrow, you're out."

"You're accusing me without any evidence whatsoever. No court in the land would convict me."

"That's not true. The court of Jill Maxwell is happy to take just my word, so if you know what's good for you, you'll bring back that yarn."

Before he could respond, my phone rang.

"Jill, it's Rita Reed."

"Hi, RiRi — err — I mean, Rita."

"You left a message for me to call you."

"Yeah, I've spoken to Kathy and she's up for a night out next week. Wednesday would work best for us if that's okay for you?"

"Wednesday's fine. Where and when?"

"Let's say eight o'clock, and I don't mind where. Why don't you choose?"

"What about the new bar that's just opened in Wash Square. Have you seen it?"

"No, but then I haven't been down there for a while."

"It looks okay from the outside. It's called Wash Upon A Time."

"Okay, let's give it a try. See you next week."

***

I'd agreed to visit Doug Duggan's widow, Elizabeth. I was a little nervous because it was only a couple of days since her husband had been found face down in the pool, and I wasn't sure what to expect.

Her semi was on a quiet cul-de-sac in Long Wash. I had to park a little way down the street because there were already three cars parked outside her house. A tall man sporting a short kilt answered the door.

"Yes?" he barked.

"I'm here to see Elizabeth."

"She isn't accepting visitors at the moment. You may not be aware of this, but her husband died in tragic circumstances earlier this week."

"Actually, she called yesterday and asked me to come over."

"I see. What's your name?"

"Jill Maxwell."

"Would you mind waiting there while I go and check with her?"

"No problem."

He closed the door and left me standing on the doorstep. After five minutes, I was beginning to think he'd abandoned me, but then the door opened, and the same man beckoned me inside. I could hear voices coming from the lounge.

"Elizabeth is upstairs in her bedroom. She told me to send you up. It's the first door on the right."

"Thanks."

I made my way upstairs and knocked on the door. A quiet voice came from inside. "Come in."

Elizabeth, who was in her dressing gown, was sitting on the bed. Her hair was dishevelled, her complexion pale, and her eyes blotchy. She had a half-empty box of tissues on the bed beside her, and the wastepaper bin at her feet was overflowing with them.

"Thank you for coming." She sounded hoarse.

"Are you sure you feel up to this? We could leave it for a few days if you like?"

"No, I want to do it now. Why don't you take a seat?" She pointed to the armchair next to the bedside cabinet.

"I'm very sorry for your loss, Elizabeth."

"Thank you. I still can't believe what's happened." She began to sob. "The night before he died, Doug told me he was going to call you. He said you were a private investigator?"

"That's right."

"He said that Debbie had told him you'd been asking questions about the owners of the lido."

"Debbie said she didn't know who the new owner was, but that her salary was being paid by a company called Reptile Holdings."

"That's right. Things started to go wrong when they took over."

"What do you mean?"

"Before the change of ownership, Doug had worked at the lido for over fifteen years, and he loved every minute of it. He started out as a lifeguard and worked his way up to manager. But then the previous owner decided that he wanted to take early retirement and sell the business. The first Doug knew about it was when he came around to say goodbye to everyone. That's when everything changed."

"In what way?"

"The first thing the new owners did was to get rid of half the staff. Then they cut the wages of those left behind, so they were doing twice the work for less money."

"Doug can't have been very happy about that."

"Of course not, but he still loved working at the lido, so he soldiered on. Then the rumours started."

"*Rumours*?"

"That the lido was going to be closed down, and the land built upon."

"Was Doug upset?"

"He was more angry than upset. Angry that they would do something like that without saying anything to the staff. That's when he began to investigate Reptile Holdings. He was determined to find out who was behind the company so that he could try and convince them of the error of their ways."

"And did he? Find out who it is, I mean?"

"Yes."

"Who?"

"I don't know."

"Didn't he tell you?"

"No. He said it was better that I didn't know because it could put me in danger. To be perfectly honest, I thought he was exaggerating, but then—" Her words faded away for a few seconds. "Sorry about that. He said he was going to tell you everything, but he never got the chance."

"What have the police said about his death?"

"They're treating it as an accident. They reckon he must have slipped and hit his head as he fell into the pool. But that's rubbish. Doug was an experienced lifeguard and always incredibly careful. Someone did this to him, and I want you to find out who it was."

"I—err—I'm not sure—"

"If it's the money, Doug had life insurance. As soon as that comes through, I'll be able to pay you."

"It isn't the money."

"Please, will you help me? I have to find out who did this to Doug and make sure they're brought to justice."

"Of course I will."

Chapter 9

After running the figures, I'd come to the conclusion that I was spending way too much money on coffee and cake.

What do you mean, you could have told me that years ago?

I was dying for a cup of tea, but I didn't want to spend any more money today. Nor did I want to go back to the office and have to listen to Mrs V complaining about Winky and her missing yellow yarn. So, instead, I decided to try my luck down at Kathy's shop—the first in her vast empire. There was no guarantee she'd be there because these days she seemed to spend most of her time at home.

I got lucky; she was there, talking to her manager. When she spotted me, she beckoned me inside.

"I assume you're after a cup of tea, Jill."

That sister of mine could read me like a book.

"Why would you think that?"

"Because that's the only time you come down here."

"That's not true." It so was. "I actually came to tell you about the arrangements for our girls' night out next week, but seeing as how you're offering, a cup of tea would be most acceptable."

"I didn't."

"You didn't *what*?"

"Offer to make you a cup of tea."

"Please, Kathy, I'm parched."

"Come on, then."

"Have I ever told you that you're my favourite sister?"

I followed her into the small office at the back of the shop.

"Have I ever told you that you're a creep?"

"Often, but I know you don't mean it."

Kathy switched on the kettle. "Do you think we should still call her RiRi or did we ought to call her Rita now?"

"Rita, I suppose."

"Yeah, I think you're right. I mean, no one calls you Beans anymore, do they?"

"Nobody's ever called me *Beans*."

"Yes, they did." She laughed. "Everyone at school used to call you that because you always had a Beanie Baby with you."

"You've just made that up."

"If you say so. So, what are the arrangements for next week?"

"We're going to meet at eight o'clock on Wednesday night outside Wash Upon A Time."

"Is that the new bar in Wash Square?"

"Yeah, that's the one."

"Have you been in there?"

"No, I didn't even know it was there until Rita mentioned it."

"I'm really looking forward to a night out." Kathy yawned. "Sorry, I'm shattered."

"I don't see how you can be tired. You don't get up until midday most days."

"Don't talk nonsense. Who do you think gets the kids off to school every day?"

"Peter?"

"Some chance. He's long gone before they've even had their breakfast. No, it's muggins here. I'm tired because I didn't get a wink of sleep last night."

"Peter feeling amorous, was he?"

"No chance. He was fast asleep, snoring his head off."

"What kept you awake, then? Are you worried about the business?"

"No, nothing like that. I told you that we had new neighbours, didn't I?"

"Yeah, you said you thought they seemed okay."

"They did, but last night they were playing music until all hours. That's why I couldn't sleep."

"Didn't it keep Peter awake too?"

"No, that man could sleep through anything. When I told him about it this morning, he said it can't have been all that bad because it didn't wake him up."

"You should have a word with them and tell them it's unacceptable."

"I plan to do just that. It wouldn't have been so bad if the music had been something I liked, but it was jazz. I mean, who likes jazz?"

"Are you sure that's what it was?"

"Of course I am; I know jazz when I hear it."

Oh bum!

"Maybe it would be better if you didn't say anything to your neighbours yet."

"You just said I should go around there."

"I—err—was a bit hasty. Perhaps it was a one-off? It might not happen again."

"I shouldn't have to put up with that noise."

"I know, but you did say that they've only just moved in. You don't want to risk falling out with them, do you? There's nothing worse than being at war with your neighbours."

"That's true."

"I'd give it a few days and see what happens."

"You're probably right, but if it continues, I'll have to do something about it."

It was time to change the subject. "How's Lizzie's leg?"

"It's fine. She went back to school this morning."

"Already?"

"Yeah. The doctor said it was okay if she took it steady on her crutches."

"And how is she? Apart from her leg, I mean."

"Okay."

"No problems at school or anything?"

"What makes you ask that? She didn't say something to you the other day, did she?"

"No, I would have said. What about Mikey? How's he doing?"

"Your guess is as good as mine. He barely talks to me these days. I'm lucky if I get the occasional grunt out of him. He spends all his time on Snapchat, TikTok or whatever social media app is flavour of the week."

"Don't you worry about that?"

"Of course I do, but there's a limit to what I can do about it. When Florence is a teenager, you'll have all this to deal with."

"I can't wait. At least I only have to cope with caterpillars at the moment."

We hadn't been chatting for very long when the manager popped her head around the door to ask if Kathy could help with a difficult customer. Kathy said I should stay put, but I'd finished my tea, so I made my excuses and left.

What on earth was Henry thinking, playing jazz all hours of the night? I would have to have a serious word with that young elf, and I'd need to do it quickly, before

Kathy picked a fight with her new neighbours.

Why was nothing in my life ever straight forward?

***

As I walked past Coffee Rock, I happened to glance through the window, and I spotted Daze and Blaze.

They were jiving!

And boy, those two could certainly move. I'd been watching them for a couple of minutes when Daze saw me and gestured that I should go inside.

"I had no idea you two were so talented," I said.

"Daze and I have won the Rogue Retrievers jive competition for the last two years in a row," Blaze said.

"Colour me impressed."

The three of us took a seat close to the jukebox.

"Can I get you a drink, Jill?" Daze offered.

"No, thanks. I've just had a cup of tea at Kathy's shop. Is it your day off?"

"No such luck. We're just on our break. We've been trying to track down the Canary Brothers all week."

"Who are they?"

"A couple of wizards. Nasty pieces of work, both of them."

"Why are they called the Canary Brothers?"

"Because—" Daze's phone rang. "Yes. Okay. I understand. We'll be right there. Sorry, Jill, but we have to shoot off. It's an emergency."

"Okay, see you."

***

I'd had more than enough for one day, so I called Mrs V to tell her I was headed home. I parked outside the old watermill, but before heading inside, I wanted to update Grandma on the lido situation.

When I walked through the hotel entrance, who should I bump into but Mr Ivers.

"Hello, Jill. If you're here for your movie newsletter, I'm afraid you're a week early."

"Actually, I'm here to see my grandmother. How are things with you, Mr Ivers?"

"Top-notch. Couldn't be better."

"Are you sure? You seemed a little out of sorts the last time I saw you."

"Really? I don't remember that. I'm tickety-boo."

"That's good to hear. And how are you enjoying working here?"

"I love it. I get to meet lots of people, and there's always something to do."

"No problems, then?"

"None."

"And nothing unusual has happened?"

"*Unusual*? Not that I can think of. Except for the ants, but your grandmother said I wasn't to talk about those."

"Great."

By the time I reached the desk, the receptionist had already called Grandma. "Your grandmother says you can go straight to her office."

"Right. Thanks."

"I hope you have some good news for a change, Jill." Grandma was sporting a curly wig.

"Err—not really." I couldn't take my eyes off her hair.

"Why are you wearing that?"

"Wearing what?"

"That wig?"

"It's not a wig. This is my own hair. I've had it restyled."

"O—kay."

"Have you found out who owns the lido yet?"

"It's a company called Reptile Holdings."

"And who are they when they're at home?"

"I don't know yet."

"Why not? What am I paying you for, exactly?"

"You aren't paying me."

"Don't split hairs. Have you made any progress at all?"

"I spoke to the manager's widow."

"What did she have to say?"

"She believes her husband was killed because he was trying to find out more about the owners of the lido."

"What did I tell you? Something decidedly fishy is going on there, and the sooner you find out what it is, the better."

I'd eaten the last two custard creams that morning, so I called in at the village store to replenish my stock. Much to my surprise and relief, they were in the same spot as the last time I'd purchased them, which meant I was in and out of the shop much quicker than I'd expected.

As I stepped outside, I almost ran straight into the vicar, who was wearing a scarf wrapped so tightly around his neck, I was amazed he could breathe, let alone talk.

"Hi, Jill." He glanced at the five packets of biscuits under my arm. "I see you're keen on custard creams."

"They are the king of biscuits, Vicar."

"I'm more of a Jammie Dodger man myself. By the way, I'm grateful that you'll be helping out next week."

"Sorry?"

"At the village fete. I bumped into Jack when he was taking your little girl to school. I mentioned that we were looking for volunteers to man the stalls, and he said you and he would be happy to help out."

"Did he? That was nice of him. When exactly is the fete, Vicar?"

"A week on Sunday. Let's hope the weather holds out."

"Yeah. Fingers crossed."

I was almost home when who should I bump into, but my good friend, Stewart.

"Jill, I'm glad I've seen you." That made one of us. "You've got an awful lot of custard creams there."

"Did you want something, Stewart, because I'm in a bit of a hurry."

"I need Buddy."

"You may need a buddy, Stewart, but I don't think you and I could ever be friends. Not after the stunt you pulled."

"I didn't mean I need *a* buddy. I need Buddy the Chihuahua. I want him back."

"What? Why the sudden change of heart?"

"I'm missing the little guy. I didn't think I would, but the house seems empty without him."

"That's not what you said the last time I saw you. You sounded like you were glad to see the back of him."

"I was wrong. So, can I have him back? Please."

"I don't see why not."

"Great. Shall I come and get him tonight? Say, seven

o'clock?"

"Sure."

I'd be pleased to see the back of the little monster.

As soon as I walked through the door, Florence came running over and gave me a big hug.

"Mummy, I found a caterpillar. It's red with yellow spots."

"Are you sure about that, darling? I don't think there are any red caterpillars around here."

"There are, Mummy. His name is Archie. Do you want to come outside to see him?"

"Maybe later. I have to talk to Daddy first. You go out and play and I'll join you in a few minutes."

Jack looked up from his newspaper. "Has Florence told you about Archie?"

"She has. That girl is obsessed with caterpillars. But never mind about them, I have some great news."

"Have we won the lottery?"

"No, something almost as good. Stewart wants Buddy back."

"What?"

"I bumped into him in the village just now. He says he's missing the little dog."

"Well, he can't have him."

"What do you mean? This is our chance to get rid of him."

"Are you insane, Jill? Florence loves her dog. She'd be devastated."

"Are you sure? She doesn't like feeding him. She always says his food smells bad."

"I'm telling you. If you give her dog away, she'll never

forgive you."

"I suppose you're right. Pity. Anyway, I've got a bone to pick with you."

"What have I done now?"

"The vicar has just thanked me for volunteering to man one of the stalls at the annual village fete."

"I saw him earlier. He said they were shorthanded, so I thought you and I could help out."

"Don't you think you should have asked me first?"

"I knew you wouldn't mind. And besides, Florence will want to go to the fete, so we can take turns manning the stall and being with her."

"But village fetes are so boring."

"It's not like we've got anything better to do on a Sunday, is it?"

"We could watch paint dry instead."

He glanced at the biscuits. "Do you think you've got enough of those?"

We'd just finished dinner when Jack's phone beeped with a message.

"I've been waiting for this. Florence, come and see."

They both stared at the screen. Although I could hear music, I couldn't see what they were looking at, but whatever it was, it had them both engrossed. After a few minutes, Jack said, "What do you think, Florence?"

"Are they better than me and Mummy, Daddy?"

"No, of course not."

"What are you two watching?" I said.

"See for yourself." He handed me the phone. "I got talking to Donna when I collected Florence from school. She said she and Wendy had been practising their dance routine every evening, and she promised to send over a video for Florence to watch."

I pressed play on the video. The routine that Donna and Wendy had come up with was nowhere near as complicated as the one that Florence had devised. Their performance was faultless and put ours to shame.

"We have to practise more, Mummy," Florence said. "Otherwise, Wendy will win on Saturday."

"Okay, darling. We'll practise some more tomorrow. Probably."

"No! We have to do it tonight and we have to practise twice as long."

"Right." Great.

I'd just finished loading the dishwasher when there was a knock at the door. Jack was outside with Florence, so I went to answer it, and found Stewart standing there.

"Where is he, Jill? Where's Buddy?"

"You can't have him."

"You said I could."

"I've changed my mind. It would break Florence's little heart."

"I have to have him at least for Saturday morning."

"Why? What's happening then?"

"My mother's coming around. She was the one who bought Buddy for me. I haven't told her that I've given him away. If he isn't there when she comes, I'll get it in the neck. Please, Jill, you have to help me."

"Why should I?"

"I'll give you a tenner to borrow him on Saturday morning."

"Fifty quid."

"That's outrageous."

"Take it or leave it."

"Okay, fifty quid, but you have to have him at my place by ten o'clock."

"I will, but if you don't have the cash, I won't leave him with you."

"I'll have the money."

"Good." I closed the door.

That's what I call a result.

"Who was that?" Jack came through from the kitchen.

"Just someone selling double glazing."

Chapter 10

"Are you alright, Jill?" Jack was standing at the bottom of the stairs, watching me slowly hobble down.

"Just about."

"What's wrong with you?"

"It's my legs. They're stiff after all that dancing Florence made me do last night."

"You're walking like an old lady."

"Thanks, you really know how to make a girl feel special."

"Mummy! Mummy!" Florence came bounding across the kitchen. "I found him."

"You found who?"

"Archie."

"Is that the red and yellow caterpillar you told me about?"

"Yes. He must have been hiding last night when you came outside to look at him. Come and see him now."

"Can I have my breakfast first? I'm starving."

"Please, Mummy. Come now or he'll go again."

"Oh, okay."

She took me by the hand and practically dragged me outside.

"Look, he's over there."

Sure enough, just as she'd said, there was a red caterpillar with yellow spots. "He's very fancy, isn't he?"

"Archie is my favourite caterpillar ever."

"Why do you call him Archie?"

"Because that's his name, silly."

"Of course."

"Is that all you're having for breakfast, Jill?" Jack said, as he and Florence tucked into their muesli.

"It's what I fancy." I took a bite of my second custard cream.

"It isn't very healthy though, is it? Why don't you have some fruit, at least?"

"Cut me some slack, Jack. My legs are killing me and I'm tired. You could at least allow me to enjoy my custard creams without guilt tripping me."

"Okay, but don't blame me when all your teeth fall out."

"They're not going to fall out now, are they, Mummy?" Florence shuddered.

"They're not going to fall out at all, darling. Daddy's just being silly."

***

On my way to the office, I made a detour to Kathy's house because I wanted to have a word with Henry about his all-night jazz sessions. If they were allowed to continue, there was a real danger that Kathy would storm over to her new neighbours' house and lay into them. They, of course, would have absolutely no idea what she was talking about.

I didn't want her to see my car, so I parked on the next street and made my way to her house on foot.

At last, a bit of good luck! There were no cars on the driveway; Kathy and Peter must have both gone into work early. I hurried around the back of the house, but there was no sign of the elves.

The gnome with the fishing rod gave me a little wave.

"Hi, Jill, you spend almost as much time here as the owners."

"Not by choice. Do you happen to know where Henry and Henrietta are?"

"They're probably in the summer house, making out again." He rolled his eyes. "That's where they usually are."

"Right, thanks." I glanced back at the conservatory, to make sure the coast was still clear, then walked over to the summer house and pushed open the door.

"Jill? Hi," Henry said, all innocent-like. "We weren't expecting to see you."

"I can see that. How come you aren't stone?"

"We don't use the potion at night because it makes it difficult to get close to one another." Henry winked at me. "If you know what I mean."

"Why are you in here, anyway? You're only meant to be in the summer house during the hours of darkness."

"Is it light already?" Henrietta said.

"Yes, and it has been for an hour. You both need to turn yourselves to stone and get out in the garden before someone realises that you're missing."

"Sorry, Jill." Henry straightened his collar.

"First, though, I need a word with you about something Kathy told me."

"Who's Kathy?

"Have you forgotten already? She's my sister. The woman who owns this house."

"Oh yes, sorry. Carry on."

"She said she'd been kept awake all night by someone playing loud jazz music."

"I told you, Henry," Henrietta barked at him. "I said

that awful music was too loud."

"I do apologise," Henry said. "It's just that it's so nice to be able to enjoy jazz anytime I want, and not have to wait until someone's driving the car."

"That's as maybe, but you're going to have to keep the volume down so they can't hear it in the house. Otherwise, I'll have no choice but to take you two back to the car."

"Don't do that, Jill," Henry said. "We love it here. After all this space and fresh air, we can't go back to that claustrophobic glove compartment."

"Keep the music down, then."

"We will. I promise."

"Good. Now, take your potion and get out into the garden before someone realises you're missing."

I was halfway down the driveway when I heard Peter's voice behind me.

"Jill?"

Oh bum!

"Hi, Peter. I thought you'd gone to work."

"My van's gone in for servicing, so I decided to stay home and catch up on some paperwork. Did I just see you in the back garden?"

"Err, yeah. I thought I'd just check up on the elves that I gave Kathy."

"Check up on them?"

"Yeah, I—err—wanted to make sure they'd settled in okay."

"*Right*? And have they?"

"Yeah. All A-Okay."

"That's good." He glanced at the road. "Where's your

car?"

"I had to take mine in for a service too."

"How did you get here?"

"Jack gave me a lift."

"Where is he?"

"He—err—had to go back to take Florence to school."

"How are you going to get to the office?"

"I thought I'd walk."

"It's miles from here."

"The exercise will do me good." I started down the driveway. "See you."

"Bye, Jill."

No doubt he'd tell Kathy that her crazy sister had made a house call.

I walked slowly down the street and kept checking behind me until Peter had gone into the house, then I doubled back and hurried to the car.

***

When I arrived at the office, Mrs V had a huge smile plastered across her face.

"Good morning, Jill. What a beautiful day this is."

"Good morning. You're looking exceptionally pleased with life today, Mrs V. Any particular reason?"

"Can't you guess? I have to admit that I didn't think I'd ever see the day when you actually did it."

"Did what?"

"Got rid of that fleabag of a cat. I've been telling you to do it for long enough."

"Winky? I haven't got rid of him. Not yet, anyway."

"Well, he's gone."

"What do you mean, he's gone?"

"The food you put out for him yesterday hasn't been touched and there's no sign of him."

"He's probably just gone on one of his expeditions. He does go missing occasionally."

"How very disappointing. I really thought you'd finally got shut of him."

Just as Mrs V had said, Winky's food was still in his bowl, untouched. That didn't necessarily mean anything. He'd probably just gone to visit one of his many friends and decided to stay over. He wouldn't have just upped and left like that. Not without saying goodbye.

I was just about to take a seat at my desk when I noticed a small white envelope on the chair. I ripped it open, to find a note from Winky.

Dear Jill,

I had absolutely nothing to do with the disappearance of the old bag lady's yarn, but it's clear that you're not prepared to accept my word. Rather than suffer the indignation of being thrown onto the street, I have decided to leave of my own accord.

I wish you well and hope you can live with yourself.

Yours disappointedly,

Winky.

I slumped into the chair, feeling dreadful. It's true that I'd given him an ultimatum, but I would never have thrown him out. I was just trying to force him to return the yarn.

What if he really hadn't taken it? What if he'd been telling the truth?

I walked over to the open window.

"Winky! Winky, where are you? Winky!"

Nothing.

For the next hour, I shuffled papers around my desk while watching the window in case Winky returned, but he was a no-show.

***

I'd arranged to meet Andy, the mechanic who had worked alongside Killer at the bike workshop, which was next door to the Wash-on-Wheels clubroom.

One of the two large wooden doors was propped open. Inside, there were a number of motorcycles in different states of repair. Lying on the floor, working on one of them, was a man wearing blue overalls.

"Excuse me," I said.

He looked up. "Are you that private investigator woman?"

"That's me. Jill Maxwell."

"I'll be with you in a minute. I just need to get this nut undone, but it doesn't want to budge. Why don't you go over there and put the kettle on?"

"Sure."

On the small table were several mugs. They were all covered in grease and had the dregs of something inside them, which may or may not have been tea or coffee. I filled the kettle but decided not to bother with a drink.

"Yes! Got it!" Andy climbed to his feet, wiped his greasy hands on his overalls, and came over to join me. "Tea or coffee?"

"Nothing for me, thanks."

"Grab a chair."

I did as he said and waited until he'd made himself a cup of tea, which he poured into a mug that bore the words: **Bikers do it on two wheels**.

"I suppose you're here to talk about Killer." He wiped his nose on his sleeve.

"Yeah. Chains told me that you and Killer worked together."

"That's right. Most of the time, anyway."

"I understand that you were a member of this club before Killer."

"Several years before."

"How did you feel when Chains brought him in?"

"I thought it was unnecessary. I can do everything that Killer could. If you ask me, he was overrated."

"I take it that you and he didn't get on."

"That's not true. I wasn't thrilled that they brought him in, but I'm not the kind of person to hold a grudge."

"Were you two able to work together okay?"

"For the most part. I didn't always agree with his methods, but we always got there in the end."

"What were the two of you working on when he died?"

"We'd more or less finished all the work on the competition bike. That's it over there." He pointed to a bike at the far end of the workshop.

"It looks good."

"Good? That bike is the dog's. We'll win again this year for sure."

"When is the competition?"

"Week after next."

"If you weren't working on the competition bike that day, what were you working on?"

"I worked on several bikes. None of them were big jobs. Killer was working on his own bike because he'd had a couple of problems with it the weekend before."

"I believe you were the one who found him."

"Yeah, he was lying next to his bike."

"Any idea where his bike is now?"

"It's over there, behind that screen."

"How come it's still in here?"

"No one knew what to do with it, but Chains told me yesterday that Killer's brother is supposed to be coming to pick it up."

"Can I take a look at it?"

"Sure." He led the way across the workshop and around the screen. "Nice bike, eh?"

"I guess. I understand from Chains that the police believe Killer's death was an accident."

"So they reckon, but I don't buy it."

"What makes you say that?"

"See that workbench over there? The edge of it was covered in his blood. Someone must have thrown him against it."

"How do you know he didn't just trip and fall backwards? That's what the police believe, I assume?"

"Yeah, but they're idiots." He pointed to the floor. "There was blood all the way from the bench to his bike, where he'd managed to drag himself."

"It could still have been an accident."

"Then why did he do this?" He took out his phone, brought up a photo and held it out for me to see.

"That's this bike, isn't it?"

"Yeah. Zoom in on the petrol tank. What do you see?"

"Is that blood?"

"Yeah. It's the letter 'S'. Killer was trying to tell us who did this to him."

"That's a bit of a stretch, isn't it? It might not even be

the letter 'S'. He might just have been trying to stand up and dragged his fingers across the tank."

"That's definitely an 'S' and it stands for Slugger."

"The leader of the Loose Chippings motorcycle club?"

"Yeah. It had to be him who did it. I'd bet my life on it."

"Did you point out the blood print to the police?"

"Yeah, but they weren't interested. They'd already made up their minds that it was an accident."

"Seems I need to have a chat with Slugger."

"Be careful. That guy is insane."

***

After leaving the garage, I headed across town to the office. I'd just turned a corner, when I found the pavement blocked by workmen; they were digging a big hole. Pedestrians were being redirected across the road.

Why were they always digging holes in Washbridge? It's not like they ever actually seemed to do anything with them, other than fill them in again. I was about to cross the road when I caught a glimpse of the two workmen: Standing in the hole, ankle deep in water, were Daze and Blaze.

I leaned over the barrier. "Hey, Daze. Having fun?"

"Why do we get all the worst jobs? I'm beginning to think someone doesn't like us."

"What are you two doing down there?"

"Digging a hole. What does it look like?"

"I can see that, but I assume this is all a cover?"

"You're right. We're on the lookout for Blue Jim."

"Who's he?"

"A rogue wizard who, according to our intel, has been

plying his trade in this neighbourhood."

"I thought you were after the Canary Brothers?"

"We caught them yesterday. They're banged up."

"You were about to tell me why they're known as the Canary Brothers when you were called away."

"It's because they're obsessed with the colour yellow. They wander around the human world, stealing all manner of stuff. It doesn't much matter to them what it is, just as long as it's yellow."

"Hang on. Is it possible they could have stolen some wool?"

"If it's yellow, they'll steal it. They're like a couple of magpies. Why do you ask?"

"Mrs V had all her yellow yarn stolen the other day. She thought it was Winky who'd taken it."

"It's quite possible that the Canary Brothers took it," Daze said.

"Is there any way you could check?"

"Everything that was recovered is back in Candlefield. You can take a look through it if you like."

"Great. When can we do it?"

"I can take you there now," Blaze offered. "Anything to get out of this hole for a few minutes."

"Okay, let's go."

Blaze and I magicked ourselves to Rogue Retriever Headquarters.

"All the Canary Brothers' stuff is in that room over there," Blaze said. "Why don't you take a look through it? There's a couple of things I need to do in the office."

The room, which was little more than a cupboard, was full of stuff, all of which was yellow: clothes, jewellery, kitchen appliances—you name it and it was there. It would have taken me ages to work my way through it all, but then I caught a break. In the corner, a huge yellow teddy bear was sitting on a pile of yellow balls of wool.

That was good news for Mrs V, but it meant that I'd wrongly accused Winky, and now he'd run away.

I'd just collected all the yarn when Blaze returned.

"This belongs to Mrs V. Is it okay if I take it back to her?"

"Sure. Someone will have the job of trying to return this lot to their rightful owners, so you'll be helping them."

"Thanks."

I magicked myself back to Washbridge and hurried to the office. When I walked through the door, Mrs V's eyes lit up.

"You found my yarn. Where was it?"

"I—err—found it in the skip around the back of the building."

"What was it doing there?"

"Perhaps you put it in the waste bin instead of the yarn basket. You said yourself you've been feeling rather stressed recently. Stress can do strange things to the mind."

Chapter 11

I was trying really hard to focus on the pile of papers in front of me, but it was impossible because I was feeling so guilty about Winky. I should never have accused him of stealing Mrs V's wool without evidence. I'd made it even worse by threatening to throw him out onto the street if he didn't return the wool by the end of business today.

And now he was gone, just like that. What if something happened to him?

Who was I trying to kid? Winky had more street-smarts than all the other cats in Washbridge put together. He would be fine.

Fingers crossed.

My phone rang; it was Mad.

"Jill, I don't suppose you're free at the moment, are you?"

"Yeah, why?"

"Would it be okay if I popped over to see you?"

"Sure."

"Okay, we'll be there in a couple of minutes."

We? Was she with Brad?

I didn't have long to wait to find out because ten minutes later, Mrs V popped her head around the door.

"Madeline's here to see you, Jill. She has your niece with her."

"Lizzie? You'd better send them in."

Lizzie, on her crutches, came through the door first, followed by Mad.

"Shouldn't you be in school?" I said.

"It's only study time, which we do in the library.

Nobody will know I'm missing."

"You can't just sneak out of school. Your mother will do her nut if she finds out."

"She won't find out. Everyone does it."

"You're not *everyone*."

"This is the first time I've skipped school, honestly. You won't tell Mum, will you?"

"I should."

"Please don't, Auntie Jill."

"Alright, but only if you give me your word that you won't do it again."

"I promise."

I turned to Mad. "Did you encourage her to skive off school?"

"Of course not."

"She didn't, Auntie Jill. Honestly. I had to talk to someone, so I went to her shop."

"Okay. Sorry, Mad. You'd better both sit down and tell me exactly why you're here."

"You tell her, Mad," Lizzie said.

"The thing is, Jill, it's quite clear that Lizzie can see ghosts."

"I see them all the time. I try to block them out, but it doesn't do any good."

"That must be very scary for you."

"Not really. I'm used to it now, and most of them are friendly. That's why I want to be a ghost hunter like Mad."

"What? You can't be a ghost hunter. You're still a child."

"That's so unfair!"

"Was this your idea, Mad?"

"No, it wasn't, but I do think Lizzie is right."

"Are you crazy? She's just a kid."

"I know, and I'm not suggesting she become a ghost hunter today, but she could train to be one. If she starts now, she'll be fully qualified by the time she's old enough to take on the job."

"I can't believe I'm hearing this. Are you seriously suggesting my niece trains to be a ghost hunter?"

"Why not? There are worse jobs."

"What about Kathy? She'll think Lizzie has lost her mind if she tells her she wants to train to be a ghost hunter."

"I won't tell her, Auntie Jill."

"The training is only a couple of hours a week," Mad said. "Lizzie could do it at the weekend."

"Don't you think Kathy will notice if she goes missing every weekend?"

"She won't have to go anywhere. Most of the training can be delivered remotely these days."

"What if your Mum or Dad walk in on you when you're in the middle of a training session?"

"I'll just switch screens." She grinned. "I already do that when I'm looking at something that I don't want them to see."

"I really wish you two hadn't involved me in all of this. If Kathy finds out, she'll have my guts for garters. Are you absolutely sure you want to do this, Lizzie?"

"Positive. I can't wait to get started."

"And you can make all the arrangements, Mad?"

"Yeah, no problem, but I wanted to run it by you before I did anything."

"And you'll make sure she doesn't come to any harm?"

"Of course I will. I promise."

"Okay, then. I just hope it doesn't backfire."

"Thanks, Auntie Jill." Lizzie hobbled around the desk and gave me a big hug.

"Just one thing, I *do not* want to be updated on your progress. That way I at least have a degree of plausible deniability."

"Fair enough."

They were just about to leave when I called Mad back.

"If you happen to see Winky while you're out and about, give me a call, will you?"

"Have you lost him?"

"Kind of. Just keep your eyes peeled."

***

I made a phone call.

"Is that Fi?"

"Who's that?"

"Jill Maxwell. I spoke to you at the motorcycle club."

"The private investigator. I remember. What's up?"

"I wondered if we could have a chat?"

"Sure. Fire away."

"I was hoping we might be able to meet somewhere."

"Where?"

"I could come to your place if you like."

"That wouldn't be a good idea. Johnny's here most of the time."

"And Johnny is—?"

"My boyfriend."

"Right. I thought you and Chains were an item?"

"We are."

"Right."

"How about we meet at Big Bessie's?"

"What's that?"

"A diner on the A2186. About nine miles outside Washbridge."

"Sure. When?"

"I can't do it today because Johnny and I are just about to set off for a long weekend in Bognor."

"Okay. How about Monday, then?"

"That works for me. Meet me there at eight o'clock and you can buy me breakfast."

I'd no sooner finished on that call than my phone rang again; it was Aunt Lucy.

"Jill, could you pop over when you have a minute?"

"Sure. There's nothing wrong, is there?"

"No. It's Rhymes. He asked me to get in touch with you."

"Did he say what it was about?"

"No, just that he'd like you to pop over when you can."

"I may as well come over now."

"Okay, I'll put the kettle on."

There were at least a couple of dozen corks on the kitchen table.

"I see you're still sorting out your corks, Aunt Lucy."

"Actually, I'm trying to decide which one to enter into the competition. What do you think?"

If I'd given her a truthful answer, she probably wouldn't have spoken to me again.

"Which competition is that?"

"Candlefield Corks of course."

"Of course. How could I have forgotten?"

"I used to enter every year, but after what happened with Teresa Dropforge, I became disillusioned."

"What happened?"

"She sabotaged her main competitor's corks before the judges had the chance to view them. I was devastated when I saw what she'd done to my Little Tipper."

"You give all of your corks a name?"

"Of course not. That would be silly. Only my favourites."

"Right. Out of interest, what exactly did she do to your Little Tipper?"

"She took a Stanley knife to it. Even after all this time, it still upsets me to think about it."

"But you've decided to make a return to the competition?"

"Yes, I think now is the right time. So, which one do you think I should go with?"

"I'm no expert, clearly, but I do like that one."

"Blue Sue? I agree. I'd already narrowed it down to that one or Skinny Timmy or Long Joe. Decision made. Blue Sue it is. Would you like to come to the competition? It can be very exciting."

"When is it?"

"A week on Sunday. I've asked the twins but they're already doing something."

I just bet they were.

"What a pity, so am I."

"Maybe next year, then?"

"Definitely." Not a chance. "I'd better go and see what Rhymes wants. Is Barry upstairs?"

"No. Dolly has taken him to the park."

"Jill, you couldn't have timed it better." Rhymes looked up from the notepad he was writing on. "What rhymes with marmalade?"

"Err, barricade?"

"That doesn't work."

"Renegade?"

"That doesn't work either."

"Why don't you read me what you have so far?"

"Okay. Are you ready?"

"As I'll ever be."

"It's called an Ode to Toast."

"Great."

"Toast is so delicious,
It can be covered with jam or marmalade,
When it comes to snacks,"

"Hmm, it's very good. So far."

"That's where I'm stuck." He sighed. "I can't come up with the next line."

"Err, how about, *toast takes the highest accolade?*"

"That's genius! You didn't tell me you were a poet too, Jill."

"It's not something I like to brag about. Aunt Lucy said you wanted to see me?"

"That's right. I've had some exciting news. You'll never guess."

"I honestly have no idea."

"I've been asked to do a reading of my poems at the Tortoise Poets Society."

"That's great. I'm really pleased for you." And, well worth dragging me all the way over here.

"It's in London."

"I thought you meant here in Candlefield."

"No. That's why I wanted to see you. I need you to get me there."

"To London? Have you actually been to the human world before?"

"No, that's why I'm so excited. Do you think there'll be time to do some sightseeing too?"

"Hang on. I haven't said I can take you."

"You have to, Jill. This is a once in a lifetime opportunity. Please say you will." He gave me that pathetic little tortoise face of his. The one he knew I couldn't say no to.

"When is it?"

"In three weeks."

"I—err—"

"Please, Jill. I'll be forever in your debt."

"Okay, then."

When would I ever learn?

"Is everything okay?" Aunt Lucy asked when I joined her in the kitchen.

"Everything's hunky dory. I've just agreed to take Rhymes to London for a poetry recital."

"That's so nice of you. You're such a kind soul."

"Aren't I just?"

"Did you hear about Queen Chomp, Jill? It's so incredibly sad."

Queen Chomp was the queen of the rainbow fairies who I'd encountered several years earlier, when I'd been trying to get hold of some sap from the rainbow lily. At the time, we thought Grandma was in a coma and that the sap was the only thing that could save her. As it transpired, she wasn't in a coma at all; she was just witchbernating.

"What's happened to her?"

"See for yourself." Aunt Lucy picked up The Candle newspaper and handed it to me.

"She's dying? But she isn't very old, is she?"

"No. It's all very tragic."

"It says here that she's been taken to the Rainbow Zone. Where's that?"

"I'm no expert, but from what I understand, it's where the Rainbow fairies go to spend their final days."

"Hold on. Say that again, would you?"

"I said the Rainbow Zone is where Rainbow fairies end their days."

"Pearl is a genius."

"She's my daughter and I love her dearly, but I never thought I'd hear you say that about her. What did she do?"

"Sorry, Aunt Lucy, I have to get back. I'll explain everything another day."

"Okay, bye."

***

I charged into the house, almost knocking Jack over.

"I know where it is, Jack!"

"That's great. You know where *what* is?"

"I think I've found the—"

"What have you found, Mummy?" Florence came running out of the kitchen.

"I—err—I've found another red caterpillar with yellow spots."

"Brill!" Her little face lit up. "Is it a boy or a girl?"

"I — err — think it's a girl."

"She can be Archie's girlfriend. Where is she?"

"In the front garden."

"Show me! Show me, please!"

We went out into the garden and I made a show of trying to find the (non-existent) second caterpillar. "She seems to have disappeared."

"Where was she, Mummy? I might be able to find her."

"Somewhere around here."

Florence got down on her hands and knees and began to search the lawn and flowerbeds. I took that opportunity to go over to Jack who was standing in the doorway.

"I take it that it wasn't really a caterpillar you found?" Jack said, in a hushed voice.

"No. It's the first compass stone, and I haven't actually found it yet, but I think I might know where to look."

"Where?"

"When I showed the clue to Pearl, she said she thought part of it was missing because the paper was torn. I didn't think much of it at the time, but now I reckon she might be right."

"I still can't see the caterpillar, Mummy."

"Keep looking, darling. It must be there somewhere."

"So, where's the stone?" Jack said.

"When I was at Aunt Lucy's earlier, she showed me an article about the queen of the rainbow fairies. She's critically ill and has been moved to the Rainbow Zone."

"So?"

"That's where rainbow fairies end their days."

"You've lost me."

"What if the whole clue was actually: **Find the north**

compass stone where the rainbows end their days?

"It's a bit convoluted, isn't it? Wouldn't it have said where *rainbow fairies*?"

"That's not how clues work, Jack. They're supposed to be convoluted. Didn't you ever have scavenger hunts when you were a kid?"

"I've found it, Mummy!" Florence jumped to her feet.

"You have?"

"Look!" She came running over to us and held out her open palm to reveal the caterpillar.

"I'm going to call her Angie."

"Archie and Angie? Nice."

"Can I take her to see Archie?"

"Of course. Off you go."

"I assume you'll be paying a visit to the Rainbow Zone," Jack said.

"I might as well. It's not like I have any other leads. I may have to buy a Bakewell pudding or two first, though."

Chapter 12

"Mummy! Daddy! It's time to get up!"

I managed to open one eye, to find Florence jumping up and down on our bed.

"What time is it?" Jack yawned.

I fumbled to grab my phone from the bedside cabinet. "Ten to six. Go back to bed, Florence."

"I can't sleep, Mummy. It's the dance competition today. Let's practise."

"Forget it. I've done all the practising I can. If I do any more, I won't have any energy left for the competition."

"Aww. Can I have breakfast, then?"

"Jack, your daughter wants breakfast."

"The last time I looked, she was *our* daughter."

"Yes, but you know how to make the muesli just how she likes it."

"I suppose I'd better get it for her, or you'll give her those awful strawberry toffee pop things."

"They're Strawberrycandy Pops, and I wouldn't say no if you offered to bring me a bowl of them."

"That's not happening. We'll all have breakfast together at the kitchen table, like a proper family. Come on, Florence, let's go and get our *healthy* breakfasts."

When I eventually managed to drag myself downstairs, Buddy started to circle my legs.

"Have you fed the dog, Florence?" I already knew the answer because his empty bowl was still on the worktop.

"His food smells horrible, Mummy."

"We've already talked about this. Buddy is your dog, so you have to feed him. You know where the pouches are."

"But my breakfast will go cold."

"Muesli doesn't go cold. If you don't start feeding your dog, we'll have to give him away."

"No!" She jumped off the stool. "Please don't give Buddy away."

"Okay, but from now on you have to promise to feed him without me having to remind you."

"I promise." She emptied the foul-smelling gloop into his bowl, and then began to go through our dance routine.

"What about the rest of your muesli, Florence?" Jack said.

"I'm full, Daddy, and I have to practise the dance."

Jack looked to me to back him up, but I couldn't in good conscience encourage her to eat that revolting stuff.

Twenty minutes before we were due to set off for the village hall, Donna and Wendy came to the door.

"I hope you don't mind us coming over, Jill, but this one has been driving me mad all morning, asking how long it is until dance class."

"Of course not. Come in. Florence is out in the garden, looking at her caterpillars. Why don't you go and join her, Wendy?"

"Okay, Mrs Maxwell."

Whenever one of the kids called me that, I felt a thousand years old.

"Would you like a cup of tea, Donna?" I led the way into the kitchen.

"Do we have time?"

"There's always time for a cuppa, and Jack was just about to make one, weren't you, darling?"

"Apparently. Good morning, Donna."

"Morning, Jack. Are you coming to the competition?"

"I wouldn't miss it for the world." He looked at me and grinned.

"Hold on. I thought you were going golfing?"

"I was, but Florence said she'd like me to be there to watch her."

"You can't be there."

"Too late. I've promised her now."

Oh bum! It was bad enough having to do the dance, but knowing Jack was watching would make it ten times worse.

Wendy and Florence came running inside.

"Mummy!" Wendy whooped. "Florence has got two red caterpillars, and they both have yellow spots."

"How unusual."

"Look!" Florence held out her bucket.

"Wow! They really are colourful, aren't they?" Donna said. "Where did you find those?"

"In the garden. Archie was in the back, and Mummy found Angie in the front."

"Archie and Angie? Those are nice names."

"Why don't we have any red caterpillars with yellow spots in our garden, Mummy?" Wendy said.

"Maybe we do. You'll just have to look for them." Donna took the drink from me. "Thanks, Jill. Are you looking forward to the competition?"

"Oh yeah. I've been counting the minutes."

"I certainly have." Jack laughed.

"I'll warn you now, Jack, if I see you videoing me, I will smash your phone into a million pieces."

"Okay, you two!" Jack shouted to the girls who were still on caterpillar duty. "It's time to go to dance class."

"Yay!" Florence came rushing inside with Wendy hot on her heels.

I waited until we were halfway between the house and the village hall before making my move.

"I've left my purse behind. I'll just nip back and get it."

"You never forget your purse." Jack eyed me, suspiciously.

"Well I have. I'll only be a couple of minutes."

"You'd better not miss the competition. Florence will never forgive you."

"I won't. You lot go ahead. I'll be there before you know it."

I ran back to the old watermill, rushed inside, grabbed Buddy, and then set off down the village.

"Where are we going?" Buddy yawned. He'd been fast asleep when I picked him up.

"I have a nice little surprise for you."

"Will I like it?"

"Yeah, I'm sure you will."

"Hang on. What are we doing here? I'm not going back to this loser."

"It's only for a few hours, I promise." I knocked on the door.

"I didn't think you were coming." Stewart certainly scrubbed up nicely in his Sunday best. "My mother will be here any minute."

"I'm here now, aren't I? Where's the cash?"

"We said twenty pounds, didn't we?" He held out a twenty-pound note.

"Fifty or I take him home."

"That's daylight robbery."

"Take it or leave it."

"Okay, okay." He took another two banknotes out of his pocket. "Here you are."

"Thank you." I handed Buddy to him. "Don't forget what we agreed. I've left the gate to the back garden on the latch, so make sure you have him back there before midday."

"No worries. My mother never stays more than an hour."

"Okay. I have to go."

Jack shot me a look as I rushed into the village hall.

"Where have you been?"

"To get my purse, I told you."

"Don't give me that. I know you, Jill. You're up to something."

"Moi?"

"At least you came back. I thought you'd done a runner, so you didn't have to do the dance."

"Were you going to stand in for me?"

"I couldn't have done any worse."

"You're cruising for a bruising, buddy. Where are the girls?"

"Over there. They're making the draw to determine the order."

"I hope we're on first, so I can get this nightmare over with."

Just then, Florence and Wendy came running over. Donna was trailing behind them.

"Mummy and me are on fifth," Wendy said.

"We're number eleven." Florence handed me a slip of paper with number eleven printed on it.

"How many are taking part?"

"There are twelve couples altogether," Donna said. "You're second from last."

And so, the torture began.

As I watched the mother and daughter combos perform, it quickly became apparent that the mothers fell into three categories: There were those, like me, who clearly had no experience or aptitude for dancing.

Yes, I know I said I could have been a ballerina, but I say a lot of stuff. Surely, you've worked that out by now.

In the second category, were those mothers who clearly had some background in dancing—maybe they'd attended dance classes when they were kids—but who were now rusty, out of shape, or both.

And then there were those who looked like they worked out five times a day, went to dance class twice a week, and probably auditioned for stage musicals every weekend.

"It's Wendy's turn," Florence said.

Donna and Wendy's performance was every bit as impressive as the one I'd seen on the video.

Until.

With only a few seconds left in their routine, Wendy tripped. Although she recovered quickly, she was inconsolable when the music finished. Florence, being the good friend she was, went over to give her a hug.

It was our turn now, and my nerves were beginning to jangle. It was then that I noticed Jack take his phone out of his pocket.

"I said no videos."

"I promised Florence I'd record it."

Oh bum! I could hardly deny Florence the opportunity

to see herself in action, but the thought of other people seeing me make a fool of myself was scary. I had no doubt whatsoever that the video would find its way to Kathy, and she'd never let me live it down. And what if it ended up on YouTube? It didn't bear thinking about.

"Mummy, it's our turn." Florence grabbed my hand and dragged me out of the chair.

It was decision time.

I could have ensured victory by using magic, but what kind of example would that be to set for my daughter? The only honourable thing to do was to do my best and live with the embarrassment of having everyone see me make a fool of myself.

***

We left the village hall with Donna and Wendy who had recovered from her earlier upset.

"Where shall I put this, Mummy?" Florence held the tiny cup aloft.

"I think you should keep it in your bedroom."

"I'm disappointed for Wendy," Donna said. "But if we couldn't win, I'm glad you and Florence did."

"Thanks, Donna."

"You deserved it. Neither of you put a foot wrong. You must have put in hours of practice."

"We did, trust me."

Jack coughed and said something that sounded like *cheat* under his breath, but I ignored him.

Once we reached the old watermill, we said our goodbyes.

"Jill, what time shall I bring Wendy over tomorrow?"

"We have to be there at two, so let's say one-thirty."

"Okay. We'll see you then."

Florence went running upstairs, to find a spot to keep her little trophy. Meanwhile, Jack was giving me *the look*.

"What?"

"I don't believe you just did that, Jill."

"Did what?"

"You know what. You cheated."

"What do you mean? We won fair and square."

"With the help of magic."

"Nonsense. What makes you think I used magic?"

"You didn't put a foot wrong."

"That's because I put in so much practice."

"I saw you do it. I saw you cast the spell."

"Don't be ridiculous. There's nothing to see."

"Yes, there is. There's this certain look you have when you're casting a spell. It only lasts for a split second, but I can recognise it."

"Rubbish."

"Look me in the eye and deny you used magic to win."

"Okay, I admit it, but it was your fault."

"*My* fault? How was it my fault?"

"Because you were recording the dance. I didn't want millions of people to see me make a fool of myself. And, besides, I didn't use magic on Florence, so she won fair and square."

"I still think it was a bad message to send her."

"Anyway, I never would have done it if it had meant that we took the trophy away from Donna and Wendy, but they'd already blown their chances. Do you forgive me?"

"I suppose so."

Florence came running down the stairs and then stopped dead in her tracks.

"Where's Buddy?"

"Yeah, where is he?" Jack went through to the lounge. "He's not in here."

"Maybe he's hiding upstairs." I suggested.

Florence ran back upstairs, but came down a few minutes later, empty handed. "He isn't up there. Did you give him away, Mummy?" Her bottom lip started to tremble. "I said I would feed him."

"Of course I didn't. I would never do that, darling." I caught Jack giving me an accusing look. "I didn't, honestly. He must be out in the garden."

But he wasn't.

"Did you find him, Mummy?" Florence said when I walked back into the kitchen.

"No, but don't worry. He can't be far away. You stay here with Daddy and I'll go and find him."

"I want to come!" Florence yelled.

"No, you stay here with Daddy. I'll find him. I promise."

I headed out of the door before Jack could ask any awkward questions, and rushed down to Stewart's house. If anything had happened to Buddy, I would kill that man. Slowly and very painfully.

Moments after I'd hammered on his door, Stewart made an appearance, looking very sheepish.

"Where's Buddy? Why didn't you put him back in our garden, as agreed?"

"There's been a slight problem."

"If anything's happened to —"

"He's fine, honestly."

"Then why isn't he in our garden?"

"My mother is still here. I didn't expect her to stay so long."

"Stewart! Who is it?" The voice came from behind him, and moments later, a large woman appeared at his side. "Your tea is going cold. Who's this?"

"This? This is — err — "

"I'm Molly, the dogwalker. I've come to take Buddy on his daily walk, haven't I, Stewart?"

"Err, that's right, Mum."

"I can't believe you have a dog walker, Stewart." She shook her head. "When did you become so lazy?"

"I'll just go and get Buddy for you, Ji — err — Molly."

His mother eyed me up and down. "Is this really your job? Dog walking?"

"Yeah."

"And you can make a living doing this?"

"Just about."

Stewart returned with Buddy in his arms. "There you go, Molly."

"Thanks. Come on, Buddy, let's get your exercise."

"Am I glad to see you," Buddy said, as we made our way back to the old watermill.

"I never thought I'd hear you say that."

"You lot may be dysfunctional, but you're better than that loser."

"I'll take that as a compliment."

"You found him, Mummy!" Florence shouted when I walked through the door.

"I told you I would. Why don't you play ball with him in the garden?"

Once Florence and Buddy were out of earshot, Jack

turned to me. "Is there anything you'd like to tell me, Jill?"

Chapter 13

It was Sunday morning, and Florence was bouncing off the walls with excitement because we were going to visit Ursula, queen of the unicorns, later today.

"How much longer is it now, Mummy?" she asked for the fifth time in the last hour.

"It's ages yet. I've already told you that we don't go until this afternoon. Why don't you go and play with Archie and Angie?"

"But we might be late for the queen."

"We won't, I promise. We'll set off in plenty of time. Now, go and check that the caterpillars are alright."

"Okay." She rushed out into the garden.

"This is going to be a very long morning." I sighed.

"Hmm." Jack was looking all around the kitchen, clearly distracted by something.

"What are you looking for?"

"I was just checking that you hadn't sold the dog again."

"You're hilarious. And I didn't sell him; I just rented him out for a few hours."

"How could you possibly think that was okay?"

"If Stewart had brought him back on time, you'd have been none the wiser."

"But he didn't, and I am."

"How about I give you half the money? Will that shut you up?"

"I don't want your blood money."

"How is it *blood* money? No one died."

"I think you should spend it on Florence. Buddy is *her* dog, after all."

"I — err — I was going to do that anyway."

"Of course you were."

"I was. That was the whole point of doing it."

"Great. What will you buy her?"

"I don't know. She's quite partial to custard creams."

"Jill!"

"Only joking. Sheesh, whatever happened to your sense of humour?"

Even though Florence was obsessed with caterpillars, they didn't hold her attention for very long. She was now running around the lounge, holding a plastic cup on her head.

"I'm a unicorn. I'm a unicorn!"

"I wonder if Robbie would fancy a game of golf," Jack said.

"Forget it. If I have to cope with Little Miss Unicorn, then so do you."

"How long is it now, Mummy?"

"Five minutes less than the last time you asked. We won't be leaving until after we've had our lunch."

"Can we have it now?"

"No, we can't. It's only eleven o'clock."

"The queen might not mind if we get there early."

"She won't be there now. She told me she had to go shopping this morning."

"We could go shopping with her."

"No, we can't. You'll just have to wait until this afternoon. Why don't you go and play with your dolls' house?"

"I can't because I'm a unicorn." She began to lap the room again.

An hour later, and I could stand no more of it.

"Jack, can I have a word?" I gestured to him to follow me into the hall.

"What's up?"

"I have to nip out."

"Oh no you don't. You vetoed my golfing."

"This is different. I'm going to follow up my lead on the compass stone."

"Oh. That's different. Are you going to the Rainbow Zone?"

"Hopefully, but I have to find out where it is first. I'm going to start at the queen's palace and take it from there."

***

After a brief detour to Bakewell to purchase half a dozen Bakewell puddings, I magicked myself to the Dark Woods. After shrinking myself to fairy size, I headed north towards Rainbow Valley.

The fairy manning the checkpoint wasn't the one I'd encountered on my previous visit, several years earlier, but she had clearly attended the same charm school.

"Who are you and what do you want?"

"I'd like to see Queen Chomp, please."

"Not possible."

"I realise she's in the Rainbow Zone, so if you could just direct me there, I'll be on my way."

"You can't go to the Rainbow Zone without a permit."

"Who can give me a permit?"

"Queen Chomp."

"But she's in the Rainbow Zone."

"Correct."

"How am I supposed to get a permit from Queen Chomp if I can only go to the Rainbow Zone if I have a permit?"

"Not my problem. Was there anything else?"

"There must be someone else who can issue me with a permit. Who's in charge now the queen is away?"

"That would be her sister, Princess Gobble."

"Great. In that case I'd like to see the Princess."

"She isn't accepting visitors."

"I think she'll see me."

"And why would she do that?"

"Because I have these." I took the box out of my bag and opened the lid. "And if you call her to tell her I'm here, one of these can be yours."

"Mmm." She licked her lips. "What's your name?"

"Jill Maxwell. Tell her I did some business with her sister a few years ago."

"How do you spell that?"

"J-I-L—"

"I know how to spell Jill. I meant your last name."

"Right, sorry. It's M-A-X-W-E-L-L."

"Wait there."

She went into the guardhouse, made a phone call, and returned a couple of minutes later.

"The princess says she can spare you a few minutes." She raised the barrier. "Just follow the—"

"It's okay. I remember the way."

The fairy who greeted me at the rainbow coloured gates of the palace was the same one I'd met there on my previous visit. Unfortunately, I couldn't for the life of me remember her name.

"Welcome back, Jill. It's been a while."

"Thanks, err—"

"Felicity."

"Of course. I was sorry to hear about the queen."

"It came as something of a shock to us all, but she's in the best place now."

"Where is the Rainbow Zone, exactly?"

"I'm afraid I'm not at liberty to divulge that information. Let's go through to the great hall. The princess is waiting for you in there."

Princess Gobble was a slightly younger version of her sister, the queen.

"Where are they?" she demanded, as soon as I stepped into the hall. "Where are the Bakewell puddings?"

"In my bag."

"Give them to me."

"I'm sorry, your highness, but I need a couple of things from you first."

"What do you want? Hurry up, I'm starving."

"I need you to tell me how to find the Rainbow Zone."

"That's easy. You go back out of the gates, take a left and keep on walking along the rainbow road until you see the huge pot."

"Of gold?"

"Why would you think it was full of gold? It's just a very large pot that someone dumped by the roadside years ago. Take a right there and keep on going until you reach the Zone."

"How will I know when I have? Reached the Zone, I mean."

"You'll know. Trust me."

"Okay, but I understood that I'd need a permit too."

"How bothersome. Felicity, go and get me the permit book, would you?"

"Yes, your highness." Felicity disappeared out of the doors and returned a minute later with a small pad. "The permit book, your highness."

The princess scribbled her signature, tore a sheet from the book, and handed it to me.

"Thank you." I gave her a couple of Bakewell puddings, which she began to devour.

"Was there anything else?"

"No, that's everything. Thank you for your time."

I'd been walking along the rainbow road for almost twenty-five minutes, and I was beginning to think I'd been sent on a wild goose chase, but then I spotted it.

The giant pot.

Despite what the princess had said, I couldn't help but wonder if there might be gold in there. For the sake of a couple of minutes, it seemed silly not to at least check. The pot was so tall that I couldn't see inside, so after making sure that no one was around, I managed to clamber up the side by putting my foot on one of the handles. It was so dark that I couldn't be sure if there was anything inside it or not. If I could just grab my phone, I'd be able to use the flashlight to—ouch! I overbalanced and tumbled headfirst into the pot. Fortunately, my landing was broken by something soft.

"Do you mind!" Whatever I'd landed on, pushed me away. "That hurt."

"I'm sorry. It was an accident." I turned on the flashlight app.

"It's okay. No permanent harm done." Whoever or whatever it was, brushed himself down. "I don't get many visitors in here."

I wasn't surprised.

"I'm Jill. Sorry about this. I was looking for—err—gold." I laughed.

"Then you're in the right place. I'm Gordon Gold, and I'm very pleased to make your acquaintance."

"Err, likewise."

"What did you want to see me about?"

"I understand that you might know the way to the Rainbow Zone."

"I do indeed. Climb back out of the pot, take the next right, and keep on going."

"How will I know when I'm there?"

"Trust me, you'll know."

"Thanks. Just one more thing, and I hope you don't mind me asking, but—err—what exactly are you, Gordon?"

"I don't mind at all. I'm a pot troll."

"Is this your home?"

"Yes, what do you think of it?"

"It's very nice, but doesn't the darkness bother you?"

"No, you get used to it after a while. I'd much rather be in here than at the bottom of a well like my cousin, Timothy."

"Does he happen to live in the Dark Well?"

"Yes, how did you know?"

"Our paths crossed a long time ago. Anyway, thanks again, I'd better be going."

"Are you sure you wouldn't like to stay for a cup of troll tea? It's exceptionally good."

"I wish I could. Maybe another day."

They were right.

Both Princess Gobble and Gordon Gold had said I'd know when I'd arrived at the Rainbow Zone, and I sure did. The road narrowed until it was no more than a foot-wide path that suddenly became much steeper. It took all of my concentration not to fall as I climbed higher and higher. Pretty soon, I was so high that clouds obscured everything below me. The temperature had plummeted too, and I had to blow on my hands to keep them warm.

At long last, the narrow path started to level off, and I was just beginning to think I was through the worst of it when it began to descend sharply again. The ground was still obscured, so I had no idea what was below. If I wasn't very careful, I would fall. Gently does it— aarghh! My legs went from under me and I began to slide down the path.

This wasn't going to end well.

I emerged from the clouds, just in time to see the ground hurtling towards me. At this speed, I would surely break every bone in my body. I closed my eyes, and braced myself for the impact, but when it came, it was soft and fluffy.

I was in a large hole full of cotton wool. Relieved to be still alive, and after a few false starts, I eventually managed to climb out.

"Are you okay?" An elderly rainbow fairy, lying in a deckchair, lifted her sunglasses.

"Yes, but only thanks to the cotton wool. Do you happen to know where I can find Queen Chomp?"

"The last time I saw her, she was in the sun lounge."

She pointed to the white building at the far end of an expansive lawn.

"Thanks."

The large doors, which faced the lawn, were wide open, so I walked straight in. I'd expected to find lots of frail, elderly rainbow fairies being attended to by doctors and nurses. Nothing could have been further from the truth. The room was full of sprightly-looking fairies, mostly elderly, but all of them looking as fit as fleas. Queen Chomp was seated at a large table, playing cards with three other rainbow fairies.

"Excuse me, your highness."

"Can't you see I'm playing—oh, it's you. What brings you here?"

"I need your help."

"Are you after more lily sap?"

"No, not this time. I'm just after some information."

"That comes at a price too."

"I have Bakewell puddings."

"Shush!" She glanced around to see if anyone had heard. "If the others know you have them, they'll all want some."

"I'm a little confused, your highness."

"About what?"

"I understood you came here because you were dying."

"That's right. I am."

"You seem to have made a remarkable recovery."

"If only that were true. I could go at any minute. The same is true for all the others here."

"But everyone looks so—"

Just then, the woman who was seated to the queen's

right, *popped*. Yes, I do realise how weird that sounds, but it's the only way I can think to describe what happened. One minute, she was sitting there, and the next, POP! She disappeared into thin air.

"See what I mean?" the queen said. "Now, where are those Bakewell puddings?"

"I need an answer to my question first."

"Be quick, then. I'm ravenous."

"I was led to believe that the north compass stone is somewhere here in the Rainbow Zone. Do you know where?"

"Of course I do. Go back out the way you came. There's a fountain halfway down the lawn."

"I saw it. Is the stone in there?"

"It's in the water."

"How do I get it?"

"Just put your hand in and grab it."

"That's all?"

"Well, yes. Except for the electric eels of course."

"*Eels*?"

"Just kidding." She laughed. "Where are those Bakewell puddings?"

***

"How long is it now, Mummy?"

Despite the eventful day I'd had so far, time had of course stood still in the human world, and Florence had not developed any more patience.

"If you ask me that one more time, young lady, there'll be no unicorns for you."

"Not fair." She pouted.

"Go and play with Buddy. You haven't thrown his ball for him yet today. And you know how much he likes to chase after it."

"Okay." She hurried outside.

"How did it go?" Jack asked.

"Voila!" I held out the compass stone, which was just that, an unimpressive circular rock.

"Is that it? I was expecting something much more impressive."

"One down, three to go."

"Where are you going to put it?"

"It has to be somewhere really safe."

"You could rent a bank deposit box."

"Nah, I'll stick it in a shoe box in the wardrobe."

Chapter 14

"Why didn't you tell me, Jill?" Kathy shouted down the phone.

Oh bum! She must have found out that Lizzie had skipped school, realised that I knew about it, and was going to have a go at me for not telling her. How would I talk myself out of this one? First, I had to stall for time.

"Tell you what?"

"You know very well what."

"I — err — well, Lizzie —"

"Never mind about Lizzie. How long have you been going there?"

Huh?

"Going where?"

"To the dance studio. Which one are you going to?"

"What are you talking about? I'm not going to any dance studio."

"Don't give me that. I've seen the video."

Oh bum, and double bum!

"Where did you see it?" As if I didn't know.

"Jack sent it to me. I couldn't believe my eyes when I saw it. You and Florence were great."

"Thanks, but it was just luck. Every other time I did the dance, I messed up."

"I don't understand you, Jill. Normally, you're only too keen to brag about things, and usually without any justification. How come this time you're hiding your light under a bushel?"

"What is a bushel, anyway? I've always wondered."

"Oh no you don't. You're doing what you always do when you don't want to talk about something. You're going off at a tangent."

"No, I'm not. What's a tangent, anyway?"

"You know I've been wanting to get into shape for ages. Why didn't you tell me you'd taken up dance? I would have gone with you."

"Honestly, the only dance class I go to is Florence's, and all I do is watch."

"Pull the other one."

"Would you believe me if I said I cast a magic spell so I could dance like that?"

"Another silly tangent. Look, the next time you go to your dance studio, you're taking me with you, okay?"

"Sure. I give you my word that the next time I go, you can come with me." Which will be never.

Florence was upstairs, playing with her unicorns, and counting the minutes until it was time to see the real thing. Jack was in the lounge, adding the stamps, which Oscar had brought around earlier, to his album.

"Which country do you reckon this one is from?" He held up a stamp with a picture of a kangaroo and some kind of reptile.

"Australia, I suppose."

"That's what I thought at first, but the marine iguana is found only in the Galápagos Islands."

"How on earth do you know that?"

"I looked it up. So, where do you think I should put it?"

"That's a really dangerous question to ask me right now."

"I'm sensing you're angry about something."

"Guess who I've just been talking to."

"Don't tell me it was Ursula. She hasn't cancelled

Florence's trip, has she?"

"No, it wasn't Ursula. It was Kathy."

"What did she say to upset you?"

"She wanted to know why I hadn't told her that I was going to a dance studio. Now why do you think she would ask me something like that?"

"I—err—" He shuffled from one foot to the other.

"Go on. I'm listening."

"I thought it would be nice for her to see Florence's moment of triumph."

"But she saw me dancing too."

"So what? You should be proud of your performance. It's not like you cheated by using magic, is it?"

***

Donna and Wendy arrived ten minutes earlier than arranged.

"I'm sorry we're early, Jill," Donna said. "Wendy has been driving us crazy since six o'clock this morning."

"Snap. Come on in."

"Where's Jack?"

"He's just nipped to the store."

The two girls were running around the kitchen, holding plastic cups on their heads.

"Wendy, stop it," Donna said, more in hope than expectation.

"Florence, why don't you and Wendy go and run around the garden until it's time."

"Isn't it time now?"

"Not quite. Go outside and I'll call you."

"Okay."

"That's better." Donna grinned. "Wendy's been like that all morning."

"To be fair, it's not every day you get to meet a unicorn."

"True. By the way, congratulations on your win yesterday. You and Florence were fantastic."

"Thanks."

"I've put the video on YouTube. Have you seen it?"

"You recorded us?"

"Not just you two. I recorded the whole competition. It's had over five hundred views already."

"That's — err — great."

At long last, it was time for us to go.

"Are you sure you don't want to come too, Donna? I'm sure the queen wouldn't mind."

"No, it's okay. I'll wait here. It's not like you'll be gone for more than a few seconds."

"Okay. Come on, girls, take my hands. It's time to go and see the unicorns."

"Bye, Mummy." Wendy gave Donna a kiss then put her hand in mine.

"Let's go, Mummy." Florence grabbed my other hand.

I magicked the three of us to the entrance hall of the queen's palace. Waiting for us there was Ronald.

"Welcome back, Jill. Who are these two pretty ladies?"

"This is my daughter, Florence. And this is her best friend, Wendy."

For the first time that day, both girls fell silent; they were so stunned to come face to face with a unicorn.

"I'm very pleased to meet you, Florence and Wendy." He stomped his hoof.

"Say hello," I encouraged them.

"Hi, Ronald." Wendy was the first to speak.

"Are you really a unicorn?" Florence said.

"I certainly am. Can't you see my horn?"

"Can I touch it?"

I was horrified. "That's not very polite, Florence."

"It's okay," Ronald said. "Of course you can touch it." He dipped his head so she could reach the horn.

"It feels funny." Florence giggled nervously.

"What about you, Wendy?" Ronald turned to her. "Would you like to try?"

"Yes, please."

When the two girls had finished, Ronald took a couple of steps back. "Now, you two. Would you like your own unicorn horns?"

"Yes, please!" They chorused.

"Follow me, then." He led the way to the gold cabinet and pulled open the drawer. I expected to see the conical hats that he'd tricked me into wearing on my first visit to the palace, but it was full of realistic looking unicorn horns. Ronald must have seen the look of surprise on my face, so after telling the girls to pick one each, he took me to one side. "It's okay. They aren't real."

"Thank goodness for that."

Florence came running over. "Look, Mummy, I chose the red one."

"That's lovely, darling."

"I've got a yellow one, Mrs Maxwell." Wendy held hers up for me to see.

"That's very pretty too."

"If you want to, you can stick them on your head," Ronald said.

"Yeah!" Florence put hers on her forehead and it stayed put.

Wendy followed suit.

"They will come off, won't they?" I said to Ronald.

"Of course. Just give them a twist and they'll snap off. Right, it's time to go and meet the queen now. Are you girls ready?"

They chorused a deafening, "Yes!"

Queen Ursula was on her throne, but as soon as we walked through the door, she stepped down and trotted across the room to us.

"These must be the two prettiest girls in the human world. Which one of you is Florence?"

"I am," Florence said, as quiet as a mouse. She was clearly overawed to be in the presence of the queen of the unicorns.

"So you must be Wendy?"

Wendy could only manage a nod.

"My name is Ursula. I'm very pleased to meet you both. I see Ronald has given you your own horns. I have to say you both make excellent unicorns." That brought a smile to the face of both girls. "Would you like to know what we have planned for you today?"

"Yes, please." Florence had found her voice again.

"First, you're going to ride in the royal carriage, through U-city. Then, when you get back to the palace, there'll be a party tea for you. How does that sound?"

"Brilliant!" Florence squealed.

"Fantastic!" Wendy yelled.

"In that case, your carriage awaits. Ronald, would you escort these two young ladies?"

"It will be my pleasure, your highness."

"What about me, Ursula?" I said. "Shall I go with them?"

"You're welcome to accompany them, or you can stay here and we can chat."

Much as I would have liked to look around U-City, the thought of being stuck in a carriage with two manic young girls wasn't the least bit appealing.

"Florence, do you mind if I stay here with the queen?"

She shrugged, and it was clear she couldn't have cared less, so long as she got to ride in the unicorn carriage.

Once the girls and Ronald had left, Ursula ordered tea for two.

"Bring it through to my quarters, would you?"

"I really do appreciate you doing this today, Ursula."

"Don't mention it, Jill. It's the least I could do."

Her quarters turned out to be a room only half the size of the throne room, but every bit as spectacular. There was so much gold, I needed sunglasses; the furnishings were made from only the very best materials. Being queen of the unicorns definitely paid way better than being a private investigator.

"This is a lovely room, Ursula."

"Thanks. The throne room always feels rather ostentatious, that's why I spend most of my time in this little hideaway. It's much more homely."

"Right."

"Grab a seat, I've ordered Earl Grey tea for us, and I hear on the grapevine that you have a soft spot for custard creams."

"Where did you hear that?" I took a seat on one of the

two ginormous sofas.

"I have my spies." She grinned.

"I really am grateful you allowed Florence and her friend to pay you a visit."

"The pleasure is all mine, and besides, there's something I want to talk to you about."

"Oh?"

Before she could elaborate, Ronald brought in the tea and biscuits, and much to my delight, the custard creams were on a plate by themselves.

"I understand that you don't like your custard creams mixed with other biscuits." He put the plate on the table next to me.

"Your spies are very good. Thank you."

Ursula waited until Ronald had left us alone and then said, "I wanted to bring you up to date on the Devon *situation*."

"That's really not necessary, Ursula. He's your brother, and I understand that complicates things."

"It does, but after you left, I gave a lot of thought to what you'd said."

"I shouldn't have said anything. It's none of my business."

"I'm glad you did. I needed someone to make me see sense. I couldn't continue to turn a blind eye to Devon's antics, so I've exiled him."

"You have? I really wasn't expecting that."

"Neither was he. It isn't quite as bad as it sounds. He's living on U-Island in the lap of luxury."

"Where is that?"

"Off the south coast of U-City. It's only ten minutes by steamer. He's allowed to visit U-City one day per month, but he isn't allowed to go to the human world."

"How did he take that?"

"He wasn't happy, but when he realised the alternative was to spend time behind bars, he quickly warmed to the idea. I've promised to review the situation in two years."

"I have to say, Ursula, I'm impressed. That can't have been easy."

"It wasn't, but what kind of example would I have been setting for my subjects if I'd done nothing?"

When Florence and Wendy returned from the carriage ride around U-City, they were even more hyper.

"We went to the park, Mummy. The slide was really, really big. So was the roundabout."

"Then we saw the unicorn fish," Wendy said.

"*Unicorn fish*?"

"Yeah, they're in the lake. They have horns on their heads too."

"Fantastic."

"And we saw a giant fountain," Florence said.

"And now it's time for tea. Follow me, everyone." Ursula led the way into a huge dining room. On either side of the table, which ran the full length of the room, were lots of young unicorns, all clearly excited about meeting the two girls.

"Florence and Wendy, I've put you at either end of the table."

The two girls took their seats and were soon chatting to the young unicorns.

"Tuck in, everyone!" Ronald said.

The table was heaped high with sandwiches, cake and pop. The children (human and unicorn) didn't need telling twice to get stuck in.

***

All too soon (for the girls, not for me), it was time to say our goodbyes.

"Say thank you to the queen," I said.

"Thank you!" Wendy gushed.

"Thank you!" Florence said. "Can we come again?"

"Florence! You shouldn't say that." I was mortified.

"It's okay, Jill. I'm just glad the girls have enjoyed themselves. And yes, Florence, you're both welcome to come back again."

"Next week?"

"Maybe not that soon. Perhaps next year."

"Yay!"

"Thanks again, Ursula. And well done with the other thing. Bye."

"Bye, everyone." The queen saw us off.

"It was brilliant, Mummy!" Wendy said to Donna. "We had a ride in a carriage, and we saw unicorn fish, and we ate lots of cake."

"It sounds like you had a lovely time."

"We did, and we got these." She held open a giant carrier bag.

Ursula had given a bag full of presents to both girls just before I magicked us back to the human world. Florence was already tearing the wrapping paper off hers.

"Can I open mine too, Mummy?" Wendy said.

"Let's get back home first. You can do it there."

"You're welcome to stay, Donna," I said.

"We really ought to get back. Thanks again for today."

"No problem. I have a feeling we might be doing it again next year. Florence, say goodbye to Wendy and her mummy."

"Bye." She managed without once looking up from her haul of presents.

Chapter 15

"But Mummy, I don't feel very well."

"You're perfectly fine. You have to go, so let's hear no more about it, please."

Normally, Florence couldn't wait to go to school to be with her friends, but this morning, she was pretending to be under the weather, so that she could stay at home and play with the toy unicorns that Ursula had given her. But I was onto her game.

"Please, Mummy, I'm poorly." She forced a cough to prove the point.

"Why don't you take one of your new unicorn toys to show the children at school?"

"Can I?"

"Yes, but you mustn't tell anyone where you got it from."

"Okay. Which one shall I take?" Her cough had miraculously cleared up.

"You decide. Mummy has to go to work." I gave her a kiss, then went through to the lounge where Jack was catching up with the TV news. "I'm off, Jack."

"You're going in early, aren't you?"

"I have to meet someone at a diner on the A2186."

"Big Bessie's?"

"How did you know?"

"I've driven past it a thousand times. It looks like a real greasy spoon. I hope you aren't planning on getting anything to eat from there."

"I might risk a bacon cob. I'm starving."

"Rather you than me."

"A word of warning. Florence was trying to get out of

going to school just now."

"Is she poorly?"

"She reckons so, but she's fine. She just wants to stay home to play with her new toys. I told her she can take one of them to school with her. That seems to have placated her for now, but I wanted to make sure you don't cave in and let her stay off school."

"I wouldn't do that."

"You say that, but I know what you're like. She can twist you around her little finger."

"Rubbish."

"Just like I can." I grinned.

***

Wow! Jack hadn't been kidding about Big Bessie's. It wasn't so much a greasy spoon as a greasy ladle. It wasn't even a proper building, but instead appeared to be three old steel containers that had been welded together. It was with some trepidation that I pushed open the steel door, only to be met with the overwhelming aroma of bacon.

Mmm, I love that smell.

"Over here!" Fi shouted from the table closest to the counter. "Grab a seat. I haven't ordered yet. I thought I'd wait for you. The breakfast cobs are to die for."

With Jack's words of wisdom still ringing in my ears, I went for the sausage and bacon cob.

"Have you been here before, Jill?"

"I can't say I have."

"You're in for a treat, then. Bessie makes the best bacon cobs in this part of the country, and I should know, I've eaten my way through a few hundred."

"Bessie does actually exist, then?"

"Yeah." She grinned. "That's her." She pointed to the overweight, unshaved, bald-headed man who was hard at work at the griddle. "His name's actually Thomas, but everyone calls him Bessie. It drives him mad."

I did a double take when the food arrived.

"Big enough for you?" Fi laughed.

"This is ridiculous." The cob was so large I needed two hands to hold it.

"Take a bite."

I did, and she was right, it was the best breakfast cob I'd ever tasted. "This is delicious."

"Told you, didn't I?"

I was a little nervous about drinking from the huge mug, which clearly had never seen the inside of a dishwasher, so I closed my eyes while I drank.

"How well did you know Killer, Fi?"

"He and I were an item for a while. Almost a year in fact."

"Was that before Johnny?"

"At the same time, actually, but before Chains."

"Right. Your love life is a little complicated."

"Not to me."

"Does that mean you were seeing Killer while he was still a member of Loose Chippings?"

"Yeah, we had to keep it quiet because it wouldn't have gone down well with either club. Life became a lot simpler once he joined WOW."

"Wow?"

"Wash-on-Wheels."

"Of course. I thought for a minute, you meant—err—never mind. How did it end? Between you and Killer, I mean?"

"He ended it."

"Did he find out about Johnny?"

"No, it wasn't that. He'd always known about him."

"Why then?"

"He said things were getting stale, but I reckon he was seeing someone else. I can always tell."

"Do you know who?"

"No idea."

"And then you and Chains got together?"

"Not straight away, but yeah, a few months later."

"When was the last time you saw Killer?"

"The day before he died. I went over to the workshop to take a look at the competition bike."

"Did the two of you talk?"

"A bit. Mainly about the bike."

"How did he seem?"

"Same as always."

As Fi reached across the table for the ketchup, I noticed a small tattoo on her wrist: A red rose with a letter S on the stem.

"What does the S stand for?"

"That's for my parents: Susan and Stephen. They died within a few hours of one another."

"How awful. Was it a car crash?"

"No. My mum had been ill for years, so her passing wasn't unexpected. But that same night, my dad died from a heart attack. At least, that's what they called it. It was a broken heart if you ask me."

"That must have been terrible for you."

"It was the worst day of my life. The day Killer died was the third anniversary of their death. I was on my way back from Halifax when I heard about him."

"*Halifax?*"

"That's where my parents are buried. I visit their grave every year on that day."

"Were you close to them?"

"Very. I was a bad kid, got into a lot of trouble, but they always stood by me."

I finished the last of my breakfast cob and stood up. "Okay, thanks for taking the time to talk to me, Fi."

"For what it's worth, I don't reckon Slugger did it."

"Oh?" I sat back down again. "You never spoke up when Chains said he thought Slugger was responsible."

"Chains doesn't like to be contradicted. Particularly not by me."

"Who do you think killed him?"

"You have to promise you won't let on it came from me."

"You have my word."

"If you ask me, it was Sid."

"Why him?"

"I happen to know that Killer had lent Sid some money. I heard the two of them arguing about it. From what I could make out, Sid should have paid back the money some time ago."

"Did the argument get heated?"

"Yeah, very. There were lots of threats going back and forth. Have you spoken to Sid yet?"

"No, but I intend to."

***

I left the diner feeling several pounds heavier. I would

have to make sure I avoided this road in future in case I was tempted to try more of Bessie's delicious but calorie-loaded offerings.

On the drive into Washbridge, I began to think about Winky. Was he still wandering the streets, cold and alone? Hopefully, I'd find him sitting on the sofa; I'd apologise for misjudging him, and everything would go back to how it used to be.

"Morning, Jill." Mrs V was eating strawberries. "Would you like one?"

"No, thanks. Is Winky back?"

"No, and I hope we've seen the last of him."

"Are you sure he hasn't sneaked back in?" I started for my office. "Maybe he's hiding under the sofa."

But he wasn't. And he wasn't on my desk. Or on the windowsill.

The office was sans Winky.

I slumped into my chair, feeling totally despondent. I'd done some terrible things in my time, but this was by far the worst, and I couldn't allow it to stand. I had to find Winky, apologise to him, and ask him to come back. How to find him, though, that was the question. Posters were a waste of time. I'd tried those the last time he'd gone missing. Instead of finding him, I'd ended up with an imposter called Blinky. Besides, the world had moved on since then. Why spend hours putting up posters when I could reach millions through social media? There was just one teeny, tiny problem: I wasn't exactly the world's leading expert when it came to social media type stuff, but I knew someone who did know their way around it, so I made a call and left a voicemail asking them to call me back.

A few minutes later, Mrs V popped her head around the door.

"Jill, I have the lady from the dog grooming salon here. She wondered if you might be able to spare her a few minutes."

"Of course. Send her through."

As soon as she walked in, it was clear that Farah was hot under the collar about something. She usually had a smile on her face, but today, her face looked like thunder.

"I'm sorry to disturb you, Jill."

"No problem. Is something wrong?"

"Have you opened your post yet today?"

I glanced at the pile of unopened bills on my desk. "I haven't got around to it yet. Why?"

"I've just had a letter from the *new* landlord."

"I didn't realise we had a new landlord."

"Neither did I, but we do, and they say they're going to raise the rent by twenty-five per cent."

"They're doing what!" I grabbed the pile of letters on my desk. "What's the name of these cowboys?"

"Robert Bear & Associates."

"It's here." I ripped open the envelope and skimmed through the letter. "This is outrageous."

"Can they do this, Jill? Legally, I mean?"

"I don't know, but I do know there's no way I can afford to pay what they're asking. I can barely afford to pay the current charge."

"Neither can I. I would have to go back to working as a mobile dog groomer."

"I'm going to have a word with these jokers."

"Will you let me know how you get on?"

"Of course."

"Thanks, Jill. I'd better get back because I'm halfway through shampooing a Westie."

As soon as Farah had left, I called the number on the letterhead, and got the obligatory automated answering system.

"Thank you for calling Robert Bear & Associates. Your call is very important to us."

Translation: We couldn't give a fig about you or your call.

"We are receiving an unusually high volume of calls at the moment, but most of your questions will be answered on our website, www.wecouldntgivea.fig."

Translation: We still don't give a fig about you.

"If you wish to stay on the line, we will be with you as soon as we can."

Translation: Zero figs given here.

That was followed by hold music, which was so bad that I would have preferred to listen to jazz. Every few minutes the music halted, and for a brief moment, there was the hope that I might actually get to speak to a human being. That hope was soon dashed though.

"All our operators are busy at the moment. Please stay on the line and we'll be with you as soon as possible. Your call is very important to us."

No translation necessary.

I put up with this nonsense for almost fifteen minutes while getting progressively angrier and angrier.

And then the line went dead.

Aaaaaaarrrgggghhh!

I was just about to throw my phone through the window when it rang. Was it possible they'd seen my missed call and were ringing me back?

Of course not.

"Auntie Jill?"

"Hi, Mikey."

"You left me a message to call you."

"Yeah, thanks for getting back to me. I wanted to ask you a favour."

"Err — right?"

"You're into social media and all that stuff, aren't you?"

"I guess."

"Winky has gone missing, and I wondered if you knew how to put a post on — err, wherever it is you put a post — so that if anyone sees him they contact me."

"Sure, no problem. Do you have a photo of him?"

"Yeah."

"Do you know how to send it to me?"

"Of course I do."

"Okay. Let me have it and I'll get the post up in the next few minutes."

"Great. I'll send it straight away."

"Later." And with that, he ended the call.

Which photo of Winky should I send to him? I had so many. Probably not the one of him dressed as a pirate.

"Mrs V, I need a favour."

"Of course, dear. How much did you want to borrow?"

"Err, no, I don't need any money. I need some legal advice."

"I'll do my best, but my expertise is more in the yarn sphere."

"I actually meant from Armi."

"You realise he's retired. He's no longer a practising

lawyer."

"I know he can't act in an official capacity, but I wondered if he might be able to give me some advice. Informally."

"I'm sure he will if he can. Are you in trouble with the law again?"

"Nothing like that. Apparently, we have a new landlord who wants to raise the rent by twenty-five per cent. That's why Farah came over."

"That's outrageous. Can they do that?"

"That's what I need Armi to tell me because if that increase stands, we'll have to move out, and I have no idea where we'll go."

"We can't allow that to happen. This office is like my second home. I'll have a word with Armi tonight."

"Thanks. Oh, and by the way, I've asked my young nephew to put up an announcement on social media asking that if anyone spots Winky, they get in touch with me."

"Why would you go and do that?"

"Because I'm worried about him."

"That cat is more than capable of looking after himself."

"I just wanted to warn you in case someone gets in touch to say they know where he is."

Chapter 16

If Doug Duggan, the now deceased manager of Candlefield Lido, had been able to uncover who was behind Reptile Holdings, surely a super sleuth such as myself should be able to do the same.

What do you mean, you wouldn't bank on it?

Unfortunately, it would mean a trip to the Candlefield Library archives—not exactly one of my favourite places. To fortify myself ahead of my visit to that dusty basement, I decided to call in at Cuppy C.

These days, the twins never seemed to be behind the counter. Today, they were both huddled around a table close to the window.

"Hey, Jill!" Pearl was the first to spot me. "Come and join us."

"What are you two planning?"

"Do you remember we told you we were trying to figure out what to do with the space upstairs?" Amber said.

"I do."

"We've come up with our best idea ever."

"Oh dear."

"We really have this time," Pearl insisted. "Wait until you hear it."

"Go on, then. I'm all ears."

"They aren't all that big," Amber quipped, and the two of them fell into hysterics.

"If you're going to tell me, you'd better be quick about it because I have to go to the library in a few minutes."

"Corks," Pearl said.

"*Corks?*"

"That's right. Corks."

"I'm probably being dense, but I don't have the faintest idea what you're talking about."

"Did you know Mum collects them?" Amber said.

"I didn't until a few days ago. Apparently, she gives some of them names?"

"She's always done that."

"And you don't find it a bit weird?"

"I might. You might. But all the corkers do that kind of stuff."

"*Corkers*?"

"That's what they call people who collect corks."

"That's a stupid name."

"What do you think, Jill?"

"About what? You haven't actually told me what you're planning on doing."

"Oh yeah." Amber giggled. "We're going to open a cork museum upstairs."

"This is a wind-up, right?"

"Of course not. Corkers will come from all over Candlefield to see it, and while they're here, they'll buy lots of food and drink."

"Hmm, I'm not convinced."

"You haven't heard the best part yet."

"Which is?"

"It's not going to cost us a penny to set this up. We'll just use all of Mum's corks."

"And Aunt Lucy is okay with that?"

"We haven't actually mentioned it to her yet, but she's bound to agree. She loves to show off her collection."

"You'll still need to ask her."

"We will. We'll do it this afternoon."

"And when will the *cork museum* open?"

"If all goes to plan, it should be open within a couple of weeks."

***

Have I ever mentioned that I hate the Combined Sup Council? Well, I do. With a burning passion. Several years had passed since I was, for a very short time, a member of that esteemed institution. During my time on the council, I had tried without success to persuade them to introduce the internet to Candlefield. Since then, nothing had changed—still no internet, which meant the only way to access the archives of The Candle newspaper was by going to the library. Maybe they had introduced microfiche since my last visit—I could always hope.

As I approached the information desk, it appeared to be deserted, but then an elf appeared. Then disappeared. Then reappeared.

"Hi, can I help?" he said in-between bounces.

A glance over the counter revealed that he had large springs attached to his feet.

"Hi. I need to take a look at old copies of The Candle. I don't suppose you've transferred them to microfiche, have you?"

"I'm afraid not." He sighed. "That's a particular bugbear of mine. I pushed very hard for them to do it, but the money doesn't stretch that far."

"Are the papers still in that dusty basement?"

"I'm afraid so. We have made one improvement, though."

"What's that?"

"We've purchased a new chair. It's much more comfortable than the one that used to be down there."

"Great."

The chair might have been more comfortable than its predecessor, but it was already covered in dust. By now, I was very familiar with the way that copies of The Candle were stored, so I set about checking all those published in the last twelve months, which was no mean feat when your nose was being assaulted by clouds of dust. I was hoping to find some mention of Reptile Holdings, but I wasn't optimistic. By way of a backup, I also kept a lookout for any articles relating to controversial new property developments during that same period.

I'd only been at it for a few minutes when someone coughed. I'd assumed I was alone in the basement—no one else was crazy enough to be down there. When I glanced around, I couldn't see anyone. Maybe I'd imagined it.

"Excuse me." The tiny voice seemed to come from down near my feet. It was only when I leaned forward that I saw the tiny dust-covered creature.

"Hi."

"You're sitting in my chair," he said.

"Who are you?"

"Not that it's any of your business, but I'm Barry."

"I have a dog called Barry."

"Fascinating, I'm sure." He yawned. "But that doesn't alter the fact that you're in my chair."

"Sorry." I stood up. "I had no idea it was yours."

"Thank you." With a huge leap, for someone so tiny, he jumped onto the chair.

"Do you live down here, Barry?"

"I do. For almost four years now."

"Are you a fairy?"

"*A fairy*? Do I look like a fairy?"

"You do, actually."

"Well, I'm not. I'll have you know that I'm a sprite. A dust sprite to be precise."

"You're definitely in the right place, then. There's certainly plenty of dust in here. I'm Jill, by the way."

"What brings you down here, Jill? Are you a fan of dust too?"

"Not really. I'm hoping to find some information from these back issues."

"Why don't you tell me what you're looking for, and I'll help you."

"I wouldn't want to put you to any trouble."

"It's no trouble. I enjoy a challenge. What are we looking for?"

After I'd explained the purpose of my mission, he dived straight in. For such a little creature, Barry had no problems skimming through the newspapers. I'd given him half, and he was already further down his pile than I was.

"What about this one?"

Residents lose battle to keep community centre open.

"Maybe." The article certainly had similarities to the lido takeover. There too, no one knew who was behind the development, which had resulted in the community centre being demolished.

"Hey, Jill, what do you think about dust?"

"It makes me sneeze."

"I know. Great, isn't it? You can't beat a good sneeze. Is

it dusty where you live?"

"Not particularly."

"You're welcome to move in down here with me if you like. There's plenty of room as you can see. You'd have to bring your own chair, though."

"That's very generous of you, but I couldn't leave my family behind."

"I understand, but if you ever change your mind, the offer still stands."

It was almost an hour later when I came across another interesting article:

Children's nursery to close. Parents devastated.

It was a similar story. An unknown company had bought the building, which had housed a popular nursery, and closed it down.

"That's me done," Barry said. "I didn't find any mention of Reptile Holdings."

"Me neither, but these two articles might be worth following up. Thanks for your help, Barry."

"It was my pleasure. Much as I love this basement, it can get a little lonely down here. Will you come and see me again?"

"Maybe. It all depends what cases I'm working on."

Back at the car, I was just about to set off for home when I got a call from Jack.

"Jill, can you pick up a box of muesli on your way in, please? I've just realised we don't have enough for morning."

"Are you sure you wouldn't prefer Toffeecandy Pops?"

"Positive. I'd nip to the store myself, but Wendy and Florence are playing in the garden, and I don't like to disturb them."

"No problem."

***

"Hello, Jill," Marjorie Stock was doing another crossword. So far, she'd filled in only two answers.

"Hi, Marjorie. Have you just started that?"

"No, I've been at it since early this morning. They're much more difficult than they used to be. Take this clue for example: A seven letter word for an animal that lives in the water, beginning with an 'O'. I thought it was an otter, but that's too few letters."

"Octopus?"

"Of course. You're a genius, Jill. What about this one?"

"I'd love to stay and help, Marjorie, but I need to get back home."

"Of course. Were you looking for something in particular?"

"Jack asked me to pick up a box of muesli. I assume it'll be under 'S'?" For sawdust.

"Under 'S'? No, it's in the 'M' section."

"Of course. 'M' for mush. I should have realised."

I grabbed a box and returned to the counter.

Marjorie was still puzzling over the crossword. "Not East. Four letters beginning with a 'W'."

"West, possibly?"

"Of course. You're really good at this, Jill. You should come to my crossword club."

"*You're* in a crossword club?"

"Yes. We meet every second Thursday in the month. Would you like to join me?"

"Thanks, but I don't really think it's my scene."

"If you change your mind, let me know. We're always on the lookout for new members, particularly someone with your talent."

It was only when I stepped out of the store that I noticed the greengrocers had a new sign: Oranges' Oranges. Jack had been giving me a hard time recently about what he insisted was my unhealthy diet. Perhaps he had a point. Maybe I should eat more (or even some) fruit.

The only customers in the revamped shop were two vampires who were eyeing the blood oranges. Behind the counter was a couple in their early thirties; they both had ginger hair and freckles.

"Hi!" The man greeted me. "Welcome to Oranges' Oranges."

"Hi. When did you take over the shop?"

"Last week. I'm Craig and this is my sister, Gina. We're the Oranges."

"Orange is your name?"

"That's right. Hence Oranges' Oranges."

"I actually met a couple with the same surname several years ago."

"Really? It's quite an unusual name. Maybe it was our parents?"

"I'm just trying to remember their first names."

"Our mum's name is Rosemary, and everyone calls our dad Pip."

"Pip, that was it. Nice people."

"They are," Gina said. "They helped us to come up with the money for this place. Where did you meet Mum and Dad?"

"They came to ask me for help with their neighbour."

"Hang on," Craig said. "Are you by any chance a private investigator?"

"I am, yes."

"You're the one who gave my mum *the crystals coated with the anti-witch potion*, aren't you?"

"I — err —"

"It's okay. It worked a treat. Dad and the two of us still laugh about it from time to time."

"I probably shouldn't have billed your parents for it."

"Nonsense. Dad considers it some of the best money he's ever spent, and Mum still swears by it. She's adamant it's the only reason she hasn't had any more problems with her neighbour."

"In that case, I don't feel so bad."

"It was only last week that she told me she was getting low on the crystals, so you might be getting another visit from her soon."

"Oh dear."

"Anyway, what can I get for you? Sorry, I don't even know your name."

"It's Jill, and I'd like half a dozen of these oranges, please."

***

"Did you pick up someone else's bag by mistake?" Jack said when he saw the oranges.

"You're still not funny. I got these from Oranges' Oranges."

"Where?"

"It's the new name for the greengrocers."

"Since when?"

"Last week, apparently."

"Bit of a weird name, isn't it?"

"It's a brother and sister. Orange is their surname. And while I was getting your muesli, Marjorie Stock invited me to join her crossword club. She said they're always on the lookout for exceptional talent like mine."

"Yeah, right." He laughed.

"I don't know why you're laughing. I've always had a natural ability for solving crosswords."

"Of course you have. Just like I've always had a natural talent for the high wire."

"Now you're just being silly. Is Florence still outside with Wendy?"

"Donna came to get Wendy ten minutes ago, but Florence is still out there. She's really engrossed in something."

"I'll go and say hello to her."

"Mummy, something is wrong with Archie and Angie."

"What do you mean?"

"They've gone all funny. Look, they're underneath that branch."

"It's okay. They've just turned into chrysalis."

"I don't want them to be Christmas lists. I want them to be caterpillars."

"It's *cris-a-lis*, and all caterpillars do it."

"Why?"

"They stay inside that shell thing for a while and then, one day, they come back out as a butterfly."

Her face lit up. "Are Archie and Angie going to be butterflies?"

"Yes, they are."

"Will they still be red with yellow spots?"

"I don't know. You'll have to wait and find out."

"How long does it take? Can I stay out here and wait?"

"It doesn't happen that quick."

"How long will it be?"

"I'm not sure. Why don't you go and ask Daddy? He's an expert on caterpillars and butterflies."

Chapter 17

"Don't tell me you're going to eat another one," Jack said.

I'd just begun to peel an orange. "You were the one who told me I should eat more fruit."

"I know, but you've already eaten two."

"So what? If one is good for you, three must be three times as good."

"That's the problem with you, Jill. It's all or nothing. Have you never heard the saying, all things in moderation?"

"Have you never heard of the saying, those who wear plus fours aren't qualified to give anyone advice on anything?"

Florence, who had been unusually quiet over breakfast, piped up, "How much longer do you think it will take, Daddy?"

"I've already told you, pumpkin, I don't know. Somewhere between seven to fourteen days, according to the internet."

"But that's a *really* long time."

"I'm sorry, but there's nothing Daddy can do about it. Why don't you go outside and check on them?"

"Okay." She jumped down from the chair and dashed outside.

"Thanks for telling Florence that I was an expert on caterpillars." Jack gave me a look.

"Don't mention it."

"What are you up to today?"

"I'm going to talk to someone about the motorcycle club murder."

"Are you going to wear leathers? I bet you'd look good in them."

"That's exactly what Winky said."

"Has there been any word yet on the cat?"

"No, nothing. What if something has happened to him?"

"It won't have. Winky can look after himself. I would have thought you knew that by now."

"Yeah, you're right. I hope."

***

The Loose Chippings HQ had clearly once been a barn. When I pulled up outside, it was surrounded by at least twenty motorbikes.

Standing outside the double doors was a bunch of bikers. The tallest (and ugliest) of them never took his eyes off me as I crossed the road towards the building.

"Look what we have here, guys." He sneered. "Little Miss Prim."

The other men laughed and made comments under their breath.

"I'm here to talk to Mr Rainer."

"*Mr Rainer*?" The tall guy scoffed and took a few steps forward until he was right in my face. He had bad breath, and what looked like a home-made tattoo of a snake on his arm. "Why don't you talk to me? Aren't I good looking enough for you?"

"I want to speak to Mr Rainer. Get out of my way, please."

"We've got a feisty one here, boys. And what will you do if I don't get out of your way, honey?"

"I'll put you on the floor and walk over you."

They all seemed to find that hilarious.

"Look, honey." Tall guy put his hand on my shoulder. "I don't think you —"

He didn't get a chance to finish the sentence because, with the help of the 'power' spell, I put him on his back, then walked across his chest and headed for the doors. That seemed to silence the other men who stepped aside.

"Very impressive." The man who had appeared in the doorway was several years younger than the others. Undeniably handsome, with blond hair that was combed back, he had a huge grin on his face. "Get up, Billy, you're embarrassing yourself."

Billy picked himself up, said a few choice words under his breath and walked away.

"I'm looking for Mr Rainer."

"That's me, but only my probation officer calls me Mr Rainer. You can call me Slugger. And what should I call you?"

"My name is Jill Maxwell. I'd like to talk to you about Cecil Cole."

"Killer? What's your interest in him?"

"I'm a private investigator. I'm looking into his death."

"A PI, eh? I didn't realise they came in such pretty packages."

"Is there somewhere we can talk?"

"I was just on my way out."

"This is important."

"In that case, why don't you jump on the bike and we can talk as we ride."

"On a motorbike?"

"Are you coming or not?" He started towards the row

of bikes.

"I don't have a crash helmet."

"I've got a spare one. Come on."

If I'd allowed myself time to think it through, I'd have told him no, but it all happened so quickly that the next thing I knew we were speeding down the road. We were able to talk through the comms built into the helmets.

"You okay back there?"

"Not really."

"Not a biker, then?"

"Definitely not."

"I apologise for Billy. He's one heck of a mechanic, but he has a habit of shooting his mouth off."

"Forget it."

"Where did you learn to fight like that? Not many guys could put Billy on his back."

"Can we talk about Killer?"

"Sure, what do you want to know?"

"Did you murder him?"

"Wow!" He laughed. "You get straight to the point, don't you?"

"Did you?"

"No, I didn't." He pulled the bike into a layby where there was yet another roadside café, which was only marginally more salubrious than Big Bessie's. "Come on, I'll buy you a coffee."

Once Slugger had the drinks, we took a seat at one of the plastic tables outside.

"The guys at Wash-on-Wheels are sure you did it," I said.

"Chains and co? I'd be surprised if they didn't think that, but they're wrong. The truth is that Killer and I were good pals. We went back a long way."

"You can't have been happy when he jumped ship and joined Wash-on-Wheels?"

"You're right. I wasn't, but I understood why he'd done it. Killer wanted to win the competition, but we don't have the same resources as WOW. Here's the thing, though, he soon realised that there's more to life than winning a cup."

"What do you mean?"

"He wasn't happy at WOW. He admitted to me that he'd made a mistake, and said he didn't fit in over there."

"When was this?"

"A few weeks ago. He asked how I'd feel about him coming back to Loose Chippings."

"What did you say?"

"That I'd be glad to have him back."

"Are you telling me Killer planned to quit WOW to re-join your lot?"

"Yeah."

"Can you prove that?"

"Billy was there when Killer and I discussed his coming back, but I'm not sure if he'll be in the mood to talk to you. Not after what you just did to him." Slugger took a long drink from the mug. "I don't imagine someone like you slums it like this very often."

"Then, you'd be wrong. I was in Big Bessie's only yesterday."

"I'm impressed. We'll make a biker of you yet."

***

My numerous attempts to contact the new landlord had

got me precisely nowhere because I couldn't get past their obnoxious call handling system. It was time for a different approach, so after parking my car in Washbridge, I headed for their offices. Robert Bear & Associates were located on the third floor of Cloverleafs, one of the newest office buildings in Washbridge. The faceless steel and smoked glass structure had been built on the site of the old Washbridge main post office.

The ground floor was taken up with a huge reception area in which there was more foliage than there was in my garden. The two receptionists: one male, one female, looked lost behind the desk which ran the full length of one wall.

"Hi, I'm here to see someone from Robert Bear & Associates."

"Can I ask your name, please?"

"Jill Maxwell."

"And the name of the person you have an appointment with?"

"I don't actually have an appointment."

"I'm not sure that's going to work. They don't usually see anyone without an appointment."

"Would you give them a call, please?"

"Sure." She picked up the phone. "Hi, it's Rachel on reception. I have a lady down here without an appointment. She'd like to speak to someone. Yes, that's what I told her. Okay, thanks." She ended the call and gave me a shrug.

"I take it that's a no."

"Sorry. I did try."

"Sure."

If at first you don't succeed, bring out the magic.

I nipped out of the building, found a secluded spot, made myself invisible, and then headed back inside. I figured I'd probably freak someone out if I called the lift, so instead I waited until someone else did it. I didn't have to wait long until two young women pressed the 'Call' button. When the lift doors opened, I slipped in beside them. Fortunately, they pressed the button for the third floor.

"Have you seen what Carol is wearing?" the first woman said.

"You mean that top?" said the second woman.

"Yeah. Where do you reckon she found it? She must have been to the car boot sale again."

"What about Linda's shoes?"

"I know. It wouldn't be so bad if she could actually walk in them."

When the doors opened on the third floor, all three of us got out. As we did, another woman walked by.

"Hi, Carol," the first woman called. "I love your top. Is it new?"

Wow! Just wow!

There were several companies located on that floor; the landlord's office was the third door I came to. After a quick check to make sure there was no one else in the corridor, I reversed the 'invisible' spell, and then walked confidently inside.

Behind a much smaller reception desk sat a young man wearing a blue suit, a brown shirt and a pink tie. Clearly, he did not possess a mirror.

"Can I help you?" He sure managed to pack a whole lot of attitude into those four words.

"I want to see whoever is in charge."

"May I ask what it's about?"

"I've just received a letter that says my rent is being increased by twenty-five per cent."

"And?"

"*And*, it's outrageous."

"If you wish to register a complaint there is a formal procedure for doing so."

"Does that involve me having to listen to the world's worst hold music and a message telling me how much you value my business? I've tried that already, thanks."

"The complaint procedure is online at our web site. It's www —"

"I want to speak to a human being, and I want to do it now."

"I'm afraid that's not possible. I'm the only one here today."

"How do I know you're not lying?"

"You don't, but it happens to be true."

"Okay. Let's try this another way. What's the name of the boss of this organisation?"

"That would be Mr Bear."

"Robert, I assume?"

"Actually, no. Robert Bear died about six months ago. His son, Edward, has taken over the business."

"And do you have a phone number for him?"

"I'm sorry, but I can't —"

"Forget it. Thanks for your time."

***

As I walked back to the office, I considered nipping into Coffee Animal until I saw that the animal of the day was a cat. I was still too upset about Winky to spend half-an-hour surrounded by dozens of moggies.

"Jill! Yoohoo!" Deli shouted from across the road.

There was something different about her, but I couldn't work out what. It was only when she was standing in front of me that I realised what it was: her lips. They were huge.

"Hi, Deli. How are things?"

"Couldn't be better, Jill. Couldn't be better. Have you noticed anything different about me?"

"Your hair is a little shorter."

"Something else."

"New shoes?"

"My lips. I've got new lips."

"Oh, right, yeah. They're very — err — " BIG! "Nice."

"Thanks. I thought at first that Nails might have overdone it, but I'm getting used to them now, and everyone says they suit me."

Liars. "They do. Has Nails branched out?"

"He has. Maybe I should call him Lips now." She laughed. "We've had tons of bookings for the new treatment already." Her gaze shifted to my mouth. "Your lips are a little on the thin side. Have you ever thought of having them done?"

"No. I'm happy with them the way they are."

"You should be more adventurous, Jill. Give your Jack a surprise."

I could just imagine what Jack's reaction would be if I went home with lips the size of life preservers.

"I don't think so."

"If it's the cost, don't worry. There's a fifty percent discount for family and friends. I told Madeline yesterday."

"Is she having hers done?"

"She said she'd think about it."

I just bet she did.

***

"Any sign of Winky, Mrs V?"

"You'll be pleased to hear—"

"He's back?"

"That he's still missing."

"Oh." I sighed.

"I asked Armi about the rent situation last night, Jill."

"What did he say?"

"That it depends."

"On what?"

"The terms of your lease. He said if you let him have a copy, he'd take a look through it for you."

"Right."

"You do know where the lease is, don't you?"

"Err, yeah, of course." I didn't have the foggiest idea. "I'll dig it out and let you have it."

My office seemed so empty without Winky. I missed the banter and his cheeky ways. What if I never saw him again? I checked my email to see if anyone had contacted me about the posts that Mikey had put up, but there was nothing.

"It's a bit late to be sorry now, isn't it?"

The little voice seemed to come from my desk, but I couldn't see anyone. It was only when I got closer that I spotted the small spider.

"Sorry? Were you talking to me?"

"It's your own fault. You were the one who drove Winky away."

"Who are you, anyway?"

"Albert."

"Where did you suddenly pop up from?"

"I've lived here for months. Not that you've ever noticed. You're much too preoccupied with yourself."

"That's a bit harsh. I can't be expected to know every insect in the place."

"Winky did. He took time to get to know us all. We all miss him terribly."

"I miss him too."

"If it wasn't for you, he'd still be here. How could you accuse him of something like that?"

"I — err — "

"Never mind. I don't have time to listen to your lame excuses." And with that, Albert scurried away.

Leaving me feeling even worse.

Chapter 18

I was wondering when the next disgruntled insect might crawl out of the woodwork when my phone rang.

"Jill, I'm sorry to bother you."

"It's no bother, Aunt Lucy, I wasn't doing anything important."

"Rhymes has been pestering me all day to call you, to check that you haven't forgotten you've promised to take him to the recital in London."

I'd been trying very hard to forget about it. "No, of course not. Tell him I'm looking forward to it."

"He said to tell you it's the week after next."

"Don't worry. It's in my diary."

"Great. I'll tell him. I'd better let you get back to your work."

"You must be thrilled about the corks."

"What about them?"

"That everyone will be able to see them in the cork museum."

"I'm sorry, Jill, but I have no idea what you're talking about. What cork museum?"

"Didn't the twins talk to you?"

"I haven't spoken to them for a couple of days."

"Oh? Never mind, then. I should get on."

"Hold on. You can't leave it like that. What's all this about a cork museum?"

"It might be better if you heard it from them."

"Jill!"

"Okay. When I was in Cuppy C yesterday, they told me about their plans for the rooms upstairs."

"And?"

"And they're going to open a cork museum. They reckon it will attract corkers from all over Candlefield."

"I do hate that word."

"*Corkers*?"

"Yes. It sounds ridiculous. Sorry, you were saying."

"Just that they plan to open a cork museum and that they were going to — err — hoping to put all of your corks on display."

"Are they now? And yet, this is the first I've heard of it."

"I'm sure that's just an oversight on their part. They definitely told me they were going to give you a call."

"I'll look forward to that. Thanks for the tip-off. Bye, Jill."

"Err, bye."

Oh bum! The twins were going to kill me.

***

I had planned to drop in at Cuppy C on my way to see Lillian Wrongplant, the witch who had been in charge of the community centre at the time it was taken over by developers. After my conversation with Aunt Lucy, I changed my mind about visiting Cuppy C because I had a feeling that the twins might be after blood. My blood.

Lillian Wrongplant lived in a mushroom. Not literally, that would be silly. Her tiny cottage was shaped like a giant mushroom. The brass knocker on the door was also in the shape of a mushroom. The woman obviously had a thing for them.

"You must be Jill." She answered the door wearing an apron covered in — wait for it.

Elephants.

"Thanks for agreeing to talk to me. Is it okay to call you Lillian?"

"Everyone calls me Mushy."

"On account of the mushrooms, I assume?"

"Actually, no. It's because I'm rather partial to mushy peas."

"O—kay."

She must have seen me glance at her apron because she said, "My mushroom apron is in the wash, so I had to make do with this one. Come inside, Jill, we'll go in the parlour. Can I get you anything to drink?"

It took me a moment to respond because my senses were overwhelmed by the mushroomness.

What's wrong with *mushroomness*? I think it's a great word, and I challenge you to come up with one. All suggestions on a postcard to the usual address.

"Sorry, Lill—err—I mean, Mushy, it's just that I've never seen anything quite like this."

"That's what everyone says."

"The wallpaper, the carpet, and where did you find all those mushroom ornaments?"

"I started collecting them when I was a child, and I've never stopped. My friends and relatives buy them for me on my birthday and at Christmas. Now, about that drink? Is tea okay?"

"That'll be lovely, thanks."

Mushy disappeared into the kitchen and returned a few minutes later with two cups of tea and a biscuit barrel, decorated with pictures of mushrooms.

"You mentioned on the phone that you wanted to talk about the old community centre."

"That's right. I've been looking back through old issues of The Candle at the library, and I came across an article about the community centre. I believe it was bought by property developers?"

"It was, and it still makes me angry to think about it, even after all this time. May I ask what your interest in it is, Jill?"

"Someone has bought the lido and there's a rumour going around that they intend to close it down and build on the site. I'm trying to find out who's behind it. So far, all I know about them is their name: Reptile Holdings. I looked in the archives at the library, to see if I could find any info on them, but drew a blank. That's when I came across your story. It was a longshot, but I don't have anything else to go on, so I thought I'd check to see if there was any connection."

"I've never heard of Reptile Holdings, but I'm happy to tell you what happened in our case if you're interested."

"I am."

"The community centre was loved by everyone. All kinds of activities were held there, for children and adults. It was a real focal point for the community. Then, suddenly, out of the blue, we heard it was being sold. Just like that—no warning, nothing."

"What did you do?"

"We tried to stop it. We started a petition, went to see the council, even had a sit-in. None of it did any good, though."

"Did you find out who bought it?"

"We never did, but it wasn't for the lack of trying. Whoever it was had hidden behind an army of solicitors. One night, just before we had to give up the keys, I did see a big guy, dressed in a smart suit, in a fancy car parked outside the building. He stood out like a sore thumb. I tried to have a word with him, but as soon as he saw me approaching, he drove away. He might not have had anything to do with the takeover, but I've always thought maybe he did."

"Could you describe him?"

"Not really. Like I said, he drove off before I could get close. I did notice he had a scar on the left side of his face, though."

"What happened after you handed over the keys?"

"The place was demolished within a week."

"They didn't hang around."

"They sure didn't. The thing that makes me most angry is they didn't even use the land to build housing. They put up some faceless office building. And do you know the worst part, Jill?"

"What's that?"

"That building is still standing empty. I ask you, what was the point?"

***

I'd just left Mushy's mushroom cottage when my phone rang, and I made the fatal mistake of answering it without first checking caller ID.

"Thanks very much, Jill!"

"Yeah, thanks a bunch!"

It was the twins on speakerphone.

"Hi, girls."

"Why did you have to go and shoot your mouth off to Mum?" Amber barked.

"Hold on. When I was with you two yesterday, you specifically said that you were going to call Aunt Lucy in the afternoon, so naturally I assumed she'd know all about your plans."

"We didn't get the chance," Pearl said. "We got distracted."

"Anyway, what's the big deal? It's not like Aunt Lucy is going to refuse you, is it?"

"She just did."

"Oh. You two will be able to talk her around."

"I doubt it. She was pretty annoyed. She said she didn't want any Tom, Dick or Harry handling her Blue Sue."

"I'm really sorry, girls, but you did bring this on yourselves. You should have cleared it with your mother before you ploughed ahead with your plans. You'll just have to come up with another idea for the rooms upstairs."

"No chance," Amber said. "The cork museum is still a brilliant idea."

"Maybe, but it won't be much of a cork museum without any corks, will it?"

"We'll just have to get them from somewhere else," Pearl said.

"Where?"

"We haven't worked that out yet."

There would be no free muffins for me for the foreseeable future, that much was clear. After I'd finished on the call, I checked my email and was shocked by what I saw. There, in amongst all the usual spam, was an email with a one-word subject line: **Winky**.

Nervously, I clicked on it; the contents were brief and very alarming.

We have Winky.

If you want him back in one piece, place two-hundred pounds in a brown envelope, and put it in the bin in the layby next to Wash Woods, by four o'clock today.

What was I supposed to make of that? It could be a hoax; anyone could have seen Mikey's posts. But what if it wasn't? What if they really did have Winky? I couldn't risk ignoring it, so I headed for the nearest ATM, and withdrew the cash, then headed for Wash Woods.

If the catnapper really did have Winky, there was nothing to guarantee that they'd honour their part of the bargain by releasing him once they had the money. But I had a plan.

Can you guess what kind of plan it was?

Cunning? No, much better than that.

Devious? Nothing so obvious.

What I had come up with was nothing less than a *master* plan. Truly the king of all plans. Impressed? I thought you would be.

I pulled into the layby, got out of the car just long enough to drop the envelope containing the cash into the bin, and then drove away. Half a mile down the road, I parked in another layby, turned myself invisible, and used the 'faster' spell to leg it back to the bin. I arrived there just in time to see a wizard, dressed in tramp-chic, dip his hand into the bin. Was he the catnapper or just someone down on his luck? He pulled out the envelope, and without even opening it, shot off into the woods. Even though I was invisible, I followed at a distance in case he heard my footsteps on the brush-covered path. After a few minutes, he left the path, and made his way through the undergrowth. Eventually, he reached a clearing, in the middle of which, a small tent had been pitched. A tent that looked strangely familiar.

"It's me," the wizard said.

One of the tent's flaps opened, but I was at the wrong angle to see who was inside. The wizard handed the envelope to someone, and then waited. Moments later, whoever was inside handed the wizard a bank note, and then the wizard went on his way. Should I follow him? I decided not to because all of my instincts told me that he was just the go-between. The catnapper must be inside the tent, and hopefully, Winky would be in there too.

I reversed the 'invisible' spell, walked over to the tent, and pulled back the flap. Whoever was in there was about to wish they had never been born.

"Winky?"

"Jill?"

"Are you okay? I've been worried sick."

"I'm fine."

"Where is he? Where's the catnapper? Just wait until I get my hands on him."

"He — err — left. You just missed him."

"But I didn't see—" That's when the penny dropped. "What are you hiding behind your back?"

"Nothing."

"Show me your paws. And the other one. Now both of them together." I stared at the pile of bank notes. "It was you! You're the catnapper."

"Don't be ridiculous."

"I suppose the catnapper asked you to look after his money while he just nipped out for a while, did he?"

"Err, yeah. That's exactly what happened."

"I'm not a complete idiot. This is your tent! Why would you do something like this?"

"Okay, I admit it, but you drove me to it, by accusing me of something I hadn't done and forcing me out of my home."

"I know, and I'm really sorry about that."

"I didn't quite hear that."

"I said I'm sorry, but that still doesn't excuse you trying to get ransom money out of me."

"How about we call it quits? You forget about the fake kidnap, and I'll forget about the way you made me homeless?"

"Okay, that's fair."

"Great, so let's get back to the office. I'm dying for a bowl of salmon."

"Hold on. Aren't you forgetting something?"

"What?"

"The ransom money. I want it back."

"That wasn't part of the deal."

***

Florence was out in the garden, watching the two chrysalises like a hawk, just in case Archie and Angie emerged as butterflies. Meanwhile, Jack was staring at his phone, and looking very puzzled.

"Has Candy Crush got you confused again?"

"I was just checking the bank app. Did you draw out some cash today, Jill?"

"Err, yeah."

"Two-hundred pounds?"

"Yeah, give or take."

"What did you need all that for?"

"I — err — it was for Winky."

"Is he back?"

"Yeah."

"So, what happened?"

"It's a funny story. You'll laugh when I tell you."

"I'm listening."

"He'd been catnapped."

"Really?"

"As it turned out, no. Not really. He'd catnapped himself."

"I don't understand."

"He pretended to have been catnapped and sent me a ransom demand."

"The two hundred pounds?"

"Yeah."

"You're saying you paid Winky two hundred pounds to set himself free?"

"I didn't know he was the catnapper when I drew out the cash."

"But once you did, you kept hold of the money?"

"No, because I didn't find out what had happened until I'd already handed over the money to an intermediary."

"But when you did find out, you demanded the money back."

"Of course."

"So you have the two hundred pounds."

"Some of it."

"How much of it?"

"Seventy-five pounds."

"Why only seventy-five?"

"What can I say? Winky is a tough negotiator."

Chapter 19

The next morning, the three of us were at the kitchen table.

"Can I go outside, Mummy, please?" Florence had just gobbled down her marmalade on toast.

"It looks a little cold out there."

"But I have to check on Angie and Archie."

"Okay, but you'd better put your coat on."

"I hope nothing happens to those two caterpillars," Jack said. "She'll be devastated."

Before I could respond, I got a phone call from Kathy.

"What are you wearing, Jill?"

My sister had always been the weird one, but that question was strange even by her standards.

"My PJs. Why?"

"I didn't mean what are you wearing now, numpty. I meant tonight."

"Tonight. Err—?"

"Don't tell me you've forgotten we're going out with Rita."

"Of course I haven't. I just haven't decided what I'm going to wear."

"I treated myself to a new dress yesterday."

"I can't afford anything new. I've already had to fork out a small fortune for the cat this week."

"How come?"

"I—err—had to take him to the vets."

"Is he okay?"

"He's fine. Look, I have to get going. I'll see you tonight."

"Okay. Bye."

"You'd forgotten you were going out tonight, hadn't you?" Jack grinned.

"Totally. Kathy's had a new dress for the occasion."

"You could have had one too if you hadn't given all our money to that cat."

"Don't rub it in." Out in the hall, the letterbox rattled. "It's too early for the post."

"Probably more double-glazing leaflets." Jack went to check. "It's a note from the vicar."

"Please tell me they've cancelled the village fete."

"Nope. It's just a list of who's manning which stall."

"Which one have we got?"

"The coconut shy."

"What? Those things are dangerous."

"I'm only joking. We're on the refreshments stall."

"That doesn't sound too bad."

"It doesn't mean you can help yourself to everything on there."

"As if I would."

Snigger.

***

Mrs V looked down in the dumps.

"Are you alright, Mrs V?"

"Not really. I'm feeling a little down in the dumps, actually."

There I go again. They should call me Jill Sixth-Sense Maxwell.

"What's wrong?"

"He's back."

"Who is?"

"That cat."

"Isn't it great?"

"Are you crazy? These last few days without him have been perfect. When did he come back?"

"I—err—have no idea. I'd better go and check on him."

"Did you find the lease for Armi to take a look at?"

"Not yet. I'll dig it out later today."

Winky was perched on my desk, cleaning his paws. Normally, I would have had something to say about that, but I figured I should take it easy on him, at least until he'd settled in again.

"Morning, Winky. How are you?"

"Okay, I suppose, although my joints are giving me some gyp. I reckon it must be spending time outside in all weathers."

"You were in a tent."

"The wind whistled through that flimsy thing."

"Maybe I should take you to the vet for a check-up."

"There's no need for that. I reckon double helpings of salmon will have me right as rain in a week or two."

"A week or—okay, I guess I could run to that."

"Could you carry me to the sofa? I don't want to risk injuring myself by jumping down from here."

"Err, sure." I took him over to the sofa and put him down gently. "There you go."

I spent the next two hours going through every drawer in my desk and filing cabinet, but I couldn't find a copy of the lease. I must have had one, but I had no idea where else to look for it. How was I going to fight the proposed rent increase if I couldn't find it? Then I had a brainwave.

"I'm just nipping down to Bubbles, Mrs V."

"Alright, dear. Ask Farah if she wants to adopt that

awful cat, would you?"

"Hi, Jill." Delilah was behind the reception desk. "Do you have one of your dogs booked in? I don't have anything on my computer."

"No, not today. I'd like a quick word with Farah. Is she free by any chance?"

"Her next appointment isn't for fifteen minutes. I'll just check if she can see you."

"Thanks."

Moments later, she returned. "She says you can go through."

Farah was standing next to the grooming table. "Hey, Jill, do you mind if I carry on getting things ready while we talk?"

"Of course not. Delilah said you have another appointment soon."

"Yeah, with Tiny. He's always something of a challenge."

"What is he? A Chihuahua? A Yorkie?"

"An Irish Wolfhound. His owner thought the name was ironic."

"Right. Ever since you told me about the rent increase, I've been trying to get hold of the landlord."

"Any joy?"

"None so far. I was wondering if you could let me see a copy of your lease?"

"I haven't got it."

"How come?"

"When they handed over the keys, they said their printer was on the blink, but that they'd post the lease over to me the next day. It never arrived, and to be honest,

I've never got around to chasing them. What did you want it for?"

"Mrs V's husband used to be a solicitor. He said he'd look through my lease, but I can't find it at the moment. Not to worry."

"I can't help but worry, Jill. If that increase goes through, I could be finished."

Delilah popped her head around the door. "Tiny is here, Farah."

"I'll get going," I said. "Try not to worry."

Tiny might have been many things, but *tiny* certainly wasn't one of them. It took me all my time to squeeze past him.

***

Although I had an address for Jasmine Nodringer, I'd been unable to find a contact phone number, so I was planning to turn up on her doorstep, in the hope that she'd be prepared to talk to me. Jasmine had run the day-nursery that had been forced to close when the building in which it was located was bought by property developers.

I'd visited a few unusual houses in my time, including Mushy's mushroom cottage, but this one took the biscuit. On either side of it were conventional houses, which made the lighthouse look even more out of place.

I knocked on the bright red door and a few seconds later, there was the sound of footsteps on stone steps. The wizard who answered the door was wearing a smart grey uniform and matching cap.

"I'm sorry it took me a while to get to the door, I was just cleaning the light."

"I have to ask, why is there a lighthouse here? We're miles from the coast."

"I used to work at the lighthouse at Candle Point. When they decommissioned it, I took early retirement and set about building this place."

"Do you actually live here?"

"I do."

"That's amazing. Are you Mr Nodringer?"

"That's me. Ned Nodringer at your service."

"I'd like a word with Jasmine if that's possible."

His smile faded. "Jasmine died three months ago."

"I'm so sorry. I had no idea."

"Are you a friend of hers?"

"No. My name is Jill Maxwell. I'm a private investigator."

"Why did you want to see Jasmine?"

"I wanted to talk to her about the nursery she used to run."

"You realise that closed down some time ago?"

"Yes. I was hoping to find out more about the property developers who bought it."

"I might be able to help with that. Would you like to come in?"

"Yes, please."

"Follow me. The living quarters are just below the lantern room."

"I'm guessing that's near the top of the building."

"That's right. There's only one-hundred and fifty steps, though."

"Is that all? Great."

"Would you like something to drink, Jill?" Ned asked

when we finally made it to the living quarters.

It was difficult to talk because I was too busy gasping for breath. "Water, please."

Ned, who was at least twenty years older than me, seemed unaffected by the climb, but then he probably did it several times every day.

"Are you okay, Jill?" He handed me the water.

"Absolutely." Other than feeling like my heart was about to explode at any second.

"You said you were interested in the property developer who took over the nursery. Can I ask what your interest is, exactly?"

"Of course." I told Ned about the lido and my search through The Candle archives.

"And you think the same people might be involved?"

"It's a longshot, but I have no other leads."

"I'll be happy to tell you everything I know, but I'm not sure if it will help."

"It's worth a shot."

"The nursery was Jasmine's life. We weren't able to have kids, so she treated every child at that place as though they were her own."

"Did she actually own the nursery or just manage it?"

"It was her business, but she never treated it like one. She wasn't interested in making huge profits. As long as we had enough to live on, she was happy. I can still see her face the day she came home after hearing that the landlord had sold the building out from under her."

"Could he do that?"

"Seems like it. She only rented it on a month-to-month basis, and there was no way she was going to find anywhere else as cheap."

"She must have been devastated."

"She was, but Jasmine wasn't the kind to give up without a fight. She was determined to try and talk the buyer out of the purchase. Or at least persuade him to let her continue to run the nursery from there. She thought if she could show them what the place meant to the community, and especially the kids, that they could be persuaded."

"What happened?"

"I'd never seen her so driven. She thought about nothing else, and it paid off in the end because she managed to find out the name of the company behind the takeover. They were called Reptile Holdings."

"That's the people who bought the lido. Did Jasmine manage to find out anything about them?"

"I'm not sure. I think she might have, but—" His words faded away.

"Ned, are you okay?"

"Sorry, yes. I didn't tell you how Jasmine died. She called me one day, really excited. She said she'd made a breakthrough. I asked her to tell me about it there and then, but she said she was on her way home and would tell me when she got back." He hesitated again. "But she never did. I knew something was wrong when she still wasn't home two hours later. I called her a thousand times, but she didn't answer. The next thing I knew, two policemen came to the door, and told me Jasmine's body had been found underneath Candle Bridge."

"That's terrible. I'm so sorry."

"The police said it was suicide, and of course there were plenty of people ready to testify that she'd been depressed because of the nursery closure. But I know different.

When I spoke to her on the phone that day, she wasn't depressed. Far from it. She was jubilant about whatever it was she'd discovered."

"Do you think someone killed her?"

"I'd bet my life on it. And I'm positive it was someone connected to Reptile Holdings."

"Did you tell the police that?"

"I told anyone who would listen, but it hasn't done any good so far. Do you think you'll be able to bring these people to justice?"

"Hopefully, but I have to track them down first and that isn't proving to be easy."

***

Something very bad was going on. Initially, I'd simply been trying to find out who had taken over the lido, but it had now developed into something much more serious. Two people were dead, and they had both died under suspicious circumstances: Doug Duggan, an experienced lifeguard and manager of the lido, had supposedly fallen into the pool and drowned. And, according to the police, Jasmine Nodringer had committed suicide. Yet, only minutes before, she had called her husband who insisted she'd sounded upbeat and excited to share some news with him. The common denominator was Reptile Holdings who, as yet, I had been spectacularly unsuccessful in tracking down.

After leaving Ned Nodringer, I decided to take a look at the site where the nursery had once stood. In its place was an unremarkable office building. There was no sign to indicate who occupied it, and the mirrored windows made it impossible to see inside.

"Ain't no one in there, love."

I turned around to find an elderly wizard, walking an equally elderly Labrador.

"Hi. How do you know that?"

"I live right over there." He pointed to the row of houses that faced the office block. "There's not been anyone through those front doors since they finished building it. Don't know why they bothered putting it up."

"That's strange."

"It's not the only strange thing."

"Oh?"

"There's a van comes to the building in the early hours of the morning. I'm only a light sleeper and it wakes me up every time."

"How often?"

"Most nights."

"I thought you said no one had been through the doors."

"I said no one had been through the *front* doors. The van pulls around the back. There's another door there."

"Do you have any idea what they're doing?"

"Not a clue. I just see the van go down the alley around the back. It's usually there about an hour or so."

"Okay, thanks."

"Don't I know you from somewhere? Aren't you that Gooder woman?"

"I used to be, but that's some years ago. My name is Jill Maxwell now."

"I thought I recognised your face. How come you haven't taken part in any of the tournaments recently?"

"I have a daughter now, so I've retired from all

competitions."

"Pity. You were always entertaining."

"Thanks." I think.

***

I was in two minds whether or not to risk a visit to Cuppy C. The last time I'd spoken to the twins, they'd been on my case because I'd let it slip to Aunt Lucy about the cork museum. In the end, my craving for blueberries encased in a muffin was stronger than my fear of facing their wrath.

"Look who it isn't," Pearl said. "The town crier."

"You've got a nerve, showing your face in here." Amber was tapping her fingers on the counter.

"I've said I'm sorry, girls. What else can I do?"

"You could persuade Mum to change her mind about letting us use her corks."

"What makes you think she'll listen to me?"

"She always takes more notice of you than us."

"I could try, I suppose, but I can't guarantee she'll change her mind."

"Good. That's the least you can do under the circumstances."

"Does that mean I can have a coffee and a muffin?"

"I suppose so," Pearl said, somewhat begrudgingly I felt.

Chapter 20

I went straight from Cuppy C to Aunt Lucy's house, to try to change her mind about the corks. Fortunately, I was blessed with incredible powers of persuasion.

"No. Definitely not."

"But, Aunt Lucy, I really think—"

"I know the twins have sent you over here to try and butter me up, Jill, but they should have had the courage to come and ask me themselves."

"They've already told lots of people about the cork museum. What are they going to do if there are no corks in it?"

"That's not my problem. They should have thought about that before they made their plans without checking with me first."

"If they come over here and ask you themselves, might you say yes?"

"I might." She grinned. "Then again, I might not."

"I think you're enjoying this."

"The twins have taken me for granted all of their lives. It won't do them any harm to realise my sole purpose in life isn't to pander to them."

"Fair enough."

"Anyway, enough about the twins. How are you, Jill? If you don't mind me saying so, you seem a little on edge."

"I'm fine. Just really busy."

"And what about Florence?"

"She's obsessed with unicorns and caterpillars at the moment."

"And dancing." Aunt Lucy smirked.

"She is, but what made you mention that?"

"No need for modesty. I've seen your competition-winning routine."

"How?"

"Grandma showed it to me. She said she'd downloaded it from something called YouTube, I think."

"Great!"

I waited until I'd left Aunt Lucy's house before calling the twins.

"What did she say?" Pearl said.

"That if you want her corks, the two of you have to go around there and ask her in person."

"Can we have them?" Amber shouted from somewhere in the background.

"She told Jill that we have to ask her in person. If we do what she asks, Jill, do you think she'll let us have them?"

"I don't know. She just said she'd think about it."

"Mum's never like this." Pearl sighed. "I don't know what's got into her."

"Maybe she's tired of you two taking her for granted. Anyway, it's over to you now. There's nothing more I can do."

As soon as I ended the call, my phone rang. I assumed it would be the twins again, but it turned out to be Elizabeth Duggan.

"Jill, I've just found something in one of the pockets of Doug's jacket. It's a note in his handwriting that says AnonFront. I just wondered if that name meant anything to you?"

"No, it doesn't. Is that one word or two?"

"One."

"Okay. I'll check it out and see what I come up with. Thanks, Elizabeth."

***

I'd arranged to meet Sid, Chains' second-in-command. At his request, we were meeting in the grounds of Washbridge College—a curious choice of venue, I thought.

He hadn't grown any less ugly since our last encounter, but his attire was certainly different. Instead of the leathers he'd sported at the Wash-on-Wheels clubhouse, he was wearing a shirt, smart trousers and a pair of brogues.

"I almost didn't recognise you in that get-up," I said.

"The college don't approve of the leathers."

"You're a student here?"

"A mature student, yeah. Why so surprised?"

"I guess I'd expected you to work in a garage or something. What are you studying?"

"English lit. Can we crack on? My next class is in twenty minutes."

"Sure. I mainly wanted to ask how you got on with Killer?"

"Okay, although to be honest, I didn't have a lot to do with him. I love bikes, but I'm only interested in riding them. I've never understood the appeal of taking them apart and putting them back together again. Too much like hard work if you ask me."

"Did the two of you ever socialise?"

"Only as part of the whole club."

"Never just the two of you?"

"No. We didn't really have anything in common."

"Did you ever have any bust-ups with him?"

"It sounds like you think I had something to do with his death, and I didn't. You should be talking to Slugger."

"I've already spoken to him. I don't believe he had anything to do with it."

"He's worked his charm on you, I see. Slugger always was good with the ladies."

"Not at all. Apparently, Killer was going to re-join the Loose Chippings club."

"Says who? Slugger? I wouldn't believe him if he told me rain was wet."

"You said you and Killer weren't close, but I understand that he lent you some money."

"Who told you that?"

"Did he?"

"Yeah, but that doesn't mean we were buddies or anything. It was strictly a business arrangement."

"I also heard you and he had argued because you were late repaying the loan."

"It was Fi who told you, wasn't it? She should keep her big mouth shut."

"Is it true?"

"Yeah, I was late, but I gave him a gold ring in full payment."

"And he was happy with that?"

"More than happy. That ring was worth more than I owed him, and he knew it."

"Can you prove that's what happened?"

"How am I supposed to do that? No one else knew about the arrangement." Sid took out his phone and brought up a photo of a ring with a skull on it. "This is it. I loved that ring."

"Let's for a minute assume it wasn't Slugger who murdered Killer. Is there anyone else who might have wanted him dead?"

Sid shrugged. "Maybe one of Fi's fellas—there's enough of them. Did you know she'd had a fling with Killer?"

"Yeah, she mentioned it."

"Maybe that boyfriend of hers, Johnny or whatever his name is, found out."

"No one else you can think of?"

"No, I've already told you that Slugger is your man."

***

Back at the office, Mrs V was too busy meditating to notice my arrival. I couldn't begin to imagine what a client would think if they arrived at the office, only to find her sitting cross-legged on the desk, humming.

Winky had company.

"Jill, can I introduce you to two of my best friends. This is Augustus."

"A pleasure to meet you, Jill." Augustus, a black and white cat, sporting a monocle and a walking stick, took a little bow.

"Hi."

"And this is Bertram."

"I'm very pleased to make your acquaintance, Jill." Bertram, a ginger cat, tipped his boater.

"Likewise."

"Augustus, Bertram and I were just discussing world affairs," Winky said.

"Right."

"Perhaps you'd care to join our discussion, Jill," Augustus said. "We would value a two-leggeds take on matters."

"Err, thanks, but I have a lot of work to catch up on."

"Another time, maybe?"

"Maybe."

"Before you sit down, Jill," Winky said. "The three of us are rather hungry. Do you think you could see your way clear to breaking out the salmon?"

Under normal circumstances, I would have told him and his posh pals to do one, but I was still feeling guilty at having forced him onto the streets with my unfounded accusations.

"Sure. No problem."

"Red not pink."

"Obviously."

While Winky and his snooty friends tucked into their salmon, I ran through everything I knew so far about Killer's murder, which if I'm honest, wasn't much.

Or should that be: *Witch* if I'm honest?

The big question was whether the 'S' shaped blood print on the tank of Killer's bike was significant or not. If it was, and Killer had tried to leave a clue to the identity of his murderer, then he hadn't narrowed the field by much. Slugger and Sid were both candidates by virtue of their names, but then so was Fi because of the tattoo on her wrist.

Sid had tried to suggest that I'd fallen for Slugger's charm offensive. What nonsense. I'm a total professional who would never allow my judgement to be clouded so easily.

Mind you, he was kind of cute.

According to Slugger, Killer had asked if he could return to Loose Chippings, and Slugger had welcomed him back. Unfortunately, the only person who could verify that was Billy, and the last time I'd seen that particular individual, I'd decked him and walked across his chest.

And what about Sid? He admitted that they had argued because he had failed to repay a loan to Killer. Had he really settled the debt by giving Killer his gold ring? I only had his word on that.

I wasn't sure what to think about Fi. Her love life was certainly colourful. Was it possible that jealousies had arisen? Was Killer's death a crime of passion? I probably wouldn't have considered her as a suspect if I hadn't spotted her tattoo. She claimed to have been visiting her parents' grave on the day that Killer was murdered. If that were true that gave her an alibi.

There was of course another possibility. What if the so called 'S' on the petrol tank was a red herring? What if Andy had made the mark himself to put me off the scent? I needed to have another conversation with him.

Mrs V popped her head around the door. "Jill, I didn't realise you were back."

"You were meditating, and I didn't like to disturb you."

She glanced across at the three cats. "What are *they* doing in here?"

"They're just Winky's friends. Actually, Mrs V, there's something I'd like you to do for me."

"Does it involve those cats?"

"No, of course not." I scribbled Fi's name on a slip of paper and handed it to her. "According to this young woman, her parents both died on the same day, three years ago, and are buried in Halifax. Would you see if you can find any record of them, and if you do, will you try to confirm the date they died?"

"I'll do my best."

***

It was time for my night out with Kathy and Rita.

"Aren't you taking the car?" Jack said.

"No, I want to be able to have a drink. I'll get a taxi."

"Shall I wait up for you?"

"There's no need. I doubt I'll be late, but who knows."

The taxi from Middle Tweaking to Washbridge cost a small fortune and would be even more expensive on the way back. This night out had better be worth it.

Kathy and Rita were already outside Wash Upon A Time when the cab dropped me off.

"Late as usual." Kathy tapped her watch.

"Sorry. The taxi was late."

"That's what comes of living out in the sticks."

"I didn't realise you were living in Middle Tweaking, Jill," Rita said. "Charlie and I looked at a property there, but we decided it was a bit too far out."

"Let's go inside." Kathy opened the door. "A girl could die of thirst out here."

"I'll get the first round." Rita took out her purse. "What's everyone having?"

"We should have cocktails," Kathy jumped in before I had the chance to speak.

"Cocktails it is." Rita headed for the bar.

"What do you think of this place?" Kathy looked

around.

"It's a bit much." The bar looked like it had been designed by a team of hipsters on a bad day.

"I like it. It's cool."

"You wouldn't know cool if it crept up behind you and bit you on the bum. I assume Charlie is Rita's partner. Is she married?"

"Yeah. Apparently, they moved here for his job."

"Oh? I assumed it was Rita who wanted to move back."

"Here you are ladies." Rita handed us both a green coloured cocktail. "The barman assured me this is the best drink in the house."

Kathy needed no encouragement to try it. "Mmm. That's good. Try it, Jill."

I took a sip. "It's got quite a kick."

"Okay, you two," Rita came to sit in between us. "I want to know what you've been up to while I've been gone."

The next hour was spent with Kathy and me bringing Rita up to speed. We told her about our families, our homes, and of course our careers.

"It sounds like your business is doing really well, Kathy. How many shops do you have now?"

"Seven with another two in the planning stage."

"I'm impressed. And your job sounds fascinating, Jill, but isn't it dangerous?"

"Not really. It's quite boring most of the time. Anyway, enough about us. What about you? Kathy told me that you moved back here because of your husband's work?"

"That's right, but I'm afraid I can't talk about it."

"Now I'm really intrigued." Kathy drank the last of her cocktail. "What does he do, Rita?"

"Kathy," I snapped. "She's just said she can't talk about it."

"Sorry, girls. All I can say is that he works for the government."

"Is he a spy?" Kathy eyed my cocktail. "Are you going to drink that, Jill?"

"No, he isn't a spy." Rita laughed.

"Jill?" Kathy gestured to my drink.

"You can have it. It's too strong for me. Kathy said you have a coin shop, Rita?"

"That's right. I've been interested in coins ever since I was a kid. A few years ago, Charlie suggested I turn the hobby into a business. Until now, I've only traded online, but when Charlie told me about the move, he suggested I open a shop here. I think he did it to sweeten me up because he knew I was happy living where we were."

"But you're glad to be back, aren't you?" Kathy said.

"Yeah. I'm really excited to see how the shop does, and of course it's been nice to reconnect with you two."

I'd expected us to move on to another bar, but the other two seemed perfectly happy to stay put. Kathy appeared determined to try every cocktail in the place. After a couple of glasses of wine, I moved onto orange juice. I was too old for hangovers.

It was almost ten-thirty, and I was just thinking about calling a taxi when raised voices at the bar caught our attention.

"That big guy has had way too much to drink," Kathy said. The irony of her comment was clearly lost on her.

"It looks like it could turn violent," Rita said.

She was right. The barman and the unruly customer

looked as though they were about to come to blows, but that wasn't the only thing that had caught my attention. The drunk guy was a werewolf, and he was showing all the signs of being about to shift. If that happened, there would be a bloodbath.

"Stay here, you two!" I stood up.

"Don't get involved, Jill!" Kathy shouted after me, but I was already homing in on the inebriated werewolf.

"Raymond, fancy seeing you here." I took the werewolf's arm. "Can I have a quick word?"

"I'm not Raymond." He managed to slur.

Ignoring his protests, I used the 'power' spell to drag him out the back exit into the alleyway.

"What are you doing, lady? I told you I'm not Raymond." As he spoke, he started to transform.

"My mistake." I cast the 'shrink' spell, picked up the tiny werewolf, and put him in a half-empty industrial size rubbish bin. "Sleep it off in there."

"Are you okay, Jill?" Rita said when I re-joined them.

"Yeah, I'm fine."

"You could have got yourself punched," Kathy said. "Where is he?"

"I told him he was making a fool of himself and that he should go home."

"And he left? Just like that?"

"Yeah. I can be very persuasive when I want to be."

Chapter 21

The next morning, as soon as Florence had finished her breakfast, she headed outside on caterpillar watch.

"From what you said, it sounds like Kathy is going to have a thick head this morning." Jack grinned.

"Serves her right. She must have tried every cocktail in that place."

"What did you think of that new bar?"

"It was a bit too hipster for my liking. There's a limit to how many bare ankles I can take in one night."

"What do you reckon your friend's husband's top-secret job is?"

"I've no idea, but if he works for the government, it'll be something boring, that's for sure."

"It's a good thing you were there last night, or the situation might have turned nasty with that werewolf."

"What an idiot. He's the kind who gets sups a bad reputation."

"Are you going to let him out of the bin?"

"I suppose so, although I'm tempted to let the garbage men take him to the landfill."

"Archie and Angie are still sleeping, Mummy." Florence was standing in the doorway, hands on her waist. "It's been ages."

"It's only been a few days. You'll just have to be patient."

"But what if they come out while I'm at school?"

"They won't. I had a word with them yesterday."

***

After parking the car, I headed over to the alleyway behind Wash Upon A Time. As I approached the huge bin, I could hear a tapping sound coming from inside.

The tiny werewolf, who had resumed human form, had to shelter his eyes from the light.

"Help me, please. Someone threw me in here."

"That would be me."

He blinked a few times until his eyes became accustomed to the light. "Why would you do something like that?"

"Because you were drunk and just about to shift."

"I would never do that in the human world."

"Maybe not when you're sober, but trust me, it happened. Fortunately, I was able to get you out of the bar before anyone saw you."

"What else did I do?"

"You were mouthing off and threatening the bar staff."

"I'm really sorry. My fiancée broke off our engagement yesterday, after five years."

"*Five* years? She was probably fed up of waiting for you to marry her."

"That's what she said. I only went out to drown my sorrows."

"You were lucky there were no rogue retrievers around."

"I'm really grateful for what you did."

"Just don't go making a habit of it."

"I won't. I promise. I'm Jonathan, by the way."

"Jill."

"Do you think you could get me out of here?"

I reversed the 'shrink' spell. "You can climb out yourself now."

Once he was out, he brushed himself down. "I stink, and I have a thumping headache."

"It's no more than you deserve. Anyway, I have to get going."

"Thanks again."

Mrs V had a large bag of marshmallows on her desk and, judging by the way she was struggling to speak, she had at least a couple of them in her mouth.

"Sorry, Mrs V, what did you say?"

"I do apologise, Jill. Mary Merry bought these for me and they're extremely moreish. Would you like one?"

"No, thanks." I could no longer look at a marshmallow without thinking about those pesky wood nymphs.

"I managed to track down the information you wanted."

"About Fi's parents?"

"Yes. It actually proved to be much easier than I expected. I can confirm they are buried together in Halifax, and that they did die three years ago on the same day."

"And was it the date I gave you?"

"That's right."

"Thanks, Mrs V."

"Are you sure you wouldn't like a marshmallow?"

"I'm positive."

"Why didn't you get a couple for me?" Winky said.

"A couple of what?"

"Marshmallows."

"Cats don't like marshmallows."

"This one does."

"Sorry, but it's too late now."

"Never mind. I do have a favour to ask you, though."

"What's that?"

"This sofa."

"What about it?"

"Just look at it. It's had it."

"It looks alright to me."

"You wouldn't think so if you had to sit on it all day. I think you should buy me a new one."

"I can't afford a new sofa."

"I wouldn't ask, but those days I spent on the street have brought on my rheumatism, so I need something comfortable to sit on." From behind his back, he produced a small glossy brochure. "Something like these."

"Feline Sofa World?"

"They're the country's leading feline sofa specialists."

"These prices are insane."

"You can't put a price on your health."

"I can, and this is way too expensive."

"How about if I find something a bit cheaper from one of the high street shops?"

"If you find something *a lot* cheaper, I'll think about it."

Based on what Mrs V had just told me, I could rule out Fi as a suspect, which left me with just three candidates: Slugger, Sid and Andy. With Killer out of the picture, Andy would once again be the top mechanic at Wash-on-Wheels. Could that have been motivation enough for him to commit murder? I needed to have another conversation with him.

"Andy, it's Jill Maxwell. I wondered if we could have another chat, please?"

"I've told you everything I know."

"I only need a few minutes of your time, I promise. I could come over now if that works for you."

"I'm just on my way to the dentist. One of my fillings dropped out last night."

"How about later? Would two o'clock be okay?"

"I guess so."

"Okay, I'll see you then."

***

Another visit to Candlefield Library was called for.

"Hello again." The young elf bounced across the room to greet me.

"Hi. Doesn't it get tiring, bouncing around on those springs all day?"

"It does, actually. I've put in a request for a pogo stick, but getting approval for new equipment can take ages."

His mention of the pogo stick reminded me of Janice who often frequented Little Jack's corner shop in Smallwash.

"That sucks."

"Tell me about it. I'm Orlando by the way, but everyone calls me Orland."

"Oh?"

"No, just Orland. Without the 'O'."

"Oh?"

"Precisely. The nickname started at school, and it kind of stuck."

"Oh. I mean right. I'm Jill."

"Do you want to take another look in the archives? I spoke to Barry after you left, he said you were great company."

"That was very nice of him, but actually I'm hoping to find information on AnonFront."

"What's that?"

"Your guess is as good as mine. If this were the human world, I could simply Google it."

"Goo what?"

"Google. It's an internet thing."

"I've heard about the internet. Someone said the Combined Sup Council were looking into introducing it to Candlefield."

"I wouldn't hold your breath. Do you have any suggestions where I should start my search?"

"AnonFront? Hmm, do you think it could be a company name?"

"That would be my first guess."

"Okay, let me check the Candlefield Company Register. They're down the other end."

And off he sprang with me in hot pursuit.

"Shall I get it?" I offered, as he tried in vain to reach the top shelf where the twenty-six volumes of the register were kept.

"Yes, please. The sooner I get that pogo stick the better."

"No problem." I grabbed volume 'A' of the register and flicked through the index. "Here they are."

I made a note of the company's address and then put the book back on the shelf.

"Is there anything else I can help you with today, Jill?"

"No, that's all I need, thanks."

"Before you go, could I trouble you to sign my petition?"

"What petition is that?"

"The *buy Orland a pogo stick* petition."

"Of course. I'll be glad to."

***

AnonFront were based in a small office, sandwiched in between two sandwich shops. Once through the door, I was confronted with a narrow empty room. To my left was a small sliding window with a bell next to it. Just in case anyone couldn't work it out for themselves, there was a useful sign below the bell that read: **Ring bell for attention**.

I did as instructed, and moments later, the little window slid open.

"Yes?"

"Yes?"

"Yes?"

There was not one, but three tiny elves peering through the window.

"Hi, there. I was hoping you might be able to help me."

"We'd be happy to," said the second elf. "Which of our service packages did you require?"

"I—err—haven't quite made my mind up yet. Remind me again of the options, would you?"

"There are three levels," the first elf said. "Bronze, silver and gold."

"What exactly would I get in the gold package?"

"Total anonymity. We would provide a mailing address, including post forwarding, and a telephone answering service twenty-four hours a day."

"I see. And no one would be able to track down my true address?"

"That's correct."

"And how much does that cost?"

"Three thousand pounds a year."

"That sounds very reasonable."

"Would you like me to get the forms for you to complete?" The second elf was clearly eager to seal the deal.

"In a minute, maybe. First, though, it's important to me that I only do business with ethical companies."

"You have no worries on that score," the first elf assured me.

By now, it was clear that the third elf was taking a back seat in this conversation because he'd said nothing beyond his initial greeting.

"That's good to hear. So, for example, if a company, which was using your services, was acting illegally, you would be prepared to give up their real identity and whereabouts."

"Absolutely," the second elf said without hesitation.

"Great. In that case, I'd like to know who is behind Reptile Holdings."

The elves all fell silent for a moment, and then the second one said, "Are you here to purchase one of our services or not?"

"No, I'm here to find out who Reptile Holdings are. Those scumbags are ruining people's lives, and they may even be guilty of murder."

"Sorry, we can't help you, lady."

"You just said that if one of the companies using your services was acting illegally, you would give up their real identity."

"To the authorities, and only then if they have a court

order. We're not going to give that information to any Tom, Dick or Harriet who walks through the door."

"These people have been responsible for closing down a community centre, a children's nursery, and they're about to do the same to the lido. And I'm pretty sure they've already murdered two people who tried to expose them."

"Really?" The second elf appeared moved by that revelation.

Or maybe not. Because he and the first elf began to laugh.

"Get out of here," the first elf snapped. "You're wasting our time."

I was so enraged that it took all my willpower not to do something unspeakable to those two elves. Instead, I let them know what I thought about them and the way they conducted their business, and then stormed out of the office.

I was fuming, so I decided to take a stroll around the park, to try to calm down before magicking myself back to the human world. Those elves at AnonFront were clearly only interested in making money; they didn't give a monkey's if innocent people were being hurt by the companies whose ID they were protecting.

"Excuse me." Someone tugged at my leg.

I looked down to see the third elf standing there.

"What do you want? I don't have time to hang around listening to your lame excuses for not doing the decent thing."

He passed me a slip of paper. "This is what you're after."

"G&D Enterprises?"

"They're the people behind Reptile Holdings."

"Oh, right. Thanks."

"The others don't know I'm doing this, and I'd appreciate it if you didn't tell them."

"Sure. What brought on the change of heart?"

"I've used the lido ever since I was a kid. I adore that place. The thought of these people tearing it down makes my blood boil. Do you think you'll be able to stop them?"

"I don't know, but I have a much better chance now that I know who they are. Thanks for this."

"No problem. I'm Alf, by the way."

"Jill."

"I'd better get back before the others miss me. See you, Jill."

***

Feeling a little more optimistic, but rather peckish, I magicked myself back to Washbridge. Animal of the day at Coffee Animal was a caterpillar (did a caterpillar even count as an animal?). I'd need to be sure not to tell Florence, or she would want to know why I hadn't taken her with me.

"Hi, Jill." Dot had a beauty spot on both cheeks. One day, I really would have to ask her how she did that. "Your usual?"

"Actually, I'm quite peckish. What sandwiches do you have?"

"Cheese. Ham. And cheese and ham."

"Is that all?"

"We have toasties too."

"What do you have in toasties?"

"Cheese. Ham. And cheese and ham."

"Right. I'll have a cheese and ham, please."

"Plain or toasted?"

"Just a plain sandwich, please."

She put the coffee and sandwich on a tray, and handed me a small plastic cage with a caterpillar inside.

As I looked around for a free table, I spotted Mad, so decided to go and join her. Before I had the chance to sit down, she'd pulled her scarf up over her mouth, and stood up.

"Sorry, Jill, I can't stay. Err—Brad just called to say he needs me back at the shop straight away."

"Are you okay?" I gestured to the scarf.

"Err, yeah, I've just been to the dentist. Sorry, got to go." And with that, she shot off.

"Do you always have that effect on people?" the caterpillar said.

"What do you mean?"

"As soon as you turned up, she legged it."

"Do you think I could have a bit of peace and quiet while I eat my sandwich?"

"What about a bit of lettuce for me?"

"I don't have any, sorry."

"Typical. No one cares about the lowly caterpillar."

"That's not true. In fact, my daughter and I have been looking after two caterpillars at home—they're red with yellow spots. They're in the chrysalis stage at the moment and we're waiting for them to turn into butterflies."

"Now I know you're lying. There isn't such a thing as a red caterpillar with yellow spots."

Chapter 22

The first thing I noticed when I arrived at the Wash-on-Wheels workshop was that Killer's bike had gone.

"Hey, Andy, what happened to the bike?"

"Killer's brother came to pick it up yesterday."

"I'd like to speak to him. Do you have his number by any chance?"

"Yeah, he gave it to me in case anything else belonging to Killer turned up. Tools, that sort of thing."

"How's the tooth?"

"Sore. The dentist had to extract it. Want to see?"

"I'm good, thanks."

"Did you talk to Slugger?"

"Yeah, I did."

"And?"

"And I'm not convinced that he had anything to do with Killer's death."

"Turned the charm offensive on, did he? I should have known." Andy sneered. "He's always been able to wrap women around his little finger."

"Not this woman. Anyway, the more I think about it, the more I come to the conclusion that the person who had the most to gain from Killer's death was you."

"And how do you work that out, little miss detective?"

"You had your nose put out when Chains brought Killer in. Until then, you'd been numero uno. That can't have been an easy pill for you to swallow."

"I told you last time, I wasn't thrilled, but I just got on with it."

"Are you sure you weren't angry? Maybe a little bit?"

"Not even a little bit. I showed you the blood print on

the bike's tank. Why would Killer have done that if it wasn't to let us know that Slugger was the one who attacked him?"

"We can't be certain he was the one who put the print on there, though, can we?"

"What do you mean?"

"You could have done it, to point the finger of blame at Slugger."

"I've had enough of this. You can think what you like, but I had nothing to do with Killer's death. Why don't you sling your hook?"

"I'm just saying that—"

"I don't care what you have to say. Just get lost, will you?"

***

Chains' second in command, Sid, had freely admitted that he had failed to repay a loan to Killer, but he insisted he'd given him a gold ring in full settlement. Was that true? There was one way to find out. I called the number that Andy had given me for Killer's brother.

"Hi. Is that Cecil Cole's brother?"

"Who wants to know?"

"My name is Jill Maxwell. I'm a P.I."

"I heard that they'd brought in some kind of investigator. I didn't realise it was a woman, though. Have you come up with anything yet?"

"Nothing so far, but I'd really like to talk to you if that's possible?"

"Sure, if it's going to help bring Cecil's killer to justice."

"I could pop over now if that's alright?"

"Okay. I've just come off duty. I should be home in about twenty minutes, traffic permitting."

"Are you a policeman?"

"No, a paramedic."

"Right. If you give me your address, I'll meet you there."

I knocked on the door at the address Killer's brother had given me, but there was no reply. The exterior of the terraced house was well-kept, unlike its immediate neighbours. I took a seat on the low wall in front of the house, and a few minutes later, a motor scooter pulled up in front of me.

The man took off his helmet. "Jill?"

"That's me. I'm sorry, I don't know your name."

"It's Richard, but everyone calls me Dick." He pulled the scooter up onto the pavement. "I'll just put this in the shed. If I leave it out here, some toerag will nick it."

Once he'd locked the scooter in the shed, he led the way around the back of the house and let us into the small kitchen.

"I'm going to make myself a brew. Would you like one?"

"Yes, please."

Once we had our drinks, we went through to the lounge. "Sorry for the mess. The missus left me three years ago, and I don't have much time for housework. Grab a pew."

"Were you and Kill—I mean Cecil, close?"

"It's okay, you can call him Killer." He smiled. "Everyone did except for me. And I only called him Cecil because I knew it wound him up. Were we close? As kids, yes, but when we got older and he got into bikes, we drifted apart. I was always much more interested in sport. We argued all the time, but we always had each other's back."

"Andy told me that you'd collected your brother's bike."

"I kept putting it off, but then I figured I'd have to do it sooner or later. There's barely enough room for my little scooter in the shed now."

"What will you do with it?"

"I honestly don't know. Sell it eventually, I suppose. Not yet, though. It just wouldn't feel right."

"I have to ask you something which is a little delicate."

"Fire away."

"Were you given all of your brother's personal effects?"

"What few there were, yeah."

"Would you happen to know if there was a gold ring amongst them?"

"To be honest, they gave them to me in a small plastic bag, and I haven't been able to bring myself to go through them yet. Why do you ask?"

"Do you know Sid from Wash-on-Wheels?"

"No. The only people I know over there are Chains, and Andy the mechanic."

"Sid is Chains' second in command. Apparently, Killer loaned him some cash that he couldn't pay back. According to Sid, he gave your brother a gold ring in full settlement of the debt. I just wanted to check if he's telling the truth."

"I'll go and get them."

"Don't do it if it's going to be too painful for you."

"It's okay. I won't be a minute."

When he returned, he was holding a small, blue plastic bag.

"Are you sure you're okay to do this?" I said.

"It's fine." He emptied the contents onto the coffee table.

I spotted it immediately. The gold ring was lying next to a watch. "May I?"

"Help yourself."

I picked it up to take a closer look, and sure enough, it was in the shape of a skull.

Dick and I chatted for a while longer. Or at least, he talked, and I listened. Although the two siblings had drifted apart, it was clear he'd been badly affected by his brother's untimely demise. On my way out, he thanked me for my efforts to bring his brother's killer to justice, and I promised to keep him posted.

The presence of the gold ring amongst the personal effects seemed to corroborate Sid's story, and remove any motive he might have had for wanting to get rid of Killer. I'd already eliminated Fi as a suspect because she'd been in Halifax on the day Killer was murdered. I was beginning to think that maybe I'd ruled out Slugger too quickly. He'd told me that he'd agreed to Killer returning to Loose Chippings, and that everything between them was hunky dory. Was that true? Slugger had mentioned that his mechanic, Billy, had overheard that particular conversation, and that he would be able to confirm that Killer had indeed been accepted back into the fold. Unfortunately, Billy and I weren't exactly what you'd call bosom buddies.

If I was going to get him to open up to me, I'd have to

turn on the old Jill Maxwell charm offensive.

What do you mean, good luck with that?

***

Mrs V looked puzzled.

"I'm puzzled, Jill."

Uncanny or what?

"Why are you puzzled?"

"Why would you order so many sofas?"

"What do you mean?"

"There's been a steady stream of deliveries all morning. They're all in your office."

She wasn't exaggerating.

My office was full of sofas of all shapes and sizes. Winky was jumping from one to another, seemingly oblivious to my arrival.

"What's going on, Winky?"

"I'm trying them out."

"There must be ten of them."

"Don't exaggerate. There's only eight."

"That's okay then. Why are they all in here?"

"I took on board what you said about shopping around, and I figured the best way to decide would be to try them first."

"Don't you normally do that sort of thing in the shop?"

"As a two-legged, you might be able to do that, but how am I supposed to?"

"Point taken, but I still don't understand how you got them to bring them here for you to try out."

"I didn't actually tell them that I was testing them. I bought them all online."

"You actually *bought* them? All of them?"

"Don't panic. I'll pick the one I like best, and return the others for a refund. Genius, eh?"

"And what am I supposed to do in the meantime? I can't even get to my desk."

"You can step from one to another, but you'll have to take your shoes off first."

"It doesn't look like I have much choice, does it?" I slipped off my shoes and stepped from one sofa to the next until I reached my desk.

"Which one do you like best?" Winky was lying on a green and yellow striped sofa.

"I don't care. Just pick one and get the others sent back."

"I quite like this one, but I don't want to rush my decision."

Mrs V popped her head around the door, took one look at the sofas and gave a huge sigh. "Your brother is here, Jill. Can you spare him a few minutes?"

"Of course. Send him through, would you?"

I'd been trying to contact Martin ever since I'd retrieved the first compass stone, but I'd had no joy. I'd begun to fear something might have happened to him.

He took one step into the office, then stopped dead in his tracks, with a puzzled look on his face.

"Why do you have so many sofas in here, Jill?"

"You wouldn't believe me if I told you."

"I'm not sure I can get all the way over there."

"Why don't you just sit on the sofa closest to you?"

"Okay. I wanted to check if you'd made any progress with the first compass stone?"

"Yeah, I've got it."

"You have? That's brilliant."

"I've tried to call you a thousand times to tell you, but your phone just rang out."

"Sorry. Things have been rather hectic. Did you have any problem getting it?"

"Nothing I couldn't handle. Do you know the name of the guardian of the second stone?"

"Not yet, but I'm getting close. Hopefully, I'll have something for you in the next few days. What have you done with the first stone? It's somewhere safe, I hope."

"Of course. There's no need for you to worry on that score. Just get the name of the second guardian to me as soon as possible."

"Will do."

"Do you want a drink?"

"No, thanks. I can't stay. I just wanted to see how things were going. Whatever you do, make sure you keep that stone safe."

"Don't worry. It's somewhere no one will ever find it."

***

"Look what I found, Mummy." Florence had the compass stone in her hand.

"Where did you get that?"

"It was in a box in your wardrobe."

"Why were you looking in my wardrobe?"

"I wanted a box for my beetles."

"What beetles?"

"Jen and Ben."

"I thought you liked caterpillars."

"I do, but Angie and Archie are still asleep. Daddy said

I could only keep the beetles in the house if I put them in a box."

"Did he now?"

"He said you had some boxes in your wardrobe. That's when I found the stone. Why was it in the shoe box, Mummy?"

"I put it there to keep it safe. Give it to me, please."

"But, Mummy —"

"Now, Florence."

"Okay." Somewhat reluctantly, she handed it over. "Can I keep the box for Jen and Ben."

"I guess so."

"Yay!" She went charging outside.

Moments later, Jack came through to the kitchen.

"What are you doing with that?" He gestured towards the stone.

"Florence had it."

"Why?"

"Because someone told her to look for a box in my wardrobe."

"Whoops. Sorry. Did she tell you that she's collecting beetles now?"

"She did. I don't understand her obsession with insects. She certainly doesn't get it from me."

"What are you going to do with that stone now?"

"Yes, what are you going to do with it?" Grandma said.

"You can't just walk into our house like this." I snapped. "Have you never heard of knocking?"

"I did knock, but you two were too busy arguing to hear me."

"We weren't arguing," Jack said.

"Have you found a job yet, Jim?"

"His name is Jack!" I snapped. I really wasn't in the mood for this. "Did you want something?"

"I came to tell you that the lido closed today. If you don't get this thing sorted soon, it will be too late."

"I'm doing my best."

"I hope so because the clock is ticking. So, what are you going to do with that compass stone?"

"How do you know what this is?"

"Martin told me all about it."

"*Martin*? Why would he do that? I told him not to tell anyone. Just wait until I get my hands on him."

"It wasn't his fault. He doesn't know that he told me. When he suddenly reappeared after all that time, I sensed something was afoot, so I tracked him down and used a little magic to persuade him to reveal all. Not that he'll remember any of that." She cackled. "What I'd like to know is why *you* didn't see fit to tell me."

"Because I'm perfectly capable of dealing with this situation by myself. I don't need your help."

"I wouldn't be helping you. I'd be doing it for my great-grandchild. Now, shall I take the stone for safe-keeping?"

"No, thanks, I'd rather hang on to it."

"Great-Grandma!" Florence came running back into the kitchen, shoebox in hand. "I've got two beetles."

"I love beetles. What are their names?"

"Ben and Jen."

"What fantastic names. Are you going to show them to me?"

"She can show you them outside." I ushered the two of them into the garden.

"She does it on purpose, you know," Jack said. "The name thing."

"Of course she does. She's just trying to get a reaction. You mustn't bite, whatever you do."

"Don't worry, I won't. By the way, if you spot Barbara Babble in the village, I'd give her a wide berth."

"I always do. Any reason in particular?"

"Yeah, she's totally lost the plot this time. She cornered me in the store and made me promise not to say a word to anyone about what she was about to tell me."

"Which was?"

"According to her, government agents have been sent to the village."

"What does that mean, exactly?"

"Your guess is as good as mine. The woman is a picnic short of a sandwich."

"I think you'll find that the saying is — never mind."

Chapter 23

"Mummy, Daddy, Jen won't wake up," Florence said.

"Who's Jen?" I'd only just come downstairs and I wasn't even half awake.

"My beetle." She held up the shoebox.

"Let me take a look, pumpkin." Jack took the box from her, glanced inside, then turned to me and made a subtle shake of his head.

Oh bum! If Florence realised that one of her beloved beetles had died, she'd be really upset, which was the last thing we needed just before she was due to go to school. Better to wait until she came home to deliver the bad news.

"Let me look." I took the box from Jack and put my ear to it. "Jen's fast asleep. I can hear her snoring."

"She's such a lazybones, isn't she?" Florence took back the box, seemingly satisfied with that explanation.

"Why did you go and tell her that?" Jack said, once Florence was outside and out of earshot.

"I didn't want her to be upset before she went to school."

"You do realise that I'm going to have to tell her the truth when she comes home, don't you?"

"Unless you find another *Jen* while she's at school. There must be hundreds of them out there."

"Florence will know the difference."

"Of course she won't. Seen one beetle, seen them all."

I was just about to get into the car.

"Jill! Wait!"

Oh no! I'd recognise that voice anywhere.

"Morning, Barbara. Sorry, I can't stop. I'm late for an appointment."

"You have to hear this, Jill. You'll never believe what I'm going to tell you."

"Like I said, I really do have—"

"I've seen three of them now."

"Three what?"

"Shush!" She glanced around. "They might be listening."

"I have no idea what you're talking about, Barbara. Who might be listening?"

"The government agents."

"Jack said you'd mentioned something about that."

"There were only two of them at first, but another one joined them yesterday."

"And what exactly are these *agents* doing?"

"That, Jill, is the seventy-six thousand dollar question. If you ask me, they must be on the trail of spies."

"Spies in Middle Tweaking?"

"I suspect the vicar is one of them."

"Why would you think that?"

"Haven't you noticed his peculiar behaviour?"

I had a sudden mental image of the vicar, walking down the middle of the road in the rain, wearing a dressing gown and a pair of flip-flops, with a pug under his arm.

"I can't say I have."

"Definitely suspicious if you ask me. It wouldn't surprise me if those agents were to arrest him soon."

"Right. Anyway, I really do have to get going. It was lovely to speak to you, as always."

That woman was as nutty as a fruit cake.

"Armi asked if you'd found your lease for him to look at yet," Mrs V said.

"I've looked high and low, but I can't find it anywhere. I even asked Farah from Bubbles if I could take a look at hers, but it seems she was never actually given a copy."

"Isn't that rather unusual?"

"Very, and a little suspicious if you ask me."

"What are you going to do, Jill?"

"Without a copy of the lease, I'm not sure what I can do."

"Does that mean we'll have to move out?"

"Over my dead body. Don't worry, Mrs V, I'll get it sorted."

"I do hope so, dear. I noticed the sofas are still next door. I assume you intend to do something about them?"

"They'll be out of here by Monday, I promise."

Winky had guests again. This time, instead of the two snooty male cats, there were three females.

"Good morning, Jill. Can I introduce you to Mitsi, Suzy, and Candy?"

"Hi, ladies."

The three of them chorused a quick hello.

"The girls have come over to help me make a decision on the sofa."

"I expected you to have made your mind up by now."

"These things can't be rushed."

"I like the blue one," Candy said.

"No. The green leather one is much better," said Mitsi.

"Neither of you have any taste," Suzy said. "The pink and red one is head and shoulders above the rest."

"Do you think the girls and I could have some salmon, Jill? Choosing a sofa is hungry work."

"I—err—suppose so." Winky was beginning to try my patience, but I kept reminding myself that I had to make up for the great injustice I'd done him.

Thirty minutes later, Winky's friends had left, but he was no closer to making a decision on the sofa.

"This can't go on, Winky. I need these sofas out of here by Monday morning."

"Don't worry. I'll make my mind up by the end of the day and have the rest out of here by next week."

"You better had."

Mrs V popped her head around the door. "Your two friends with the catsuits are here."

"Daze and Blaze? Send them in, would you."

Daze was sporting a rather understated navy blue catsuit. Blaze, on the other hand, was wearing a red one covered in sequins.

"Wow, Blaze, you look—err—"

"*Ridiculous* is the word you're searching for, Jill." Daze shot her sidekick a disapproving look. "We're supposed to be inconspicuous."

Walking around in catsuits? Hmm.

"Take a seat. There are plenty to choose from."

"This may be a daft question, Jill, but—"

"Why are there so many sofas in here?"

"Yeah."

"Let's just say I'm repaying a debt and leave it at that."

"Fair enough."

Daze parked herself on a brown upholstered sofa. Blaze and his sequins found a sofa that matched the colour of his catsuit.

"To what do I owe this pleasure, guys?"

"Our worst fears have been realised, Jill," Daze said, deadly serious now.

"What fears?"

"About your village."

"Are you talking about Grandma's hotel? I spoke to her at length and as far as I'm aware, she has it all in-hand now."

"Perhaps, but I fear she may have been too late implementing those measures."

"Why? What's happened?"

"We have our people working undercover in strategic organisations here in the human world, to give us a heads-up if any major problems arise. A couple of days ago, we received word that DOPA have sent some of their agents to Middle Tweaking."

"DOPA? What's that?"

"The Department of Paranormal Activity."

"I've never heard of it."

"That's hardly surprising. Officially, it doesn't exist."

"How did they get to hear about what's going on in Middle Tweaking?"

"That's what I'd like to know."

"So what happens now?"

"We have to make sure they don't find any evidence of paranormal activity."

"And how do you do that?"

"We should start by sending all of the guests at your grandmother's hotel back to Candlefield."

"Are you serious?"

"Deadly."

"Good luck with getting Grandma to go along with that."

"Actually, that's why we came to see you."

"Hold on. You're not here to ask me to tell her, are you?"

"It would be better coming from you."

"She won't listen to me. I doubt she'll listen to anyone for that matter."

"She has to this time. The DOPA people don't mess around."

"What can they actually do, though?"

"In the past when this has happened, sups have been known to disappear and never be seen again."

"What do you think happened to them?"

"We honestly don't know. That's the scary part. So, will you have a word with your grandmother? Please."

"Okay, but I don't think it will do any good. What about me?"

"What about you?"

"In case you've forgotten, I'm a sup too."

"You'll be fine unless you start casting spells in broad daylight. I'm not worried about you because you've lived among humans for so long that you fit in. It's all those first-time visitors at the hotel I'm concerned about."

"Alright. I'll talk to Grandma."

"Thanks, Jill." She stood up and turned to Blaze. "Come on, glitterball, we have work to do."

"I'm coming. Hey, you forgot to tell Jill about the Canary Brothers."

"Oh yeah. We struck a deal with those yellow guys. A

slightly reduced sentence in return for them telling us where they got all the stolen goods from, so that we could return them to their rightful owners."

"Mrs V was certainly pleased to get her yarn back."

"That's the interesting part. We gave the Canary Brothers photos of the stolen goods, and they're adamant they didn't steal the yarn."

"Why would they bother denying that? It doesn't make any sense if they've admitted to stealing the rest."

"I know, which is why I'm inclined to believe them. They reckon they found it in a dumpster in an alleyway, and from the description, I'm pretty sure they're talking about the one behind this building. They said they remembered because when they checked the dumpster, a cat jumped out and scared them to death."

"Did it now?" I glanced across at Winky who was leaping from sofa to sofa, heading for the open window.

"Anyway, we'd better get going, Jill." Daze started for the door. "Make sure you let your grandmother know how serious the situation is."

"I will." I waited until they were out of the door. "Winky!"

It was too late; he had already bolted. That feline was a dead cat walking.

I tried calling Grandma to warn her about the DOPA people, but she wasn't picking up. I'd just have to go over to the hotel after work and hope I wasn't too late.

***

According to Grandma, the lido had closed its doors, but maybe there was still time to rescue it before someone bulldozed it, and replaced it with yet another empty office building. All my hopes now hinged on getting in touch with the people behind Reptile Holdings who, courtesy of Alf the elf, I now knew to be G&D Enterprises.

They were based in a building which had once housed the local council offices, but which had been converted into units for small businesses. G&D Enterprises were on the first floor, next to a company with the intriguing name of Spider Hire.

There was no one behind the reception desk at G&D, and no bell or buzzer to call for attention. After a few minutes, my patience was beginning to run out.

"Hello! Is there anyone here?"

That seemed to do the trick because a witch, who judging by her face was halfway through applying her makeup, appeared through the door behind the desk.

"Yeah?" She was clearly a woman of few words.

"Is this G&D Enterprises?"

"That's what it says on the door, isn't it?"

And a charmer to boot.

"It's just that I thought it might be the offices of Reptile Holdings."

She tried to maintain a poker face, but I saw the brief tell that confirmed I'd struck a chord.

"Never heard of them," she lied.

"Would you mind telling me who G&D are?"

"Alistair Gator and Mr Dial."

"Let me guess, Mr Dial's first name is Crocker."

"No, it's Fred. Look, what do you want?"

"I'd like to speak to Mr Gator."

"He isn't in today."

"Okay, I'll speak to Mr Dial."

"He's not here either."

"When will they be in?"

"I'm not sure."

"What exactly is it that G&D does?"

"Import/Export."

"Of what?"

"Sorry?"

"What do they import and export?"

"Lots of things. Now, I really am very busy, so if there's nothing else."

"No, that's it. I'll let you get back to your makeup. Thanks for your help."

Did I believe any of that? Not a chance, which is why I called in at the offices next door. I was barely through the door before an eager young vampire greeted me with a toothy smile (no fangs, thankfully).

"Welcome to Spider Hire. My name is Becky. How can I help you today?"

"I'm looking to — err — hire a spider."

"That never gets old." She laughed.

"Look, can I be honest?"

"Of course."

"I have no idea what you do."

"We hire out office furniture."

"Why are you called *Spider* Hire?"

"The owner's name is Stephen Spider."

"I see."

"If you didn't know what we do, how come you're here?"

"I was just wondering if you knew anything about the business next door?"

"G&D? Not really. Why?"

I told her about the lido, the community centre, the nursery, and my suspicions regarding her neighbours.

"And you think G&D might actually be these Reptile people?"

"Yes."

"That's terrible. My gran goes to the lido every Sunday. She's going to be devastated when she finds out it's closed."

"Have you ever seen the people who work next door?"

"I see Mildred occasionally, but she rarely says more than hello."

"What about the two men? Mr Gator and Mr Dial?"

"I've only ever seen one man, and then only when I passed him in the corridor. I said hello but he blanked me. He was wearing a smart suit, and I remember thinking he looked a bit of a thug."

"Oh?"

"He's a big guy. Looks like he works out a lot. Oh, and he had a scar on his face." She pointed to her left cheek.

That pretty much sealed the deal for me. Lillian Wrongplant, AKA Mushy, had told me that she'd seen a big man, dressed in a smart suit, on the site of the community centre. He too had a scar on the side of his face. It was clear that G&D Enterprises was a front for Reptile Holdings, but I still had no idea why they were taking over buildings, only to erect offices that remained empty. According to the elderly wizard, who I'd seen walking his Labrador, a van visited the office building most nights of the week. Why would it do that? If I could find the answer to that question, maybe I'd be closer to discovering what Mr Gator and Mr Dial were up to.

Chapter 24

I was feeling rather peckish, so I stopped off at Cuppy C. The twins had pushed two tables together at the rear of the shop and, at first, I couldn't make out what they were doing, but then I realised that the tables were covered in corks of all shapes and sizes.

Once I had my sandwich and drink, I went over to find out what they were up to.

"Where did you get those corks from?" I asked.

"From Mum of course." Pearl grinned. "We knew she'd cave."

"We didn't realise she had so many of them." Amber picked up one of the larger corks.

"What are those?" I pointed to a pile of small cards on the next table.

"They were pinned to the corks."

I picked one up. "This is a detailed description of the cork."

"Yeah, we know." Pearl seemed to be arranging the corks by size. "The cards were making it difficult to sort out the corks, so we took them off. We'll put them back when they're out on display."

"Err, right. And how will you remember which card goes with which cork?"

Pearl turned to Amber who just shrugged.

"Oh dear." I laughed.

"It'll be fine," Amber insisted. "And besides, no one will know if we get a few mixed up."

"I can think of one person who will."

***

I was back in the human world, and I definitely wasn't looking forward to the next hour or so. I was on my way to speak to Billy, the man I'd humiliated on my first visit to Loose Chippings Motor Cycle Club.

Having more or less eliminated all the other suspects, my focus was now firmly back on Slugger. Was it possible that he'd murdered Killer because the mechanic had left Loose Chippings, to help Wash-on-Wheels win the competition? Slugger had said he didn't hold any grudges, and that when Killer had asked to re-join Loose Chippings, he'd welcomed him back. According to Slugger, Billy was present when that particular conversation took place, but I wanted to check that for myself. I certainly wasn't expecting him to welcome me with open arms.

"Oh, it's you again." The guy who answered the door had the word BAD shaved into his hair on one side of his head. On the other side, was the word SAD. He must have seen my reaction, and clearly felt the need to explain. "My barber's a bit hard of hearing. I asked him for BAD and MAD."

"Oh dear. Still, it'll grow out."

"If you're here to see Slugger, he isn't in today. I can tell him you called if you like."

"Actually, I'm here to see Billy."

"You're not going to beat him up again, are you?" He laughed.

"No, I just want a word with him."

"He's been keeping a low profile since you put him on his back." The man glanced around to make sure no one was within earshot. "I thought what you did to him was hilarious. He's always been too big for his boots."

"Is he here?"

"Yeah, he's in the workshop, around the back. Do you want me to take you to him?"

"It's okay. I'll find him."

Billy was hard at work on a chopper bike, and he didn't hear me come into the workshop because of the rap music, blaring out of the radio on the workbench.

"Billy!" I walked over to where he was working. "Billy!"

He looked up, and the expression on his face confirmed my fears.

"What do you want?" He turned the radio down.

"Aren't bikers supposed to like heavy metal music?"

"I asked what you wanted."

"First off, I wanted to apologise for what happened the other day."

"Nothing happened." He shrugged. "I just tripped, is all."

"Right. Anyway, I hope I didn't cause you any embarrassment."

"If you're looking for Slugger, he's not here."

"You're the one I came to see."

"I'm busy."

"This will only take a minute, then I'll be on my way."

"Spit it out, then."

"It's about Killer."

"I figured that much."

"Slugger told me that Killer had asked to re-join Loose Chippings."

"That's news to me."

"Slugger told me that you were there when the two of

them discussed it."

"Nah. Last I heard, Slugger wanted nothing to do with Killer. He said if the guy showed his face around here again, he'd regret it."

"I see. Why would Slugger lie to me about it?"

"How would I know? He can be unpredictable. You don't want to get on the wrong side of him."

"He seemed okay when we went for a coffee the other day."

"He can turn on the charm when he wants to. You aren't going to tell him what I've said, are you?"

"Of course not. That's between you and me."

***

"Mrs V, I need you to do something for me, please."

"Will it wait until I've found this dropped stitch because I promised Walter that I'd have these socks finished for him by Sunday."

"Who's Walter?"

"Our gardener."

"You have a gardener?"

"Didn't I tell you?"

"Definitely not."

"He started a couple of months ago. Armi and I aren't getting any younger, and we were finding it difficult to keep on top of everything. My friend, Judith, recommended Walter, and I have to say, he's been working wonders. I can let you have his details if you'd like to use his services."

"Thanks, but our finances won't stretch to a gardener. And besides, Jack loves gardening."

"I didn't know that."

"Neither does he. Anyway, about that little job. I've been trying to contact this person for the last hour, but he isn't answering his phone. I've sent him a couple of texts too, but either he's not seen them or he's ignoring me. Will you keep trying his number and if you get through, ask him when would be a good time for me to meet with him." I handed Mrs V a slip of paper.

"*Slugger*? Oh dear. If he asks, what shall I tell Mr Slugger you want to talk to him about?"

"Just say it's about Killer."

"You worry me sometimes, Jill. Should you really be associating with men called Slugger and Killer?"

"Don't worry, Mrs V, I can look after myself."

Winky was on the phone. "Tomorrow morning will be fine. Okay, bye." Having finished on the call, he turned his attention to me. "Don't worry. I've picked the sofa I want, and the rest of these will be out of here by Monday morning."

"That's good news. And which sofa did you choose?"

He jumped over to the red and pink one. "This one. What do you think?"

"Err, it's okay, but I think there's a better one."

"Oh? Which one?"

I weaved my way through the sofas. "This one."

"But that's the old one."

"I know, and unless you intend to pay for a new one out of your own pocket, it's the only one you're going to be getting."

"What about my rheumatism? You said you'd buy me a new sofa to make up for unjustly putting me out on the streets."

"That was when I believed my actions had been unjust, but we both know that wasn't the case, don't we?"

"I have no idea what you're talking about."

"You know precisely what I'm talking about. The Canary Brothers didn't break in here and steal Mrs V's yellow yarn. You stole it and threw it in the bin behind the alleyway."

"You can't prove that."

"I don't need to. It's written all over your face. What I don't understand is why you did it? What possessed you?"

"I was provoked."

"Provoked how?"

The old bag lady came in here one morning and threw me out into the rain for no reason whatsoever."

"I highly doubt that."

"It's true. She's vindictive, that one."

"So you stole her wool?"

"She was lucky I only took the yellow. It was all I could carry."

"And as if that wasn't bad enough, you then proceeded to guilt trip me. You had me feeding salmon to your snooty friends."

"They are not snooty."

"And to those ditzy girls."

"They are not—okay, maybe they are a little ditzy, but you owed me. Sleeping in that tent was no fun."

"And you had the audacity to make me hand over a ransom. I want the rest of that money back by the way."

"Are you really not going to let me have a new sofa? What if I say pretty please?"

"With sugar on top?"

"Yeah, pretty please with sugar on top."

"No."

"You're a hard woman."

Winky spent the next hour contacting the sofa companies to arrange collections, and giving me the cold shoulder. Like that bothered me.

"I'm leaving now, Mrs V. I have to call and see Grandma at her hotel."

"How is her new business venture doing?"

"Really well." But maybe not for much longer.

"I managed to get hold of Mr Slugger."

"You did?"

"Yes. He sounds surprisingly nice. He said he'll be in Big Bessie's tomorrow morning at seven o'clock."

"But tomorrow's Saturday."

"I'm only telling you what he said."

"Okay, thanks." Florence's dance class was at ten, but I should be back long before that. So much for my weekend lie-in. "By the way, Mrs V, did you put Winky outside one day recently?"

"I did, dear. I found him scratching your desk, and I know how much that desk means to you so I threw him out. I thought that would teach him a lesson. Why do you ask?"

"No reason."

***

I left my car outside the old watermill and walked across the village to the hotel. On the drive home, I'd been trying to figure out how I was going to persuade Grandma that she should send all her guests back to Candlefield until such time as the men from DOPA had left the village. It wasn't going to be easy.

"Hi, Jill." The receptionist, Verity, and I were now on first name terms.

"Is she in her office?"

"Your grandmother isn't in today."

"Is she *really* not in or is that just what you've been told to tell everyone?"

"No, I promise. She's gone to London on business."

"What kind of business?"

"I have no idea. She doesn't tell me that kind of stuff."

"Okay. Are you on duty tomorrow?"

"Yes, I am."

"I've got a couple of things happening in the morning, so I won't be able to get over until midday-ish. Will you tell Grandma that it's very urgent that I speak to her?"

"Of course."

Florence came running to greet me as soon as I walked in the door.

"Mummy, Jen has shrunk!"

"Beetles can't shrink, darling."

"But she has. Come and see." She led the way into the kitchen and lifted the lid on the shoebox. "See, Jen's smaller than she was this morning."

"She does look a little smaller. Perhaps it was all that sleeping."

"Will I shrink if I sleep too much?"

"No, you won't. It's just a beetle thing."

That seemed to satisfy her, and she headed outside to

check on the caterpillars. Jack, who had been listening to that brief exchange, was preparing dinner.

"Couldn't you have found a beetle the same size as the dead one?" I said in a hushed voice.

"I did try, but there just aren't that many beetles in the garden. I thought I'd got it just about right, but she noticed the difference straight away."

"Something smells nice."

"That's my new aftershave. It's called Jock."

"I was talking about the food. And *Jock*? Seriously?"

"Take a sniff." He leaned towards me.

"It smells exactly the same as your old one."

"Rubbish, this one is much more —"

"Jocky?"

"I was going to say musky. According to the ads, I'll have women swooning over me."

"O — kay." I laughed. "I have to go out on a stakeout tonight."

"Do you need me to read Florence's bedtime story?"

"No, it's okay, I can do it. I won't need to leave here until midnight, and besides, the job is in Candlefield, so you'll hardly notice I've gone."

"What's the job?"

"I'm still working on the lido thing for Grandma, but it's turned rather sinister now. Unless I'm badly mistaken, the people behind the lido closure may be responsible for two murders."

***

Jack went up to bed just before eleven. I had planned to watch some TV before magicking myself over to the site of the old nursery, but I dozed off. It was almost one in the morning when I woke up with a crick in my neck, feeling like death warmed up. I was sorely tempted to forget the stakeout and just go to bed, but I knew that when I saw Grandma later that day, she would demand a progress report.

The elderly wizard, who lived across the road from the new office block, had told me that a van came to the building most days, in the early hours of the morning. Hopefully, it would turn up tonight and I hadn't already missed it.

There was nowhere in the alleyway at the rear of the office building from where I would be able to get a good view of the door without being spotted, so I made myself invisible. To pass the time, I daydreamed about all the things I'd do if I won the lottery.

You might be wondering why I didn't just magic myself a gazillion pounds? There's a very good reason for that and it's called MERRY. That acronym stands for the Magical Ethics, Rules and Regulations Yearbook, which as its name suggests is updated annually. Any witch or wizard found in contravention of that particular publication will find themselves in deep doodoo. If you'd like a copy of the book, please send a cheque for five-hundred pounds to the usual address.

Trust me to pick the coldest night of the year so far. Hopefully, no one would notice my breath, which was still visible even though I wasn't. That's if anyone turned up, which was beginning to look doubtful. The only thing that kept me going was the thought of the warm bed waiting for me back home.

At two-forty, headlights came around the corner of the building, and a plain white van stopped just beyond the doors. The wizard who climbed out of the passenger side had the physique of a bodybuilder and a scar on his left cheek. He opened the double doors and guided the driver as he reversed the van into the building. I had to be quick in order to get inside before the doors closed behind us. We were in some kind of loading bay, which seemed completely out of place in this office building. A second wizard got out of the driver's side and joined his colleague. Mr Gator and Mr Dial, I assumed.

The two of them stood next to the van and stared into the shadows. They were clearly waiting for something, but what? Moments later, I had my answer, when a small wooden trolley rolled into sight. It was being pushed by four tiny creatures who were covered in blue dust. They weren't elves or pixies. In fact, I'd never seen anything quite like them, with their long noses, big ears and huge feet. The two wizards wasted no time in unloading a number of wooden boxes from the back of the van, into which the weird creatures started to load the blue stones.

What on earth was going on?

When the boxes of stones had been put into the van, the wizards climbed into the vehicle, and one of the small creatures threw the switch to open the doors. I slipped outside just in time to see the van drive away. I hadn't been sure what to expect from the stakeout, but this most definitely had not been it.

Chapter 25

"Why are you getting up so early, Jill?" Jack sat up in bed. "It's Saturday."

"I have another meeting at Big Bessie's."

"Is that just an excuse to have a greasy-spoon breakfast?"

"No, it's not. I have a meeting with the leader of Loose Chippings Motorcycle Club, but I might indulge while I'm there."

"Will you be back in time for Florence's dance class?"

"Definitely."

"How did your stakeout go last night?"

"It was kind of weird. Not what I was expecting at all. There isn't time to go into it now, but I'll tell you all about it later. Give Florence a kiss for me, would you?"

"Will do."

***

Slugger was waiting by his bike in the layby.

"Before we go inside, I should warn you that they don't serve muesli in here." He grinned.

"Just as well. I detest that stuff."

"I'm surprised. I had you down as a muesli and camomile tea woman. I'm having the full English, care to join me?"

I was sorely tempted, but I settled for a sausage cob, which was a meal in itself.

"Who was that old lady who called me yesterday?"

"That was Mrs V, my PA."

"That woman is pretty fearsome. She threatened me

with all kinds of things if I laid a finger on you."

"Mrs V is very protective."

"Judging by the way you dealt with Billy, I wouldn't think you need much protection."

"It's Billy I want to talk to you about. Amongst other things."

"I'm listening."

"There are a few people who had a grudge against Killer."

"Am I supposed to be surprised by that?"

"Andy, the mechanic at Wash-on-Wheels, had his nose put out when Chains brought in Killer, but I'm satisfied he didn't murder him. Chains' second-in-command, Sid, borrowed money from Killer, but failed to pay it back. I ruled him out once I was able to confirm that he'd paid the debt by giving Killer his gold ring."

"And you're telling me all of this why?"

"Because there's still one person with reason to have a grudge against Killer, and so far, I haven't been able to rule him out."

"Let me take a wild guess. Would that person be me by any chance?"

"Got it in one."

"I've already told you that Killer and I had buried the hatchet, and that I'd agreed he could re-join Loose Chippings."

"That's what you said, yeah. I'm just not sure I believe it. Everyone I've talked to says you have a temper, a flair for violence, and that you hold a grudge."

"I've never hit anyone who didn't deserve it. Anyway, I told you that Billy was there when Killer and I discussed him returning."

"That's not what Billy says."

"What?"

"I spoke to him yesterday and he's adamant that he never heard the two of you discussing Killer's return."

"He's lying."

"Why would he do that?"

"I have no idea. Maybe it's his way of getting back at you for what you did to him. He was pretty embarrassed."

"How does him lying harm me? If anything, you're the one who's damaged by his failing to corroborate what you said."

"Who knows how Billy's mind works."

"Isn't the truth that you went over to Wash-on-Wheels that day to try and persuade Killer to re-join Loose Chippings, and that he turned you down flat?"

"Is a vivid imagination a prerequisite in your job?"

"When he refused your offer, you lost your temper and struck out."

Slugger mopped up the remains of his tomato juice with a sausage, popped it into his mouth, and stood up. "It's been a blast, Jill, but I really do have to go. My old Mum is expecting me."

"I'm going to find the evidence I need to prove you did this, and when I do, the police will be knocking at your door."

"I won't hold my breath."

***

"How was the full English?" Jack asked when I got back to the old watermill.

"I didn't have time for one, so I had to settle for —"

"Muesli?"

"I reckon if you asked for that in Big Bessie's, you'd be lynched. Actually, I just had a couple of slices of toast."

"How did it go?"

"It didn't. Slugger is still sticking to his story that he and the murder victim had reconciled their differences. I'm just not sure I believe him." I glanced around. "Where's Florence? On caterpillar watch?"

"No. She's over at Donna's house."

"How come?"

"Donna came over about an hour ago to tell us that the dance class had been cancelled. They've got a burst water pipe at the village hall, so they've had to cancel all activities this weekend. Donna said she was planning to take Wendy into town later, and she asked if Florence wanted to spend the day with them. Needless to say, Florence was all for it. That means we have the whole day to ourselves. What are we going to do, sexy?" He gave me that look of his, which I'm pretty sure was supposed to be alluring, but he actually looked as though he was about to sneeze.

"Before I do anything, I have to go and see Grandma."

"Can't that wait?"

"No, it can't. I've already waited too long."

"Okay, what about afterwards?"

"Afterwards, you can treat me to lunch at The Middle."

"Okay, but what about after that?"

"That'll depend how nice you are to me between now and then."

***

As soon as Verity spotted me, she began to shake her head, which I took as a bad sign.

"I'm really sorry, Jill, but your grandmother is in a meeting at the moment, and she gave strict instructions that she was not to be disturbed under any circumstances."

"Did you tell her that I was coming over this morning, and that it was urgent?"

"I did, but she didn't seem very interested. Sorry."

"It's not your fault, but this can't wait, so I'm going in there."

"Please, Jill, will you at least wait here while I go and have a word with her? I don't want to lose this job."

"Sure, but tell her that I'm not going to take no for an answer."

"I'll be as quick as I can."

Five minutes later, Grandma came charging into reception with a face like thunder. A terrified looking Verity was trailing in her wake.

"This had better be good!" Grandma exploded. "You've just dragged me out of a very important meeting."

"It is, but we can't talk here. I need to speak to you in private."

"Oh, very well. Follow me." She led the way into a small office just off reception where Mr Ivers was tapping away on a computer.

He looked up. "Hello, Jill."

"Out!" Grandma barked at him.

"I haven't saved —"

"Out!"

"Of course." He scooted out of the room.

"You didn't have to be so rude to him," I said.

"You didn't have to interrupt my meeting, but you did it anyway. What's this all about?"

"You have to tell all of your guests to pack their bags immediately and return to Candlefield."

"That's very funny." She laughed in my face.

"I'm deadly serious, Grandma."

"Oh? In that case, I'll go straight out there and tell everyone to leave."

"You will?"

"Of course not. Are you insane?"

"Listen, Grandma, there are government agents in Middle Tweaking from DOPA."

"And?"

"Aren't you going to ask who DOPA are?"

"I know who they are."

"You do? I'd never heard of them until yesterday."

"I've got an idea. Why don't you come and sit in on my meeting?"

"There isn't time for that. We have to get everyone out of the hotel."

"Relax. I have it all in hand. Now, come with me."

This was madness, but Grandma was adamant that I should follow her. Seated around the circular table were three men, all dressed in grey suits.

"Gentlemen, I apologise for the interruption. This is my assistant manager, Vanessa, I hope you don't mind if she sits in on our meeting."

"Not at all," the tallest of the three said. "I'm Arthur, this is John, and that's Charlie."

"Nice to meet you, I'm sure." I managed through gritted teeth. What was Grandma playing at?

"Gentlemen, would you mind telling Vanessa where you're from?"

"We're from DOPA. You probably won't have heard of it."

Oh bum! "I can't say I have."

"It stands for the Department of Paranormal Activity."

"But surely there's no such thing as the paranormal."

"Of course not, but our department is tasked with checking any reports of such activity. Just to be on the safe side, you understand."

"I see. What brings you to Middle Tweaking?"

"There have been multiple reports of paranormal activity centred on this village, and on this hotel in particular."

"That's ridiculous."

"The reports were very convincing, but having looked around the village and the hotel, we're happy there's no substance to them."

"There isn't? I mean, of course there isn't."

"Mirabel has been quite accommodating. She has allowed us to look around the hotel and to speak to all the guests, and it's clear there's nothing amiss within these four walls."

When the meeting concluded, Grandma showed the three DOPA agents out while I waited in her office.

"How did you manage that?" I said when she returned.

"What you have to remember, Jill, is that fundamentally, most humans are stupid. Those three charged in here all guns blazing, but a little magic soon slowed them down."

"What about when your spell wears off? Won't they be

back?"

"I doubt it. Not for a few years at least. I may have accidentally poured a slow-acting potion into their tea. How did you hear about the *dopes*, anyway?"

"Daze came to see me. She was really worried."

"That young woman worries far too much. You should get Annabel to teach her meditation. Anyway, on to more important matters. What's happening with the lido?"

"What do you know about blue stones?"

"Why are you talking in riddles? What does that have to do with the lido?"

I told Grandma about my stakeout at the office building, the funny little creatures, and the blue stones.

"Long nose, big ears and huge feet, you say?"

"Yeah."

"And you're sure it wasn't a mirror you were looking at?"

"You're so not funny. Do you know what they are?"

"It sounds like the Bogdars."

"Never heard of them."

"There's no reason you should have. They live underground most of the time: in caves, sewers, that kind of thing. Are you sure the stones were blue? It must have been dark in there."

"Positive. The Bog-thingies were covered in blue dust."

"If you're right about the colour, it sounds like Candle Blue."

"What's that?"

"A semi-precious stone. Have you ever heard of Blue John?"

"Who's he?"

"Sometimes, Jill, I despair at your lack of general

knowledge. Blue John isn't a *he*. It's a mineral found in Castleton, Derbyshire."

"Now you mention it, I think I have seen jewellery made from it."

"Candle Blue is a similar thing. It's actually illegal to mine it because it's so rare."

"Are you trying to tell me that Reptile Holdings are buying up land so that they can mine underneath it? That doesn't make any sense. Why go to the expense of building an office block on there?"

"To hide what they're up to. My guess is that the interior of the building is just a shell. And as for the cost, that will pale into insignificance compared to what the stone is likely to fetch."

"But if it's illegal to mine it, how can they sell it?"

"They won't be able to sell it in Candlefield, but if they bring it over to the human world, they'll have no problem moving it. There's one sure way to prove that's what they're up to."

"What's that?"

"Check the geology of the plots of land they've taken over. I'll bet my best broom they all have Candle Blue deposits below them."

"Can you arrange that?"

"Certainly not. I have a hotel to run. You'll have to do it."

"I'm busy too, you know."

"You're so funny sometimes, Jill."

***

"I'm starving," Jack said, as we walked to The Middle.

"Me too."

"I'm not surprised if the only thing you've had all morning is a slice of toast."

"I think I'm going to have a steak with all the trimmings."

"I might have the same. It's ages since I had one."

"And sticky toffee pudding for afters."

"Yummy."

"Hi, guys." Arthur Spraggs was fiddling with the cash register. "They installed this new POS system yesterday, and I'm still trying to make sense of it."

"Don't tell me you're going all hi-tech on us," I said.

"It wasn't my idea. The brewery insisted we upgrade. Ah, that's it. Sorry about that. What can I get you?"

"I'll have a pint of lager," Jack said.

"Just a Coke for me, please. And we'd both like a steak."

"Slight problem there, I'm afraid. The oven and grill are on the blink, so we're only doing sandwiches at the moment. Hopefully, it'll be repaired in time for tonight."

My heart sank. "What sandwiches do you have?"

"Cheese. Ham. And cheese and ham."

Somewhat deflated, Jack and I were munching on our sandwiches.

"Not exactly steak, is it?" I said. "I think I should have had the ham."

"Hello, there. It's Jill, isn't it?"

It took me a moment to place the man, but then the penny dropped. "Mr Peep."

"Joe, please."

"Hello, Joe. This is my husband, Jack."

"Good to meet you, Jack."

"Is Flo with you, Joe?" I asked.

"No, she's visiting her mother."

"Joe and Flo were interested in buying Tweaking Tea Rooms, Jack. Before Miss Drinkwater's sad demise, that is."

"We may still do it," Joe said. "In fact, that's why I'm here today. I've just been talking to the solicitors handling the estate. Fingers crossed, it's looking very promising, but we don't want to get our hopes up, just in case."

"That's great news. I hope everything works out."

"Me too. Anyway, I'll let you get on with your snack. I only popped in for a quick word with Arthur."

"Joe seems nice," Jack said.

"They both are, but I should warn you they're train nuts."

"Speaking of which, I wonder how Mr Hosey is doing."

"The last time I saw him, he was working behind the bar in Bar Loco. Didn't I mention it to you?"

"I don't think so." Jack brushed the crumbs off his clothes. "So, are you ready for *afters*?"

"I don't think I'm bothered about a dessert to be honest."

"I wasn't talking about desserts."

"I should have known. You and your one-track mind. Come on, then, let's go home."

Chapter 26

"Donna? Florence?"

The two of them were standing on our doorstep. Donna was clearly stressed about something, but Florence looked fine, and was busy looking at the box in her hand.

"I was just about to call you, Jill," Donna said.

"Is something wrong?"

"It's Wendy. She started to feel poorly while we were walking around Washbridge. I've just dropped her at home with her dad."

"Is she alright?"

"Yeah, it's probably one of those twenty-four-hour bugs. I just hope she hasn't given it to Florence."

"Do you feel okay, darling?" I said.

"Yes. Look what I've got, Mummy." She held up the box. "It's a princess' carriage."

"It's a model kit," Jack said. "Cool. I loved those when I was a kid."

"I thought it might be a bit too old for her," Donna said. "But she was really keen on it."

"You didn't need to buy her anything."

"It felt like the least I could do because we'd had to cut the day short."

"Can I make my model now, Mummy?"

"Of course you can. Daddy will help you, won't you?"

"Yeah, let's go inside." Jack took her in the house.

"I'm really sorry about this, Jill. I hope you and Jack didn't have anything planned for this afternoon."

"Nothing special."

By the time I joined Jack and Florence in the kitchen,

they'd emptied the contents of the box onto the table.

"Wow, you've got a lot of pieces there," I said.

"Where do we start, Daddy?" Florence picked up the tube of glue.

"It might be best if you let Daddy glue it together."

"No, I want to do it."

"It looks like you're in for a fun afternoon." I grinned at Jack.

"Aren't you going to help us?"

"I'd love to, but I need to go and see a man about some blue stones."

"*Blue stones?*"

"I'll tell you all about it tonight. Have fun."

***

Aunt Lucy was ironing.

Her tea-towels!

"I'm glad you came over, Jill. I'd love a cup of tea, but I do hate to stop ironing once I've started. Will you pop the kettle on, please?"

"Sure. Are they—err—tea-towels that you're ironing?"

"They are. I do them the second Friday in the month."

"Right." I filled the kettle.

"Bedding is the first and third Monday, and handkerchiefs are the third Wednesday. I find it helps to have systems in place, don't you?"

"Absolutely, I swear by them."

"This is just what the doctor ordered." She took a sip of tea. "I expect you heard that I gave in, and let the twins have the corks?"

"Yes, I was in Cuppy C yesterday."

"I've told the girls that they have to take good care of them."

"I'm sure they will." Some chance.

"They should find it easy enough to set up the exhibition because I've attached a card to every cork with full details of its origin."

"That must have taken some time."

"Hours."

"The twins are lucky to have you. I popped over because I need to get in contact with a geologist here in Candlefield."

"Whatever for?"

I told her about Grandma's theory regarding the Candle Blue.

"It's a beautiful stone. My great-grandmother had a pendant made from it. That was before mining it was made illegal, obviously. Why don't you take a look in Candle Pages? There might be something in there."

I did as she suggested, and to my surprise, I found three geologists listed. The first two said they'd be happy to provide me with a consultation, but they were both booked solid for the next couple of weeks. Who knew that geologists would be in such high demand? I wasn't particularly optimistic when I tried the last name listed.

A man picked up the call on the first ring. "Walters, Walters and Walters."

"I'd like to speak to Mr Walters, please."

"Which one?"

"The geologist."

"We're all geologists. I'm William Walters."

"Hi. My name is Jill Maxwell, and I was —"

"Did you say, Jill Maxwell?"

"That's right. I was hoping to arrange a consultation. The problem is that I need it really quickly, but I don't imagine you work at the weekend."

"I don't normally, but if you're happy for me to provide the consultation at my house, I can do it right now."

"That would be brilliant. If you give me your address, I'll be straight over."

"Any luck?" Aunt Lucy said when I re-joined her in the kitchen.

"Yeah. Seems I struck lucky. I can go over there right now."

William Walters lived in one of the more upmarket areas of Candlefield, where the houses were larger and definitely more expensive.

The man opened the door while I was still mid-knock, and then he stared at me in a rather unnerving fashion.

"William?"

"Err, sorry. I just can't believe that *the* Jill Maxwell is standing on my doorstep."

"Well, here I am. It's definitely me."

"Sorry, where are my manners? Do come inside. Can I get you anything to drink?"

"No, thanks. I've actually just had a cup of tea."

"Let's go through to the living room." He gestured to the second door on the right.

I took one step inside, and then froze to the spot.

"What do you think?" He squeezed past me.

"I—err—"

"I have every poster they've ever published of you, I believe."

"And they're all on your walls. Nice."

"There are way too many to fit in this room alone. Would you like to see those in my bedroom?"

"Err, no, I'm good, but thanks for asking."

"I have this too." He picked up a large scrapbook and started to flick through the pages; it was full of press-cuttings. "There's every article ever printed about you in here. There's nothing I don't know about you. Would you like to test me?"

"That's okay. I'm very—err—" Creeped out. "Impressed."

"Thank you. I like to think that I'm your number one fan. That's why, when you called, I cancelled my plans so I could offer my services."

"That's really kind of you. I hope you're not missing anything important on my behalf?"

"It's the monthly meeting of the JM Appreciation Society."

"JM?"

"Jill Maxwell of course. The guys there are going to blow a fuse when I tell them you were in my house. Even I can't believe it. This isn't a dream, is it?"

"No, it's really me, but we do need to get down to the matter in hand."

"Of course. How exactly can I help?"

After I'd run through my theory about the Candle Blue, he brought up some weird coloured maps on his computer screen. "Okay, Jill, if you could just give me the location of the properties you mentioned."

I told him the address of the community centre, the nursery and lido.

"Check, check and check. Your hunch is correct, Jill. There are very few remaining pockets of Candle Blue, and the larger ones are all outside the built-up areas of Candlefield. There are, however, a few small deposits in Candlefield itself, and the locations you have given me, correspond to three of them."

Bingo!

"That's great. Thanks very much, William. I really do appreciate your help. How much do I owe you?"

"I wouldn't dream of taking a fee from you, but there is something you could do in lieu of payment."

"Oh?"

"Could I take a selfie with you?"

"Of course."

He snapped a couple of photos. "Thanks ever so much, Jill."

"No problem. I really must get going now, though."

"Couldn't you stay a little longer? I'd love to show you the video footage I have of you in the tournaments."

"I'd love to." Not. "But I really must be making tracks."

Lovely as it is to have fans, sometimes they can be a little *too* much. Still, my consultation with William Walters had proven to be most fruitful, and on the strength of that, I gave Daze a call.

"It's Jill. I have something that I think will interest you. Can you spare me five minutes sometime today?"

"Blaze and I are actually in a hole at the moment."

"Sorry. If you're in a fix, it can wait until Monday."

"No. When I said we were in a hole, I didn't mean we were having problems. I meant we're literally in a hole; we're digging it. You're welcome to come over and talk to me now if you like. Any excuse to get out of this muddy, wet hole."

"Okay, great."

I magicked myself to Washbridge. Daze had just climbed out of the hole and Blaze was about to do likewise.

"There's no need for you to get out," Daze said to him. "Jill is here to speak to me."

"Not fair."

"Cry me a river." Daze could be a hard woman when she wanted to be. "What have you got for us, Jill?"

"I hate my life." Blaze threw out a shovel-full of dirt, which landed suspiciously close to Daze.

"I think I've uncovered some kind of — err — I'm not sure what you'd call it. An illegal mining operation, I suppose. In Candlefield."

"That sounds like something for the local police over there."

"Yes, except that I think they're bringing the minerals over here to the human world to sell."

"Hang on. What kind of minerals?"

"Candle Blue."

"That has to be Blue Jim up to his old tricks."

"Sorry?"

"Don't you remember I told you we've been on the lookout for him?"

"Vaguely."

"That's where he got his nickname from. He peddles Candle Blue here in the human world, but so far we've had no luck tracing him."

"Do you think one of the guys I saw collecting the Candle Blue might be him?"

"I doubt it, but I'd bet my bottom dollar that they're supplying him. Fill me in on all the details, would you?"

I told Daze about the lido and the other buildings that had been taken over by Reptile Holdings, AKA, G&D Enterprises.

"That's fantastic work, Jill." She turned back to the hole. "Blaze, why are you wasting your time down there? Get up here. We have work to do."

I really hoped Daze couldn't lip read or Blaze would be in big trouble.

"Let me know how you get on, Daze, would you? I've still got Grandma on my case about the lido."

"Will do."

***

I'd no sooner walked through the door than Florence came stomping over to me, hands on her waist. "Daddy is rubbish at models!"

Jack popped his head around the kitchen door. "That's a bit harsh, pumpkin."

"Come and see, Mummy." Florence took my hand and led the way into the kitchen.

"Oh dear." It took all my willpower not to laugh. "It's not all that bad."

"It's rubbish," Florence insisted. "The wheels are wobbly, and the seat is upside down."

I sensed a distraction was needed. "Have you checked on the caterpillars yet?"

"Not today."

"You'd better go and do it, then. You might miss them turning into butterflies."

"Okay."

Once she was outside, I turned to Jack. "What's that

thing supposed to be?"

"It was really complicated."

"I thought you said you loved model kits when you were a kid?"

"I did, but I was never any good at them. Can't you use magic to put it right?"

"Sure, I'll use the *make my model princess' carriage right* spell, shall I?"

"There might be one."

"Of course there isn't."

"You said that about the 'whistle' spell."

"They're still not butterflies." A disgruntled Florence stood in the doorway. "I think they've forgotten how to do it."

"It won't be long now."

"I've got an idea," Jack said. "Why don't we all play a game?"

"Snakes and ladders!" Florence yelled. "I want to play snakes and ladders."

"No using magic to cheat, you two," Jack said as he rolled the dice.

"We don't cheat, do we, Florence?"

"No." The huge smirk on her face somewhat undermined her credibility.

Twenty minutes later, Jack was well ahead. If it had just been him and me playing, I would definitely have used magic, but I didn't want to set a bad example for Florence. It was Jack's turn to roll the dice.

"Five!" He moved the counter. "Hang on, where did that snake come from?" He pointed to the board.

I glanced over at Florence who was giggling.

A *snake*! Of course. Why didn't I realise before?

Chapter 27

It was Sunday morning, and Jack had nipped to the village store to pick up some marmalade. In any other shop that would have taken him no more than ten minutes, but with the Stock sisters' shelving system, I told him I'd expect him in an hour or so.

I was upstairs, sorting out the laundry basket when Florence came running into the bedroom.

"Great-Grandma has fixed it!"

"Fixed what?"

"The princess' carriage. It's all fixed."

"Hang on. Where is Great-Grandma?"

"In the kitchen."

"Is she now?" I threw the laundry on the bed and hurried downstairs, to find Grandma putting on the kettle. "What are you doing in here?"

"I'm making myself a cup of tea, seeing as no one else was going to do it."

"How did you get in?"

"Through that rectangular-shaped thing at the front of the house. I believe they call it a door."

"Very funny. I *meant* who let you in?"

"I let myself in. And before you have a go at me, I bumped into Jeff coming out of the gate and he said I should go straight in."

"It's Jack."

"Do you want a cuppa?"

"Yes, please."

"How did you manage to do that?" I gestured at the photo-perfect model carriage, which Florence was now happily playing with.

"With magic of course. How else?"

"Yes, but which spell did you use?"

"The *make my model princess' carriage right* spell, obviously. Anyway, enough of that. I came to see what's happening with the lido."

While we drank our tea, I brought her up to speed on the situation.

"So, I was right about the Candle Blue. What about the lido, though? Is there still time to save it?"

"I don't know. I've handed everything over to Daze."

"And what is she going to do?"

"Make some arrests, I assume."

"You *assume*? That's not going to get the job done, is it?" She gulped down the rest of her tea. "I'd better go and light a fire under that Daisy girl, or nothing will get done." She gave Florence a kiss on the head. "Bye bye, my little poppet."

"Bye, Great-Grandma."

When Jack finally got back, he'd been gone for almost an hour and a quarter.

"I thought you'd got lost."

"That store is hopeless."

"Did you get the marmalade?"

"Eventually. It was under 'L'."

"Why on earth would it be under 'L' and not 'M'?"

"According to Marjorie, it was under 'L' for *lade*." He did a double take at the princess' carriage. "What happened to that?"

"Do you like it, Daddy?" Florence beamed. "Great-Grandma mended it for me."

"Did she?" He turned to me. "And which spell did she

use?"

"I don't think she said. Anyway, I have to nip out to see someone."

"Is this all an elaborate excuse to get out of the village fete?"

"No, I promise it's not. I'll be back long before that starts."

"You'd better be. I don't want to have to explain to the vicar why you've gone AWOL."

"I'll be back."

"That impression of yours doesn't get any better."

"Says you."

***

If this morning's plan *extraordinaire* was going to work, the execution and timing would have to be just perfect.

After parking outside the house, I double-checked my watch, and then made my way to the front door. The only part of the plan that was outside of my control was whether or not he was at home, so it was with fingers crossed that I knocked.

"What do you want? How did you find out where I lived?"

"Good morning to you too, Billy. Beautiful day, isn't it?"

"I asked what you wanted."

"A cup of tea? Why thank you. I don't mind if I do." Before he could stop me, I'd pushed past him into the house.

"Get out of here before I throw you out."

"Do you really want to try that after what happened the

last time?" I took the first door on my left, which turned out to be the living room. "Oh dear, Billy, did you choose this colour scheme?"

"Tell me what you want and then get out."

"My pleasure. I'd like you to take a trip with me to the police station."

"And why would I do that?"

"I think you already know the answer."

"I don't have the faintest idea what you're talking about."

"Okay, if that's how you want to play it." I sighed. "I know you're responsible for Killer's death. I'm just not sure if you meant to do it."

"I had nothing to do with his death. I told you it was Slugger."

"Try again. Slugger has a cast iron alibi for the time of Killer's death."

"That still doesn't mean I did it."

"You did overhear the conversation between Slugger and Killer, didn't you?"

"No, I told you that I didn't."

"Slugger says otherwise."

"He's lying."

"I don't think so. When you overheard Slugger welcome Killer back, you knew your days as the number one mechanic at Loose Chippings were over."

"That's rubbish."

"So you went to see Killer, to try to persuade him not to come back."

"More nonsense."

"When he wouldn't listen, you lost your temper. You obviously didn't hit him or that would have shown up on the autopsy. Did you push him? I reckon you did, and when he hit his head on the bench, you thought he was dead, panicked and ran away. Do you want to know the really tragic part? When you left, he was still alive. If you'd called the ambulance, he might have lived."

"I didn't do it." His initial bravado had all but drained away.

"Killer managed to hang onto life just long enough to leave a clue as to the identity of his murderer."

"What are you talking about?"

"He used his own blood to scrawl on the petrol tank of his bike." I took out my phone and showed him the photo. "Andy thought it was the letter 'S', but it isn't, is it, Billy? It's a snake, just like the one on your arm."

"You can't prove any of this."

"Maybe not, but the police will be able to when they check phone location records and CCTV nearby. They haven't bothered until now because they assumed that Killer had tripped and hit his head, but I'm confident I can convince them to think again. If it really was an accident, things will go better for you if you hand yourself in before they come looking for you."

"Or I could just leave." He pushed past me and headed for the door.

I gave him a few seconds and then followed.

"Let me go!" he screamed.

"Thanks, guys," I said. "Your timing was perfect."

"My pleasure, Jill." Chains had hold of Billy's left arm.

"Can't I just give him a good kicking first?" Slugger had hold of Billy's other arm.

"No, you can't, but you can take him to the police station."

Only when they'd left did Alison show herself. She'd been waiting around the corner, no doubt watching proceedings.

"I was convinced Slugger had killed him," she said.

"So was I for a while."

"What will happen to Billy?"

"That depends if he comes clean. If he does, and he can convince the police that it was an accident, then he'll face a lesser charge."

"What if he won't admit to it?"

"I'm pretty sure it won't come to that. He's probably more scared of what Chains and Slugger will do to him than he is of the courts."

"Thanks for everything you've done, Jill. I really do appreciate it. Killer had his faults, but he didn't deserve to die like that."

"My pleasure."

"I heard Slugger took you for a ride on his bike. Can we expect you to join our club any time soon?"

"No chance. Once was enough for me."

"You'll let me have your bill?"

"You can bank on it."

***

"See, I told you I'd be back in time," I said.

Jack checked his watch. "Only just. How did it go?"

"Fantastic. I left Billy in the capable hands of Chains and Slugger, the leaders of the two motorcycle clubs. They were accompanying him to the police station so he could make a full confession."

"Are you sure they won't just dish out their own brand

of justice?"

"They know if they do, I'll turn them both in."

"How did you work out who did it?"

"To be honest, it was the game of snakes and ladders that did it."

"You're going to have to explain that."

"Killer left a blood stain on the petrol tank of his bike. It looked like an 'S', and for a while there, I was convinced Slugger had killed him. Then, yesterday, when we were playing that game, I saw the snake that you landed on, and everything made sense."

"You mean the snake our daughter magicked there, so that I'd lose?"

"Let's gloss over that for a minute. It made me realise that the blood print on the tank wasn't an 'S'. It was a snake. And guess who has a tattoo of a snake?"

"Billy."

"Got it in one. For what it's worth, I don't believe he meant to murder Killer. I think there was an argument, Billy pushed him, and he fell backwards and hit his head."

"Mummy! Daddy!" Florence came running in from the garden. "Come and see!"

"What is it?"

"Angie and Archie are butterflies."

And so they were.

"They're pretty, aren't they, Mummy?"

"They're very pretty."

They were exactly the same colours as they had been as caterpillars: Yellow with red spots.

"Can I take them into the house?"

"No. You have to leave them outside so that they can

fly."

"But they might fly away."

"They probably will eventually, but at least you've seen them turn into butterflies. Shall I take a photo of them for you?"

"Yes, please."

"Okay."

"We'd better get going." Jack tapped his watch. "Or we'll be late for the fete."

"What about Buddy?"

The little dog was fast asleep on the other side of the garden.

"We may as well leave him out here. It's not like he can get out, and the weather forecast is good."

"Okay. Let's go."

***

"I want to go on the hook-a-duck," Florence said, as soon as we arrived at Tweaking Meadows where the village fete was being held.

"Your Daddy is an expert at hook-a-duck. Mummy has to find the refreshment stall."

"Swap in thirty minutes?" Jack shouted as Florence dragged him away.

I gave him the thumbs up and then went in search of my stall. It was next to a carousel, which was playing the same awful tune on loop, at a ridiculously high volume.

"Hi, Jill." The vicar had to shout to be heard.

"Sorry I'm late."

"No problem. We've only been open a couple of minutes. I thought I'd hold the fort until you arrived.

Everything is priced, so you should be good to go. Give me a shout if you need anything."

"Will do."

There were so many cakes, all home-baked, and looking delicious. I was like a child left alone in the sweet shop. I told myself that I must resist, but those eclairs looked so tasty. Just one wouldn't hurt.

And yes, I did pay for it. Sheesh, what do you take me for?

If I'd expected an easy ride on the refreshments stall, I was sorely mistaken. I soon had a queue of people, all eager to sample the delicious wares.

"Hi, Jill." Olga appeared at my side. "The vicar asked me to come and lend you a hand."

"Thanks, I certainly need one."

After half an hour, Jack took over from me.

"Look what I've won, Mummy." Florence held up a small stuffed toy.

"A giraffe. It's lovely."

"It's a penguin."

"Oh, yeah, of course."

"I've decided to call him Hooky because I won him on hook-a-duck."

"That's a great name."

"Can I have a toffee apple?"

"I'm not sure. They're hard to eat and very sticky."

"Please, Mummy. Wendy had one."

"Is Wendy here?"

"Yes, she's with her mummy. She said she was feeling better."

"That's good. Let's go and get you that toffee apple."

I insisted that we sit down while Florence ate it, to try and avoid her getting into any more of a mess than necessary. As we were seated, I heard a familiar voice; it was Mad together with Brad.

"Mad!" When she turned around, I could see that she had a scarf pulled up over her mouth again. "Florence, Mummy is just going to talk to her friend. You stay here and finish your toffee apple. I'll only be a minute."

"Okay, Mummy." She had already managed to get red toffee over Hooky, the giraffe-shaped penguin.

"Hey, you two. Who's watching the shop?"

"We set on a new assistant," Brad said. "This is our first day off together since we opened."

"Are you okay, Mad? Do you have toothache?" She shook her head, somewhat unconvincingly. "Are you sure you're okay?"

She sighed beneath the scarf, and then slowly lowered it from her mouth. "Don't you dare laugh, Jill."

"What happened to your lips?"

"*Nails* happened to them."

"Oh dear." I stifled a laugh.

"Mum assured me he knew what he was doing, but it's my own fault for agreeing to it."

"They don't look too bad," I lied.

"Yes, they do, but at least they'll only be like this for a couple of weeks, according to Mum."

"I don't want any more of this." Florence appeared at my side, and pushed her half-eaten toffee apple into my hand.

Mad and Brad made a fuss of her for a few minutes and then went on their way.

"Why on earth would you buy one of those horrible

things?" Jack was staring at the half-eaten toffee apple.

"It's not mine. It's Florence's."

"I told her she couldn't have one because they were bad for her teeth."

"Sorry, I didn't realise. Who's manning the refreshment stall?"

"Olga volunteered to watch it by herself for the rest of the afternoon. There's barely anything left to sell, so I didn't feel bad about leaving her to it."

"I want to win a goldfish, Mummy." Florence pointed to the stall across the way.

"But you've already got Buddy. We don't need any more pets."

"Please! Please!"

"Hello, poppet, are you having a nice time?" Grandma had appeared out of nowhere.

"Yes, but I want to win a goldfish."

"I bet your daddy will win one for you if you ask him nicely, won't you, Jeremy?"

Jack shot her an ice-cold look.

"Will you, Daddy?"

"I'll try, pumpkin."

"Yay!" Florence yelped. "Great-Grandma, my caterpillars have turned into butterflies."

"Have they? Well, isn't that exciting?"

"They're the same colour as before. Yellow with red spots. Mummy has a photo of them."

I took out my phone and showed the butterfly photos to Grandma.

I'd expected her to make some frivolous comment, but instead her face fell. "Off you go with your daddy, poppet, and try to win that goldfish."

"What's wrong, Grandma?" I asked after Jack and Florence had left. "What's with the face?"

"It's those butterflies."

"What about them?"

"The caterpillars must have been brought here from Candlefield."

"How can you possibly know that?"

"Yellow butterflies with red spots? There's only one place you'll find those, and it isn't in the human world."

"So what?"

"They're called Death Wings."

"Why would anyone call a beautiful butterfly a Death Wings?"

"Because they're carnivores."

"Don't be ridiculous. And even if that were true, so what?"

"Death Wings can eat a hundred times their own body weight. They will attack any small creature they see. Mice, rats, even—"

"Tiny dogs? Buddy! Tell Jack I had to go home, would you?"

I shot out of the village fete and ran all the way to the old watermill.

"Buddy! Buddy! Where are you?" There was no sign of him. Florence was going to be devastated if her butterflies had eaten her dog. "Buddy!"

"What's all the noise about?" Buddy appeared from underneath a bush. "I was fast asleep."

"Are you okay?" I swept him into my arms; I couldn't see any wounds.

"I was fine until you woke me up. Put me down, would you?"

"I can't. It might not be safe." I opened the door and took him into the kitchen. "You can stay in here."

Just then, my phone beeped with a text message. It was from Grandma.

Death Wings – ha, ha, ha.

You're so gullible.

Underneath the text were three emojis: a dog, a butterfly and a laughing face.

When would I ever learn?

ALSO BY ADELE ABBOTT

The Witch P.I. Mysteries
(A Candlefield/Washbridge Series)

Witch Is When... (Season #1)
Witch Is When It All Began
Witch Is When Life Got Complicated
Witch Is When Everything Went Crazy
Witch Is When Things Fell Apart
Witch Is When The Bubble Burst
Witch Is When The Penny Dropped
Witch Is When The Floodgates Opened
Witch Is When The Hammer Fell
Witch Is When My Heart Broke
Witch Is When I Said Goodbye
Witch Is When Stuff Got Serious
Witch Is When All Was Revealed

Witch Is Why... (Season #2)
Witch Is Why Time Stood Still
Witch is Why The Laughter Stopped
Witch is Why Another Door Opened
Witch is Why Two Became One
Witch is Why The Moon Disappeared
Witch is Why The Wolf Howled
Witch is Why The Music Stopped
Witch is Why A Pin Dropped
Witch is Why The Owl Returned
Witch is Why The Search Began
Witch is Why Promises Were Broken
Witch is Why It Was Over

Witch Is How... (Season #3)
Witch is How Things Had Changed
Witch is How Berries Tasted Good
Witch is How The Mirror Lied
Witch is How The Tables Turned
Witch is How The Drought Ended
Witch is How The Dice Fell
Witch is How The Biscuits Disappeared
Witch is How Dreams Became Reality
Witch is How Bells Were Saved
Witch is How To Fool Cats
Witch is How To Lose Big
Witch is How Life Changed Forever

Witch Is Where... (Season #4)
Witch is Where Magic Lives Now
Witch Is Where Clowns Go To Die
Witch Is Where Squirrels Go Nuts
Witch Is Where Rainbows End
Witch Is Where Unicorns Cry

Susan Hall Investigates
(A Candlefield/Washbridge Series)
Whoops! Our New Flatmate Is A Human.
Whoops! All The Money Went Missing.
Whoops! Someone Is On Our Case.
Whoops! We're In Big Trouble Now.

Murder On Account (A Kay Royle Novel)

Web site: AdeleAbbott.com

Facebook: facebook.com/AdeleAbbottAuthor

Made in the USA
Columbia, SC
04 June 2021